Taylor Made

Taylor Made

H.L. Sweatte

Johnnie Girl Publishing
www.JGirlPub.com

Johnnie Girl Publishing

Johnnie Girl Books are published by
Johnnie Girl Publishing
39270 Paseo Padre Parkway #415
Fremont, CA 94538
www.JGirlPub.com

Taylor Made is a work of fiction. The characters, organizations, locales and incidents portrayed in this tale are either products of the author's imagination, or are used fictitiously. Any resemblance to actual persons living or dead is purely coincidental.

ISBN-13: 9780991456307
LCCN: 2014912896

Printed in the United States of America

This book is dedicated to the close family and friends who support my writing career, and particularly those who requested more of Jackson and Jasmine's love story. I hope it was worth the wait.

Chapter 1

"I don't know how much longer I can work alongside that man and not go crazy! He's like a black Clark Kent; he's probably changing into his cape and tights right now," remarked the buxom admin, glancing at the closed office door behind her.

"Girl, you *are* crazy!" replied the other admin, who had grown accustomed to hearing similarly ridiculous comments on a daily basis. Although, she had to admit, girlfriend did have a point. "I feel you though," she agreed, glancing at the door as well. "At least you have some eye candy to feast on while stuck inside this office for eight hours. My boss is old and weathered. Where's the fun in that? Yours, however, is fine and built...but he's cocky as hell."

"Well, if you looked like him, you'd be cocky too."

"Whatever," replied the more sensible one of the pair, shaking her head. "Anyway, he's taken, so you may as well just forget about it."

"That could be a temporary hurdle."

"Ooh...you are scandalous! And, *I like it.*" Giving her co-worker a sly grin, the seated admin said, "Here," and handed her a small package. "This just came in for him. Now you have an excuse to go in there."

"Thanks," replied his now very grateful assistant, as she sashayed her way over to his office. Glancing back at her cohort, she paused to smooth out the wrinkles in her knee-length skirt before lightly knocking on his door.

"Come in," he said.

"Mr. Taylor, you have a delivery," she announced, handing him a small gift box. He looked up at her and smiled. His deep, dark eyes were so intense that she swore he had x-ray vision.

"Thanks Tammy," he said, the sound of his voice causing her insides to melt.

"Sure—I mean, you're welcome," she stuttered, struggling to maintain her composure. She found it difficult to take her eyes off of his, their strong magnetic pull reeling her in. Yet, he broke his gaze to examine the box he held in his hands. She seemed to enjoy the little surprises just as much as he did, so he didn't mind the fact that she stood in front of his desk and watched as he opened it. First, he read the note attached:

For my sweetheart: I did it!

Next, he removed the bow and then the wrapping, slowly revealing one perfectly decorated cupcake.

"Someone must love you."

"I guess so," he replied with a grin that showcased his perfectly straight, white teeth. "Thanks again, Tammy."

"No problem. Just give me a buzz if you need anything."

He watched her exit his office, closing the door behind her, while he leaned back in his chair and devoured his gift.

*****

Meanwhile, Jasmine Fairchild dashed across Sproul Plaza in a hurried attempt to make it to Bancroft Avenue before her meter expired. Her sense of urgency wasn't merely tied to her desire to defeat the diligent meter maid, but rather her eagerness to get on with her day, and ultimately her life. She had just completed her last final exam, so with the exception of attending her graduation ceremony, which was just a few days away, she had no intention of ever setting foot back on campus. *No more tests, reports or exhausting cram sessions*, she thought. *I'm free!*

"Hey Jazz...baby...wait up!"

With no time for interruptions, she continued walking at a rapid pace, quickly glancing over her shoulder to see who was following. "Oh, hey Marcus."

"You still owe me a date, remember?"

Marcus, the power forward on Cal's basketball team, had been asking Jasmine out every semester since freshman year, but each time he did she respectfully declined because she was already seeing someone else. He had impeccable timing, and unfortunately for him, this time was no different.

"Sorry babe," she said, flashing him her thousand-watt smile. "You'll have to ask my boyfriend permission first."

"Oh, so it's like that, huh?"

"Yes, it's *'like that.'*"

"Dang baby, you're killing me!" he shouted, ending his pursuit. She continued her quick stroll but glanced back once more to watch as he clasped his hand to his chest, as if he were holding together the pieces of his broken heart.

"I think you'll survive," she said, grinning.

A cool breeze swept through her freshly flat-ironed locks as she finally approached the parked Mercedes CLK she had borrowed from her boyfriend for the week. With one minute left on the meter, she waved triumphantly at the meter maid who was in the process of ticketing the car right in front of hers before tossing her leopard print shoulder bag into the back seat. It was a beautiful afternoon in the spring, and she planned to enjoy it by grabbing a bite to eat before treating herself to a pedicure. Her volunteer shift at Pleasant Beginnings didn't start until six, so she had plenty of time to unwind before then.

"Jasmine, wait a second!" shouted a female voice, stalling her departure.

"Oh, hey girl," she replied upon seeing Alysha, a student from one of her literature classes, standing a few feet away near the passenger side.

"How do you think you did on the final?"

Not one for modesty, she quickly replied, "I aced it."

"Okay, good for you," said Alysha with a soft giggle. "By the way…I was wondering…" She hesitated slightly then asked, "Are you and Jackson still together?"

Jasmine noted the tense expression etched across her face as she awaited the response, a sign that told her she was dealing with yet another one of Jackson's fans. This one, however, was shy and quiet, and had therefore slid under her radar. Most of the fans she encountered were extremely bold, making it perfectly clear they were willing and ready to snag her man the moment things between them fell apart. And, most were betting that it would.

Sighing heavily, she finally replied, "Yes, we're still together."

"Oh okay," said Alysha dryly, unable to mask her disappointment. "I'll see you around."

"Yeah, see you," said Jasmine, shaking her head as she stepped inside the vehicle. That was the one thing she definitely wasn't going to miss about school: drama. Her college days had been plagued with as much foolishness and gossip as high school, and she was ready for it to end. But, just when she was about to pull away from the curb to get away from it all, the ringing of her cell phone further delayed her departure. The custom ringtone alerted her to the caller's identity, but she insisted on feigning ignorance.

"Hello?"

"Hey Beautiful."

"Who is this?"

"Very funny," replied a deep, velvety voice.

"Mr. Taylor, what a surprise!"

"I got your present."

"Great. Hope you liked it."

"I did, thank you."

"You're welcome," she said, before adding, "I just ran into yet another member of your personal fan club."

Although Jackson had graduated from grad school the previous year, there were several members of the female undergrad population that were left swooning, his good looks and charm leaving an indelible impression.

"I have no idea what you're talking about," he replied with a slight chuckle.

"Sure you don't," she said before quickly adding, "Babe, I'll call you later, okay? I gotta get going—"

"Wait."

"What?"

"Well, considering you have my car, I was hoping you could come pick me up."

"From where? I thought you were at work?"

"I am, but I want to see you."

Jasmine glanced at the time on the dashboard. There weren't enough hours in the day for her to accomplish all she had set out to do. She wanted to see him, too, but was hoping to postpone the visit. So, knowing how persuasive he could be, she attempted to offer a satisfactory alternative. "How about we meet for lunch tomorrow? I'm looking a mess right now, and I really want to get my feet done. You know I love to look good for you, from head to toe," she cooed with extra syrup in her voice.

Jackson's lips curved upwards as he held the phone to his ear. He was amused by the game his little charmer was trying to lay on him. That line may have worked on a different man, but he was a veteran when it came to seducing people with words, for he had once employed similar tactics to collect notches on his belt. Chuckling, he said, "Now you know I could care less how your toes look. Besides, what could possibly be more important than spending time with me?"

She could have named a number of things she needed to do, but chose to remain silent because she felt guilty for having neglected the one person who, for the past year, had proven to be her biggest supporter. The two hadn't spent much time together as of late because of their hectic schedules. He was busy working full time while she prepped for the future, her graduation day rapidly approaching. Having no problem using cab service to get to and from places that weren't within walking distance, she had initially refused the offer to borrow his ride. However, considering that she had a slew of job interviews lined up, he insisted she use his car to ensure she made it to her appointments on time—that and so he would have a substantial reason to see her. As usual, his persistence prevailed.

"Text me the address," she said finally, before ending the call.

Having only visited his job once, she had no idea how to get there, but knew she would have to get a move on it in order to beat the traffic coming across the Bay Bridge. The pedicure and other errands were a wash, but she still needed to make it back in time to stop by her apartment to change into her Pleasant Beginnings uniform. Peeling away from the curb, she pumped up the volume on the radio, hoping the loud music would drown out the nagging voice inside her head spouting off an endless to-do list. Not only did it include a stop at the dry cleaners to pick up a pants suit for Monday's interview, but also a stop at the post office to send her resume and burgeoning portfolio via certified mail to a few ad agencies, where she hoped to land a full-time gig. She was starting to feel stressed out about her impending interviews, not to mention the possibility of her father not attending her graduation ceremony.

Luckily, the car's GPS device perfectly guided her to the address Jackson provided. She was a little shocked, however, upon discovering she had been led to the doors of a barbershop instead of his place of business. Pulling up to the curb, she retrieved her cell phone from her purse.

"Say babe, I'm at the address you gave, but unless you've changed jobs, this isn't the same building I remember."

"Just give me a minute. I'll be out in a few," he assured.

Shutting off the engine, Jasmine leaned her head against the headrest, closed her eyes, and began nodding to the beat of the R&B slow jam pouring out of the radio. Three songs later, she opened her eyes and checked the time on the dashboard. A "few" minutes had turned into ten, and she could feel her patience waning. Sitting upright, she peered into the rearview mirror to see if Jackson was on his way out. Having parked a few feet in front of the entrance, she looked out the passenger side window to see if she could catch a glimpse of him inside, but the windows of the barbershop were frosted, and the only way she could see in was through the letters of the shop's name, The Dapper Don, which were etched out on clear glass. Since she couldn't see inside clearly from that angle, she resumed looking at the entrance of the building through the rearview mirror. Suddenly, the door of the shop flew open, and she watched as two men, dressed in business attire, exited. One held the door, while three others made their way in. She couldn't help but notice that those entering the shop looked just as sharp as those leaving, for none appeared to be in desperate need of a haircut, line up or shave.

What's taking so long... Jasmine wondered as the minutes ticked by. She shook her head in disgust because she had passed up a chance to get her nails done to see Jackson, and here he was indulging in a few grooming treatments of his own, or so she thought. As she continued to casually observe the activity outside the shop through the rearview mirror, she noticed that the two gentlemen who had exited the building were still lingering by the door chatting, as one handed over to the other what appeared to be a business card. And just as she was reaching for her cell phone again to dial Jackson about what was causing his delay, she suddenly spied a tall, voluptuous Latina exiting the building, the sight of which caused her to whip her entire torso around to get a better look from the rear window.

Long, thick, raven locks cascaded down the woman's back, stopping just short of her prominent behind, which stood out like a hump on a camel's back. Although Jasmine had only caught a slight glimpse of her face, it wasn't hard to surmise that she was very attractive, for she had the men's rapt attention, and they appeared to be mesmerized by her.

Jasmine continued to watch closely as the men grinned, then laughed as the woman flirtatiously threw her ringlets over her shoulders before stepping back inside the shop. Their gaze followed her rear-end as if they were a pride of lions stalking a gazelle, and Jasmine considered that her cue to go see why Jackson was taking his dear, sweet time.

Chapter 2

S natching the keys from the ignition, Jasmine emerged from the vehicle with her shoulders back. She placed her Chanel sunglasses—an early graduation gift to herself—over her eyes, adjusted her leopard print shoulder bag, and tossed her mid-back length hair over her shoulders before stepping onto the curb. Apparently, her hip-hugging dark wash skinny jeans, bright red blouse and matching red platform heels were eye catching, for the two gentlemen, who had just finished peeling their eyes off the curvy Latina's backside, had suddenly found a new object to ogle.

"I see the Lord is pouring out his blessings on us today," said the one on the right before nudging the other, who shook his head in agreement.

Pretending as if she hadn't heard the comment, Jasmine simply passed by them and flung the door of the barbershop open. Once inside, she raised her shades to get a better look at what was taking place inside, and couldn't believe her eyes.

"Can I help you?" asked the busty hostess behind the counter, but Jasmine was too stunned to respond and instead stood there and squinted as she took in the scene.

Unlike most back alley barbershops filled with loud men and televisions tuned to Sports Center and the like, The Dapper Don had all the trimmings of an upscale social club. The two-story loft was set up like a lounge on the first floor, with leather couches and armchairs arranged in a circular fashion around a coffee table covered with magazines. A full service bar was positioned to the far left, and Plasma television screens hung conveniently from each corner of the room. The actual barbering took place on the second floor, which could easily be seen from the lower level.

The entire shop was abuzz with men and women. Apparently, the curvaceous Latina Jasmine saw standing outside the shop was just one of several sultry sirens working inside. There were three attractive ladies serving afternoon cocktails to the men seated at the bar, and a few others assisting the barbers upstairs, each one sporting a tight black tee with the word "Dapper," emblazoned across the chest in rhinestones. The whole setup was reminiscent of the quintessential music video, the kind where men are made to look like kings while being pampered by women of all races, and have access to any extravagance money could buy. The only thing missing, she thought, was P. Diddy and a bottle of Cîroc.

"I *said*, can I help you?" repeated the hostess.

"I'm looking for my boyfriend," she replied, snapping back to the moment after being lost in the hubbub of the scenery.

"Well, if he's not here, I'm sure you can find one," stated the hostess, gesturing toward the gentlemen seated in the lounge area, who were leering at Jasmine just as much as they were at the many hostesses that were on display. Despite feeling slightly intimidated by the competition, she was definitely able to hold her own, as evidenced by her ability to captivate a man of Jackson's caliber. Yet, her good looks were only partly responsible for garnering his attention, and he, as well as the rest of the men she encountered, didn't seem to mind the extra ten pounds she was carrying, courtesy of the endorphin-producing confections she consumed to eliminate her yearning for cigarettes.

As if having heard the hostess' offer, one particular gentleman decided to make his move. "Excuse me pretty lady," he said, grabbing hold of her arm, "I know you didn't come here to get a taper fade. Please, allow me to buy you a drink."

Jasmine glanced down at the stranger's hand, which was gripping her arm tightly, then resumed eye contact. "Thanks, but I didn't come here to get manhandled either," she said, yanking her arm free from his embrace.

"Excuse me, is there a problem here?" asked Jackson, who suddenly approached. He had just finished exchanging a few words with another gentleman who, after ending their conversation with a handshake, retreated inside the private area of the shop.

"I didn't know she was with you. My bad," replied the overly aggressive patron, excusing himself as he headed toward the bar.

"You should have waited in the car," said Jackson, his dark eyes boring into Jasmine as he spoke. "I told you I'd be out soon."

"Yeah well, soon wasn't soon enough," she replied, glancing around the shop. "Besides, why is it okay for you to be in here and not me?"

Before he could respond, the curvy Latina she had seen standing outside the shop earlier approached him from the side and draped an arm around his neck. "Hey babe, long time no see," she said before planting a kiss on his cheek, a move that made Jasmine's jaw drop.

"It's been a minute," he replied, welcoming her embrace and then releasing her. Smiling, he pointed over her shoulder and said, "Carmen, this is my girl, Jasmine."

"Hello," said Carmen, turning to greet Jasmine with a smile. That smile soon faded once it met her cold glare.

"Hello," she said, stone-faced.

"Well, I'll leave you two alone," said Carmen, suddenly feeling unwelcome. "Good seeing you, sweetie. I'll see you around," she told Jackson with a wink before traipsing up the stairs.

"You ready?" asked Jasmine, trying to appear unaffected by his shapely companion, whose hips swayed back and forth with each step.

"Yes, we can go," he replied, tucking the binder he was holding underneath his arm. He rested a hand against her lower back as he guided her toward the exit of the shop.

The two made their way within inches of the door when suddenly Jasmine heard female voices sing "Goodbye Jackson," which caused her to turn around. Glancing toward the loft, she watched as the curvy Latina and another female staff member gave her boyfriend a five-finger wave, both smiling from ear-to-ear. At that, she simply rolled her eyes and headed out the door.

"So, now they're giving away lap dances with hair cuts?" she asked once they made it outside.

"Excuse me?"

"I'm not sure if that was a barbershop or a brothel. Besides, aren't you supposed to be at work?"

"Very funny," said Jackson in response to her sarcastic remark. "And to answer your question, I am at work. Perhaps if you had retracted your claws a bit then you would have noticed that I'm not the client—they are," he said, pointing toward the barbershop. "I came down here because the owner, who happens to be a good friend of mine, is looking to relocate. Business is booming, and they're outgrowing this space, so he called on me for help."

She looked down at the binder he had in his hand, the one with his employer's logo on the front, and suddenly, it all made sense. "Oh," she said, feeling slightly embarrassed for mistaking the reason for his visit. "Well, I guess I can't be mad at you for making me miss my nail appointment and other errands then," she said, wrapping her arms around his neck, a move that prompted him to slide his arms around her waist. "By the way," she continued, "what do you mean by retracting my claws? They weren't out."

"Oh really?" he asked, with raised brows. Although he stood almost a foot taller, he found it amusing how at times she seemed to stand as tall as a building given her bold and tempestuous spirit. She had entered the shop on fire, and he could tell she was annoyed by the ambiance, not to mention his interaction with Carmen, despite the fact she was trying to deny it. "You didn't seem very friendly."

"I said hello to your friend."

"Yes, you did…with daggers in your eyes," he said, chuckling.

"Well, she was flirting with you, and I had to mark my territory."

"Your territory is well protected," he assured with a smile. "Don't you trust me?"

"I trust you," she said, glancing toward the shop. "It's vultures like the ones in there I don't trust."

Jackson's smile intensified, for he found her possessiveness cute and flattering. "Well, you shouldn't worry about them," he said, squeezing her tighter. "I have no reason to flirt with anyone because I've already succeeded at snagging the most beautiful woman in the world." Jasmine rolled her eyes and sighed heavily, but he remained unaffected by her response as he peered into her eyes. "I wanted you the moment I first laid eyes on you," he admitted with complete sincerity. "But, you already know that."

Jasmine couldn't help but smile at Jackson's remarks, for he had a way with words, a way of making one believe what he said was the absolute truth. It was a skill that made him a very successful salesman, and at one point in time, a very suave Casanova. Luckily for her, however, she knew based on how they met that he wasn't just spitting game, for he had been relentless in his pursuit of her. She still clearly recalled how he stood behind her in line at Café Milano during one of their initial encounters and said with an air of certainty, *"Mr. and Mrs. Taylor, I like the sound of that,"* as if he knew they would one day be together.

"I hope you don't talk to your female clients like this," she said, suddenly fearing he was employing similar seductive tactics on others.

"How else do you think I land my sales?"

"Jackson—"

"I'm kidding," he said before shifting to a more serious tone. "And, just so you know, it wasn't my intent to disrupt your plans today. I know you have a lot on your plate, as if you haven't complained about it a million times already. It's just that you've been so busy that you barely have time for me. Do you realize that I've only seen you twice in the past month? If I hadn't loaned you my car, I probably wouldn't have gotten a chance to see you at all."

"So you admit you loaned me your car just so you could have a hold on me?"

Grinning devilishly, he replied, "Well, I had to do something. It's not a crime for a man to want to see his lady."

"You are determined, I'll give you that," she said, feeling comforted by his embrace, the warmth of his body helping ease some of the tension that had started building in her neck and shoulders as a result of the stress she was currently under. There were so many tasks she still needed to accomplish, her final shift at Pleasant Beginnings being one. In just a few short hours, she would be walking through the doors of the assisted living facility where she had been volunteering since freshman year for the last time. Unfortunately for her, the resident she was currently assigned to assist had proven to be nothing like her former companion, Missy, who was warm, loving, and playful. Although she had initially planned to quit upon Missy's demise, she ultimately agreed to carry out her volunteer duties until graduation, and was somewhat relieved her time at the facility was now coming to an end. Jackson was aware of the stress she was under and was also happy that her volunteer assignment was ending, for it had proven to be yet another obstacle standing in the way of them spending quality time together.

"By the way," she said, averting her eyes from his as she struggled to compose her words. "Thank you for supporting me and for being so understanding," she continued, still looking away. "In some ways, you've been more consistent than my father—in a lot of ways, actually."

Jackson had been dating Jasmine long enough to know that she wasn't the best at expressing her feelings, so the fact that she was now sharing her heartfelt emotions was both shocking and moving he thought. "You're welcome," he said, finally catching her eye. "And, I hope you're not still worried about your father," he continued. "I have a feeling he's not going to miss your graduation ceremony. But, if he does, you'll still have me to cheer you on."

Jasmine smiled and Jackson smiled back. His words were almost as comforting as his embrace, and she felt happy to be in the arms of the man she loved. Yet, in spite of all that, there was still a small part of her that felt slightly annoyed by the apparent flirting she had witnessed take place between him and some of the females working inside the barbershop. She had been dating him long enough to know that he could attract just as much, if not more attention as she—and that was a reality she had yet to get used to. But, she could no longer hide nor deny the fact that he was extremely desirable. With creamy, chocolate skin and full lips that were surrounded by a perfectly groomed goatee, he had all the qualities of what one would call tall, dark and handsome. Yet, there was one captivating feature that made him stand out from all the rest…his eyes. Many had tried, but few could escape the allure of those two onyx stones set against a white backdrop. Their deep, dark intensity held a certain magnetism all their own.

Donning a slate gray, three-piece suit, Jackson looked more like a banker on Wall Street than a commercial real estate agent working in San Francisco's Financial District. It had been his penchant for designer suits and unmatched level of sophistication that made him a standout on Cal's campus. It's easy for girls fresh out of high school to refer to the guys they meet in college as men, but he had proven to Jasmine that she had been amidst boys until he stepped on the scene. Six years her senior, and having graduated from grad school the previous year, he was clearly the more seasoned of the pair, and although she had matured, she still had quite a ways to go before they could level out the playing field.

"So," he said, his dark eyes staring back at hers, "how about we do lunch now, and then you swing by my place after your shift tonight."

"Lunch, yes. Your place tonight, no."

"Okay," he replied with laughter in his voice. "I'll take what I can get." Gripping her tightly, he kissed her with an intensity she could not resist, and for a while she forgot all about everything she needed to do.

Chapter 3

"Thanks so much for coming, Dad!" shouted Jasmine as she broke through the sea of fellow graduates. Donning her cap and gown and the beautiful floral lei Jackson gifted her, she raced excitedly toward her father and wrapped her arms around his neck. She was elated he hadn't backed out of attending her graduation ceremony considering there were many events he had missed because business always seemed to take precedence. Yet, nothing could have kept him from attending the graduation ceremony for his baby girl—the only woman who held his heart since his wife's passing.

"You know I wouldn't miss this for the world," he replied, holding her close.

Although she was happy to have his support, a part of her felt sad to think about the two very important people who were unable to witness her accomplishments: her mother, who died when she was only a child; and Missy, her beloved confidante, who passed during the spring semester of her junior year. Unfortunately, neither had lived long enough to see her receive her diploma, or witness her evolution. She had come a long way from being the callow youth that had entered college, and was leaving a mature, yet still blossoming young woman, fully equipped to share her talents and ambition with the rest of the world. Her feisty nature, however, never faltered, for even the love of a good man hadn't proven powerful enough to abolish that.

"My turn," said Jackson, who stood close by. Jasmine turned toward him and the two embraced. "I'm so proud of you," he said, holding her face in his hands.

"So, you guys ready for your celebratory dinner?" asked Mr. Fairchild.

"Sure," Jasmine replied. "Just give me a sec." She darted off into the crowd of fellow grads to say goodbye to a few friends and faculty members while her father and Jackson stayed behind. Just when she was almost finished making her rounds, a honey-complected Adonis suddenly appeared amidst the crowd—the one other person aside from Jackson who could make her heart palpitate.

"Congratulations!" exclaimed Stacey, sweeping her into a hug.

Stacey Fisher, the dean's son and star quarterback of the football team, had once been Jasmine's greatest pursuit in life. Although she hadn't seen him in a while, she soon remembered why she had once been so fond of him. It hadn't simply been his chiseled, athletic build or deep set dimples that had drawn her to him, for she had also found his ambitious spirit, mild temperament, and down-to-earth nature extremely appealing. And, unlike many other guys she had encountered, Stacey seemed genuine, and had therefore appeared to be the type of guy to whom she could give herself wholeheartedly, with absolutely no reservations. Her affection toward him however, appeared unrequited, as he had given up the chance to be with her in order to remain with Angel Martin, his college sweetheart.

Slightly in shock by Stacey's sudden appearance and overly affectionate gesture, Jasmine pulled away from him and said, "Congratulations to you too."

"Thanks. It's been a wild ride."

"That it has," she said, smiling. He smiled back, enabling her to catch a glimpse of his two, magnificent dimples, and she suddenly felt it best to cut the conversation short. "Well, I'd better get going," she said, glancing in her party's direction. "You take care—"

"Angel and I broke up," he blurted out, just as she was turning to leave. His announcement caused her to turn back around.

Peering into his amber-colored eyes, Jasmine saw the spark she had always known existed between them, suddenly ignite, and for a moment, she pondered the implication of his comment. But soon Jackson came to mind, so she averted her eyes and extinguished the flame.

"I'm sorry to hear that," she replied, slowly backing away. Within seconds, she was forced to take a step back even further as his usual entourage of fellow teammates and female admirers, flocked to his side.

Stepping away from the chaos, Jasmine peered into the crowd and found Jackson, surrounded by a bevy of women. She glanced back at Stacey and realized that the two scenes were very similar. Although she might not have ended up with the school's star athlete, she definitely succeeded at landing a mate who was in high demand. Jackson didn't play ball, but was young, educated, and successful with a universal sex appeal that seemingly oozed out of every pore on his body, thus attracting his own brand of groupies.

"Congratulations," she heard him say to one female admirer, who was still hovering around him as she approached.

"Thanks," replied the unidentified young lady before adding, "Let me give you my number so we can stay in touch—"

"Have I introduced you to my girlfriend?" he asked, pointing behind her.

"Oh, hey," said the young woman, turning abruptly to greet Jasmine.

"Hello," she offered with a smile.

Embarrassed, the young lady muttered, "I'll see you guys around," then scurried off toward her friend, who stood close by.

Jasmine could hear the unnamed admirer and her female companion whisper loudly to each other as they walked away:

"I can't believe they're still together!"

"I know."

"Did you hear that?" she asked Jackson, stunned.

"Don't worry about them," he said, sliding an arm around her waist as he guided her toward the exit of the Hearst Greek Theatre.

Jasmine glanced over at her father to catch his reaction, for she was certain he had witnessed the female fanfare that had swarmed around Jackson moments prior, but he appeared oblivious, as she watched him furiously type away at the keys on his Blackberry, his head tilted downward. *Constantly at work*, she thought.

Once the three of them made it out to the street, she proceeded to take the lead, forcing her father to ask, "Where are you going?"

"Toward the lot where we parked."

"I have something better," he replied, beckoning the driver of the black stretch limo that was parked a few feet from where they stood.

"You're kidding," she said, glancing at him and smiling. His presence was a big enough treat, so the fact he had planned something extravagant to help celebrate her accomplishment was the icing on the cake, and just what she needed to take her mind off the two gossipers who felt they had the right to comment on her love life.

The limo driver had already been instructed on where to go, so all the trio had to do was sit back, and enjoy the ride. Jasmine's father asked Jackson how his life was unfolding since having obtained his M.B.A. a year prior, and Jasmine tuned both of them out as she sat in awe of the plush seats, dim lighting, and small bar tucked neatly inside the limo.

"Your industry was hit pretty hard. How are things at the agency?"

"Things are going pretty well despite this dismal economy."

"That's good to hear," replied Mr. Fairchild, who was still curious about the young man who had succeeded at capturing his daughter's heart. He had met Jackson the previous summer and although they had engaged in a few conversations since, he still didn't know much about him, but was trusting of his daughter's judgment. The only name he had heard come out of her mouth during her first three years at Cal was Stacey Fisher, so naturally he was befuddled when he opened the door the previous summer to see Jasmine, who had decided to spend some time at home to mourn Missy's passing, standing in the doorway next to a tall, handsome gentleman who appeared to be a few years her senior—and was clearly not Stacey.

"There are so many folks out of work now," continued Mr. Fairchild, "so it's a blessing any of us are still employed."

"True," stated Jackson. "I've definitely been lucky."

"I believe it's more than luck that's gotten you to where you are today. You seem to have a pretty solid background in real estate, having worked alongside your father all those years. How is he by the way?"

"He's well, thanks for asking. He made some wise investments and even sold some properties at the top of the market. Business is a little slow, but he's flourishing."

"Well, hopefully his company can continue to thrive and create more jobs. It now seems having a good education isn't going to cut it. The way tuition costs are steadily mounting, some of these kids coming behind you aren't going to be able to afford it. I'm glad you and Jasmine were able to graduate before the whole system implodes."

"You're right. Although I'm still employed," he replied, crossing his fingers, "if the company I work for tanks, then I plan to leverage my investment background and move into investment banking."

"Or, you can just go work for your father," stated Mr. Fairchild with a smile.

Jackson responded to his remark with a weak grin, his silence overshadowed by Jasmine, who butted into their conversation to offer her father a drink.

"Here," she said, handing him a champagne flute.

"What's this?"

"I poured it from the bar," she announced. Since having turned twenty-one six months prior, she never passed up the chance to exercise the legal rights her age afforded her. "It's champagne, for a toast," she said, holding out another flute for Jackson.

"Shouldn't we be doing this after the meal?"

"This is a celebration, so we can do one now, and another later. To the future," she said, raising her glass up high, "and all the possibilities it holds."

"Cheers," said her father, raising the glass to his lips.

"Cheers," seconded Jackson.

Chapter 4

After a little conversation and champagne, the trio finally arrived at their destination. Anxious to see what her father had planned for the evening, Jasmine hopped out of the limo and headed toward the restaurant, where she, her father and Jackson were immediately greeted by the host, who sat them at a square table outside on the enclosed patio. "This is nice," she stated, surveying the scene.

The Waterfront Restaurant at Pier 7 in San Francisco offered magnificent views of the Bay, and thanks to Jackson's recommendation, Mr. Fairchild deemed it the perfect place to take Jasmine on her special evening. Shortly after the waiter arrived to collect their drink order, Jackson excused himself from the table to take a phone call, and Mr. Fairchild took his absence as an opportunity to connect with his daughter.

"I'm so proud of you," he said, staring at her from across the table.

"Thanks Dad."

"Not only have you earned your degree, but you've also succeeded at snagging quite a catch."

"Yeah, I guess so," she confirmed with a smile. At times she found it hard to believe that the man she had once tried to run from was now her very loving and considerate companion. True, he had been a ladies man, but the days of him playing the field were long gone, and she was the only woman who held his heart.

"Do you think he's the one?" asked her father, staring at her intently as he awaited her response.

She hesitated for a moment, knowing the answer but afraid to say it. Then, after taking a sip of water, she looked at him and said, "We'll see."

*****

"What did I tell you about calling me?" Jackson spoke sternly into his cell phone after waiting until he was out of earshot of Jasmine and her father, for he didn't want either of them to hear the conversation he knew wasn't going to be pleasant. "I don't want my girlfriend getting the wrong idea—"

"Calm down, Pretty Boy. Nobody's checking for you. Been there, done that, and, it wasn't all that."

"Yeah right," he said, sucking his teeth. "Is that why you kept blowing up my phone, begging for more?"

"Huh!" The female caller gasped uncontrollably, for she knew he was telling the truth. She just couldn't believe he had the gall to say it. "You have got to be the biggest jerk I have ever met!"

"What do you want, Bianca?" asked Jackson with irritation in his voice. He was tired of having to deal with his father's bitter office manager, the same one who had taught him to never mix business with pleasure.

"*I* don't want anything," she snapped. "I'm calling on behalf of your father—you know, the man I work for, the man you *used* to work for? He asked me to call and see if there was any way you could clear your schedule in the next week or so. He wants you to come home to discuss some very important business."

"Regarding what?"

"He didn't say. I haven't earned the keys to the kingdom yet. Like you, he's full of secrets, and didn't disclose any details."

Jackson took a deep breath then said, "Okay, well, if things go according to plan, I'll be coming home soon anyway."

"What's that supposed to mean?"

"Never mind. Just let him know I'll be in touch."

"Okay."

"And Bianca?"

"Yes?"

"Don't call my cell again. Next time, send an email."

"Go to hell," she said then hung up.

*****

"Have you decided yet?" asked Jackson once he returned to the table.

"Yeah, I think so," Jasmine replied.

The waiter returned to take their order, and once the food arrived, the three immediately began partaking in their meal. The graduation ceremony had been quite lengthy, considering the various departments, faculty members and students that had been honored, so the trio had developed quite an appetite, and weren't ashamed to satisfy it. There wasn't much conversation during the meal, and Jasmine, who had become so enamored by the whimsical scenery and fantastic views the restaurant offered, set her fork down to take it all in.

Glancing upward, she observed the cloudless sky that hung above the city. It was growing dark out, and a cool breeze swept across the Bay. Luckily, the heat lamps that were scattered about the enclosed patio in which they sat provided enough warmth to keep them toasty, and it wasn't long before she found herself admiring some of the couples that sat nearby. There was one couple in particular that caught her eye—an older pair in their late fifties or early sixties. She watched as the man reached across the table and grabbed the woman's hand, kissing it softly while she giggled then playfully yanked it away. Jasmine thought how sweet it was to see two people that age in love and acting flirtatious. She couldn't help but think of how nice it would have been had her father allowed himself to fall in love again after her mother passed away. It struck her then that she had never seen him with anyone…well, except for Miss Hall, but that was nothing.

Miss Hall was the mother of one of her elementary school classmates who happened to attend the same church she and her father attended. Even as a child, Jasmine noticed how Miss Hall had taken very little interest in her until she laid eyes on her father, who was actually an attractive man once you got past the rimless eyeglasses and Mr. Rogers sweaters he wore almost daily. Jasmine never could understand how a man with so much money, could spend so little on himself. A hardworking businessman, Mr. Fairchild rarely wore suits, opting for business casual attire that left much to be desired in his daughter's opinion. Although she shared his almond-shaped eyes, caramel complexion, and independent spirit, his fashion sense, or rather, lack thereof, was all his own.

In any case, once Miss Hall targeted Mr. Fairchild as a prospective suitor, she immediately started going out of her way to give Jasmine rides to and from school, and began arranging play dates for her and her daughter, who was really more of an acquaintance than a friend. The way her father smiled from ear to ear whenever Miss Hall came around made Jasmine cringe. The fact that this woman was trying to take her deceased mother's place while her child encroached on her territory was more than she could handle. Needless to say, she was highly relieved when Miss Hall's ex husband took a job out of state, forcing her to follow so that her daughter's relationship with him wouldn't be compromised.

As Jasmine glanced across the table at her father shoveling a big piece of juicy steak into his mouth, she couldn't help but wonder how he must have felt having gone all those years without a mate. He worked so hard that he barely had time for much if any play. Aside from work, she was the only thing he seemed to truly care about despite the fact that he never really knew how to provide her with the emotional support she needed after her mother passed away. Although at one point she may have felt threatened by anyone or anything that seemed to absorb his time and attention, she now felt a little sad knowing that he wouldn't have anyone around to keep him company. It was hard enough making the decision to leave him once she settled on a school four hundred miles away, but now that college was over, her future, and how it would impact their relationship, was unknown. For one, moving back to Los Angeles hadn't proven to be a priority given that all the interviews she had lined up were for companies located in the Bay.

Jasmine didn't know what the future held for she or her father, but in that moment, she truly felt happy. As she watched him devour his meal, a huge grin swept across her face, for she was thrilled to have him share in one of the greatest moments of her life. After taking a sip of water, she glanced over at Jackson, who she expected to see eating just as frantically as her father was, but was surprised to discover that he wasn't eating at all. Instead, he appeared to be in deep thought, as he pushed the food around his plate with a fork.

"Hey you," she said, gently nudging his arm.

"Hey," he replied, as if jolted out of a trance. He then looked at her and smiled.

Shortly thereafter, the trio finished their meal, and Jasmine thanked her father once more for making her graduation day truly special. He had the limo driver take them back to the lot in Berkeley where Jackson's car was parked, then wished the young couple a goodnight before heading back to his hotel.

"Are you tired?" asked Jackson, once he and Jasmine entered his vehicle.

"Not really."

"Good," he said before cranking the engine. "Now it's time to *really* celebrate."

Jasmine didn't know what Jackson had in store for the rest of the evening, but knowing him, she knew that whatever it was, it would be something she wouldn't soon forget.

Chapter 5

"Uggh," Jasmine cried out, reaching toward the nightstand to disarm her alarm clock. Sitting up straight, she grasped her head with both hands, which was now pounding thanks to a splitting headache. She had just glanced down at her person and noticed she was still wearing the same outfit from the previous night when Foxy, her cat, hopped onto the bed and parked herself in her lap just as she was about to let out another woeful sigh.

"Hey girl," she said, stroking the back of the cat's head. Foxy purred loudly, and Jasmine was almost certain she heard her stomach growl. "Mama's gonna get up and fix you something to eat, soon..." she said, flopping back onto the bed. She nestled her head against the pillows before grasping it again with both hands. This was her first hangover—a reminder to never drink as much as she had the previous night.

Although she was fully aware of the laundry list of things that still needed to be done, she wanted nothing more than to stay curled up in bed and wait for the pounding in her head to subside. Foxy, however, with no intention of letting her fall back to sleep, crawled on top of her and began licking her face.

"Eww," she said, wiping away her kisses. "Alright, alright, I'm getting up."

She sat up and began stroking Foxy's head again, pausing for a brief second to wipe the sleep from her eyes. Once she had finished, she looked down at her cat, and then at her hand...her left hand, which was now adorned with something big and sparkly. "Oh my gosh!" she gasped, staring at the fat rock in amazement. The sight of the magnificent ring—which she estimated at about three carats, was hypnotic, and suddenly, details of the previous night came rushing back like a flood:

"Where are we going?" she asked Jackson with one hand gripping the dashboard as his car took several sharp turns up a narrow, winding road.

"You'll see," he replied, glancing at her and smiling. "You're not scared, are you?"

"No. Just keep your eyes on the road," she commanded, to which he belted out a laugh.

About twenty agonizing minutes later, they arrived at their destination. "We're here," he said, parking alongside a dusty turnout on Grizzly Peak Boulevard.

Although she had heard stories about the majestic views offered by the stretch of road named after the Grizzly Bears that once occupied it, seeing it was awe inspiring. On a night free of fog, one could observe the entire Bay Area while standing on the peak located behind the UC Berkeley campus. The twinkling lights of the homes and cars scattered below; the body of water that separated the cities above where the Bay Bridge stood; and the dark mounds of shrub covered hills scattered along the backdrop were all clearly visible. They had surpassed the residential area of the boulevard, having stopped alongside an uninhabited area, which was a known make out spot for high school and college students.

After turning up the volume on the superior sound system inside his vehicle, Jackson grabbed Jasmine and spun her around. A picnic basket filled with chocolate covered strawberries and a few bottles of champagne accompanied the evening. "This is awesome," she said, twirling with a glass of champagne in hand.

"Glad you like your surprise."

"I love it!" She set the glass down on the hood of his car then spun herself around again and giggled while he leaned against the driver side door, admiring her and laughing. He enjoyed seeing her like this: happy and uninhibited.

"Hey, I was just wondering…" he began, his words causing her to stop dancing and look at him. "What did you and Stacey talk about tonight?"

"You saw me talking to him?"

"You see these?" he asked, pointing at his eyes. "My vision is twenty, twenty."

"I just thought you were too preoccupied with your female fan club to notice."

"I'm always watching you."

"That sounds stalker-ish," she replied with a laugh, a comment that caused him to chuckle as well. *"You know, if I weren't mistaken, I would think you're jealous. Are you jealous Mr. Taylor?"*

Jackson ran a hand across his goatee and said, "Never that."

"Oh okay," she said with a laugh. *"Well, if you must know, he just wanted to congratulate me on graduating, that's all."*

"And, he hugged you."

"Yes, he did."

"Well, luckily for him I'm not threatened. Otherwise, he'd have two broken arms to match that broken leg he suffered a while back, and his football career would be over, for good."

"Ha!" she shouted, skipping toward him then wrapping her arms around his waist. *"You are jealous. But, don't worry. I think it's cute."* He tilted his head toward the sky and Jasmine stood on the tips of her toes so she could give him a kiss on the chin. *"Trust,"* she said, gazing into his eyes as he peered down into hers, *"you have nothing to worry about."*

"Really? And why is that?"

"Because you're the one I want."

"Prove it."

"Jackson, we talked about this," she said, pulling away.

"Not that," he said, laughing as he reached for her hand and pulled her back toward him. His expression turned serious as he continued to stare into her eyes. She stared back into his and could see the moonlight dancing off the dark black pools that had always had a strong effect on her. Luckily for him, their power was working magic now. *"Marry me."*

"What?"

Removing a tiny black box from a pocket inside his suit jacket, he looked at her and said, "I'm looking forward to sharing all your accomplishments, but I have to say that one of my greatest accomplishments has been finding you." She watched him drop down on one knee, his words echoing inside her ears.

Jasmine took a deep breath, and could feel her heart pounding inside her chest. A part of her still couldn't believe how dramatically their relationship had evolved, and it seemed his effort to solidify their union was unyielding, as he was now asking for her hand in marriage.

"I—I don't know what to say," she stuttered.

"Well, I can think of one, three letter word you could say," he replied, smiling.

After closing her eyes and taking a deep breath, she finally said, "Yes."

Laughing with joy, Jackson swept her into his arms and kissed her. "Let me put it on," he said once he set her back down on the ground.

"It fits perfectly," she remarked, sounding surprised.

"Well, it helped that you just asked your father to buy your class ring. I got your size from him."

She stared down at the sparkling diamond engagement ring in amazement. A part of her still felt like daddy's little girl, so she couldn't believe that she was engaged and had her father's approval. Knowing that she had his blessing settled her nerves a bit, and enabled her to enjoy the rest of the evening, which she and Jackson spent dancing underneath the stars, only taking breaks to enjoy a few treats and libations. And in her case, one too many.

The previous night's events had seemed so perfect, magical even, to the point where she had dismissed Jackson's marriage proposal as being part of a dream. Yet, the large diamond, shining before her very eyes, was proof positive that her new status as bride-to-be was a definite reality. She hadn't at all suspected he was going to propose, and the way he had done it—underneath the clear sky in the dark of night, while standing atop a mountain that enabled them to feel like a king and queen as they stared down at the shrinking city below—made it all seem surreal.

"Oh. My. Gosh," she said once more before falling back on the bed. Foxy rushed over, ready to start licking her face again, but she put a stop to it. "Okay, I'm up," she said, tossing the covers aside as she slowly sat up, being careful not to exit the bed too quickly so her head wouldn't start spinning even faster than it already was. Before she could plant her feet onto the floor, her cell phone started ringing, and she gripped her head again, for the sound felt like two cymbals clashing in front of her face.

"Hello?"

"Hey, I'm just about ready."

Shoot! she thought, glancing over at the clock once more, this time making note of the hour. She had forgotten she promised to take her father to the airport. "Okay," she said, flustered. "I'll be there soon."

She rose from the bed and was suddenly filled with panic, for she recalled asking Jackson to borrow his car in order to escort her father to the airport, but didn't remember actually getting the vehicle. She was supposed to have dropped him off at his place the previous night, but couldn't recount any details. She didn't even remember the ride home.

Rushing into the living room, Jasmine headed straight toward the window so she could peek out to check and see if Jackson's car was indeed parked out front, but soon became startled at the sight of a large figure on her couch. Feeling a bit discombobulated, she approached the couch slowly and realized it was Jackson lying there, sound asleep. She inched her way closer until she was standing over him, unable to resist the urge to watch as he lay there, resting so peacefully.

Sleep, she thought, was one of the most vulnerable states anyone could be in, and a part of her loved seeing him like this. It reminded her of the first night they spent together, when he slept over at her apartment and literally just slept. It was the night before Missy's funeral, and she had asked him to stay because she couldn't bear the thought of being alone to suffer the loss of her dear friend. She had told him she wasn't ready to have sex with him, and he surprisingly understood. That was the same night he expressed how much he cared for her, having shared how he had never allowed himself to get to know a woman the way he had gotten to know her. After all, his player lifestyle hadn't been conducive to him finding true love. And, it hadn't been just that night, but many nights the two had spent, enjoying each other's company and establishing a solid bond, one that was filled with true intimacy, and not just the physical kind.

Jackson was the most complex man she had ever dated, and no other before him had forced her to examine herself the way that he did. Aside from her relationship with Demetri, she was used to having the upper hand. That was mainly because she wouldn't allow herself to be vulnerable with anyone. She had made that tragic mistake when she chose to give her heart, mind and body to her high school sweetheart, who in turn tossed her aside after praising her as his latest conquest. She had given him *everything*, and gotten nothing but scorn, humiliation and ridicule in return. Demetri had betrayed her in the worst way possible, and that experience still haunted her thoughts. Because of it, she avoided intimacy like the plague, and refused to become emotionally involved with anyone. After all, she had learned that it was much easier to be in control when only one's mind and not one's heart was involved.

Although she had dated a lot of men since, none had owned her— not emotionally or physically. By the time she met Jackson, she was very cynical, and could still recall the first few encounters she had with him, and how repelled she was by his arrogant demeanor. Even his scent had been a turnoff, for he donned the exact same cologne Demetri adored. The fact that these two men weren't essentially one in the same was difficult for her to comprehend, which is why Stacey, who appeared to be opposite of Jackson, had been the one she had tried to pursue. Yet Jackson was showing her, day by day, that he was nothing like Demetri. In fact, every moment she spent with him was like an emotional revival, for he had her feeling things she had suppressed, and then some.

Deciding to allow him further rest, she took a step back when suddenly he reached out and grabbed hold of her arm. "Where do you think you're going?" he asked, drawing her toward him.

"I have to get going—"

"Not so fast," he said, pulling her down on top of him. He enveloped her in his arms and immediately began showering her with kisses.

Jasmine could feel her head spinning and her insides starting to flutter, but she wasn't sure if it was because of the hangover, or him.

"Good morning," he said, once he removed his mouth from hers.

"Jackson, I—"

"Shh, don't talk," he whispered, guiding her mouth back toward his. He ran his hands up and down her spine, as her body sank further into his, but she soon felt his early morning arousal press into her, and that's when she started to pull away.

"I'm running late," she said, pushing herself up off him.

"Whatever it is, it can wait," he replied, gripping her tightly.

"It's my dad, I have to take him to the airport." She felt his grip loosen slightly, and used that as her opportunity to escape. Once back on her feet, she stumbled and tried to regain her balance.

Clasping his hands behind his head, Jackson smiled faintly then asked, "How are you feeling?" upon watching her struggle to keep a steady footing.

"Good…" she said, before feeling the room starting to spin. She then knelt back down, this time, taking a seat on the floor. "Well actually, not so much."

"Yeah, too much champagne will do that to you. You were knocked out by the time we made it back here, so I just tucked you in and crashed on the couch."

"Thanks," she said, truly appreciative of his care and concern. "At least one of us was sober." Before he could respond, she remembered what she needed to do and scrambled to get back on her feet. "I've gotta get out of here, quick!"

"Okay," said Jackson, searching the floor for his shoes. "I'm going to head home—need to shower and change. Just swing by later with the car."

"How are you going to get home?" she asked, staring at him, puzzled.

"The same way you like to get around: cab service. Don't get used to this though. I prefer being in the driver's seat."

"Okay," she said with a smile. "I'll see you soon."

He headed for the door while she headed toward the kitchen to fix Foxy a bowl of Meow Mix. Afterwards, she made her way to the bathroom for a quick shower, and was soon on her way out the door to pick up her father, who was staying just a few blocks away at the historic Bancroft Hotel.

"Good morning," she said upon exiting the vehicle to greet him with a hug. Once he released her, she dangled her left hand in front of his face.

"Congratulations," said Mr. Fairchild, admiring his daughter's ring with a smile. "Were you surprised?"

"Very," she said, mirroring his joyful response. "Wanna grab a bite to eat, to celebrate before your flight?"

"I'd love to," he said while sifting through some papers inside his briefcase. "But…"

I should have known there'd be a "but…"

"We don't have much time. Besides, I need to get back home to finalize a business transaction. You understand, don't you?"

"Yeah, I understand," said Jasmine before pulling away from the curb.

"Do you mind?" asked her father, frowning and pointing toward the sky. Jasmine loved riding around in Jackson's drop-top convertible and was so happy spring had arrived so that she could let the sunshine in. Apparently, not everyone shared that sentiment.

"Sure," she said, complying with her father's request by closing the roof.

It didn't take long for them to arrive at their destination, and after watching her father disappear through the automatic doors of the Oakland International Airport with luggage in hand, Jasmine hopped back inside the car, lowered the top, and headed to the dry cleaners to pick up the suits she needed for her upcoming interviews. Once she was finished with her errands, she headed across town to Jackson's place.

Chapter 6

"Hello Beautiful," said Jackson, greeting Jasmine at his doorstep wearing nothing but a towel wrapped around his waist.

She stood at the door, frozen, admiring his enticing form. With his legs spread shoulder width apart and his posture perfect, Jackson stood as if he had the letter "s" emblazoned across his chest—his delectably bare, hairless chest. He may not have been as chiseled as some of the athletes she once dated, but his smooth, chocolate-coated body was solid—his pecs and abdomen, well toned. After all, he could have never made it to playboy status by being a slouch.

"Did you come to finish what we started this morning?" he asked, a triumphant smile gracing his lips as he watched her eyes remain glued to his half-naked body.

"No," she replied, rolling her eyes at him. "And I'm not coming in until you put some clothes on." *He knows what he's doing*, she thought. And, he did.

Jackson knew the effect he had on women, and it seemed he insisted on being her kryptonite, steadily wearing her down until she became one big lump of silly putty sitting in the palm of his hand. Eyeing her intensely, he licked his lips then said in his deep, smooth-as-silk voice, "Babe, I just stepped out the shower and didn't want you to have to wait. I'll head upstairs and get dressed as soon as you come in, I promise." She gave him a look that told him she didn't buy it, so he said, "Scout's honor," holding up a three-finger salute.

"See, this is why I don't like coming over here," she said, stepping inside.

Jackson lived in a two-story condo in Emeryville, about fifteen minutes away from campus and ten minutes from where she lived. Although she had been to his place several times, she never quite got over how beautifully furnished it was, or how immaculate he kept it. She particularly loved the fact that it wasn't decked out in all black—the stereotypical color scheme of a bachelor. Instead, there was a very comfortable, cream-colored couch with down feathering positioned a few feet away from a burgundy accent wall. His coffee table and dining room set looked more like works of art than a place to rest one's feet or enjoy a meal. All that paired with recessed lighting made the place look like it belonged on the showroom floor of Scandinavian Designs. It was very romantic, she thought, but nothing proved more romantic than the view that could be seen from the living room window. The San Francisco Bay was just as visible from Jackson's condo as it was from the restaurant at the pier.

Just as Jasmine was about to head over to the window to take a peek at the view, Jackson grabbed her by the arm, spun her around, and pulled her body up against his. "Jackson, you made a promise," she said, feeling her shirt getting wet from the tiny streams of water that rolled off his shoulders and down his chest, as he had yet to finish drying off.

"I know, and I plan to keep it. I just want to greet my fiancée first."

"What was all that talk about Scout's honor?"

"I was never a Boy Scout," he said with a devilish grin. "Just one kiss, that's all I ask."

"Okay," she said, forcing back a smile. "One kiss—but that's it."

Jasmine could feel her heart starting to pump at a fast pace as Jackson consumed first her upper, then lower lip, suckling them both as if each had been dipped in its own unique flavor. His hands gripped her tighter as he slid his tongue inside her mouth, and she could feel the heaviness of his weight as he leaned into her. It seemed the heavier he grew, the lighter she became and after a brief moment of resistance, she let go and allowed herself to slip away into a state of sheer weightlessness.

That feeling of lightness was one she enjoyed flirting with, and she found it exciting and frightening, all at the same time. Jackson continued to drown her in kisses, and she remained submerged. It wasn't until she felt his hand creeping up the back of her shirt that she finally decided to come up for air.

"Okay, that's it. Go put some clothes on," she said, trying to contain herself.

Laughing, he maintained the firm grip he had on her while she tried pulling away. "Just one more taste," he said, as his head took a dive toward her neck.

Although she allowed him to pull her back into his world, it would only be for a moment. Jasmine may have been considered aggressive by most people's standards, but Jackson was more domineering, and knowing this, she had to fight to hold her ground with him. He had her heart—that she could no longer deny, but she refused to give him all of her...not yet at least. His kisses alone were electrifying, so she knew his sex would have the power to render her senseless.

As his fingers danced along the small of her back, his mouth drifted toward her collarbone, and that's when she had reached her limit. Tearing herself from his embrace, she heard him sigh heavily as she headed toward the window to stare out of it as originally planned. He thought she was simply enjoying the view, but she was allowing herself time to replenish the resolve she held onto so tightly.

"Okay, you win," he said, although not quite ready to give up. "But babe, can you do me a favor?"

"What?" she asked, taking a deep breath while continuing to stare out the window.

"Pick that up for me, will you?"

"Pick up what?" When he didn't respond, she turned around and gasped slightly at the image of his bare, muscular backside, which became permanently seared into her brain as he marched boldly up the stairs.

After draping the damp towel he had dropped against the back of one of the dining room chairs, she took a seat on the couch and waited for him to get dressed. It only took a few minutes before he came running back downstairs wearing a dark blue button down dress shirt and black jeans. Upon noticing his sharp yet casual appearance, she suddenly wished she hadn't come over looking so messy in her velour sweat suit and T-shirt. That combined with the fact that she didn't have on a hint of makeup and her hair was now disheveled, thanks to having driven around town in his drop-top convertible, made her feel self conscious. Yet, he didn't seem to mind her not-so-glamorous look one bit.

Dropping down onto the couch, Jackson pulled Jasmine into a bear hug and the two wrestled playfully for a moment, as she fought to push him away. "You broke your promise," she said, pouting while forcing back a smile.

"I was just playing with you," he said, chuckling while planting soft kisses along her cheek. "I would never do anything to hurt my sweet, innocent angel."

"Stop calling me that."

"What? My sweet, innocent angel?"

"Yes. I'm not that innocent."

"Alright Britney Spears," he said, referencing the pop star's hit single that included the same line. "Well, considering what I'm used to, you may as well be sporting a halo."

"Okay, fine. If I'm your *'innocent angel,'* then you're my angel too."

"How you figure? Don't you see these horns I have tucked behind my ears?"

"Don't say that," she scolded, giving his cheek a playful smack. Then, cradling his face in her hands, she looked him dead in his eyes and said, "You're my angel because you taught me how to love again. I think that deed alone earned you a new set of wings."

Jasmine noticed Jackson's eyes light up, as if he truly was touched by her words. "Well, I won't argue with that," he replied, kissing her softly on the lips.

"Mmm, by the way," she said, pulling away so she could reach inside the pocket of her sweat pants. She then handed him a set of keys and said, "Thanks again for letting me borrow your car."

"Soon, it'll be *our* car," he corrected, kissing her softly once more. "So, your father made it out okay?"

"Yeah, and he congratulated me on our engagement."

"Speaking of which, I spoke with my parents this morning to share the good news and they want us to come home for a visit. I've been wanting you to meet them, and I now have a good reason."

"Oh," she replied, feeling knots form in the pit of her stomach. Her hangover had already subsided, so she knew that was the result of sheer nervousness.

Jackson noticed her tense expression and said with a slight laugh, "Relax. They want to meet you, not *eat* you. I survived meeting your father, so what makes you think you won't survive meeting mine?"

"It's not that."

"Then what is it?"

Jasmine remained silent as she pondered the gravity of the situation. She was slowly digesting the fact that they had gotten engaged, and less than twenty-four hours later, were now planning a trip to meet her future in-laws. She couldn't help but think of how, just a little over a year ago, the mere thought of such a commitment would have sent her packing.

"I know you have a lot of interviews lined up," he continued, "so I told my mother I'd get back to her about a date."

"When were you thinking about going?" she asked, rising from the couch.

"I'll have to talk to my boss, but I'm pretty sure I can get some time off in the next few weeks. How does the second week in June sound?"

"Sure…that should work."

"Great!" he exclaimed, springing up off the couch. "I'll take care of everything. You just be ready to go." He grabbed her by the waist and leaned in for a kiss, which he had expected to be brief based on how she had fought him off earlier, but the two began kissing passionately. She loved inhaling the scent of his freshly bathed skin as it mingled with his cologne, and suddenly felt the urge to take it all in. He was the only thing she could grab hold of at the moment to soothe her rattled nerves.

Jasmine was terrified at the prospect of meeting Jackson's family, yet figured she was going to have to do so sooner or later. With or without an engagement, the two had been dating exclusively for a little over a year, and she really didn't know all there was to know about the reformed player who shockingly seemed to have a heart of gold, despite his former womanizing ways. He had already dismissed certain rumors, like the one about his family being filthy rich and owning a casino. Yet she knew from experience that gossip, even when proven false, often carried some semblance of truth. So, despite her apprehension, she figured it was high time she learned the truth about Mr. Taylor, and his legendary roots.

Chapter 7

Jasmine completed three job interviews just one week after graduation. She had applied for a junior copywriting position with a few ad agencies, two of which were located in San Francisco. Yet, the one she really wanted was for a boutique agency in downtown Oakland. She had dumped the pursuit of law for a writing career, a transition that proved flawless thanks to her English degree. It had been her American Lit professor who encouraged her to make the transition, having lauded her "extraordinary writing ability." Thus, she continued to hone her craft and figured that if she could just get on board with a small company and help take their marketing talent to the next level, the number of doors that would open for her would be countless. Jackson however felt she was making a terrible mistake, for he thought her quick-witted and argumentative nature would have made for a fantastic lawyer.

Although she had gone into each of her interviews feeling very confident, she left them full of anxiety, for she couldn't wait to see if any would result in a call back. To make matters worse, Jackson had already booked their trip to Vegas, and before she knew it, it was time to meet his family.

"I'm here to see Mr. Taylor," she informed the receptionist at the front desk of the building in which he worked, early one Friday morning.

"And whom may I say is here?"

"Jasmine."

"Okay. If you don't mind waiting a moment, I'll have his assistant come out and escort you inside his office."

"Thanks," replied Jasmine, quickly surveying the room. She took a seat in the waiting area, but before she could get comfortable, another woman entered the room.

"Hi, I'm Mr. Taylor's assistant. You can come in now."

Jasmine rose out of her seat and followed the woman inside, taking note of her tight blouse, which appeared to be on the verge of busting open. "Thanks," she said once his assistant opened the door to his office, allowing her to enter.

"Hey, I'll be ready in a minute," said Jackson, as he placed some papers inside his briefcase.

"So, that was your assistant?" she asked, glancing back at the door. "Let me guess, when she comes in to give you your copies, does she lean over the desk like this?" Jasmine leaned forward and pouted, while raising one foot behind her.

"Um, no," Jackson replied, quickly dismissing her sexy impersonation.

"Well, good," said Jasmine, "because if she did, her boobs would be spilling all over the table. It looked like the buttons on her blouse were holding on for dear life…where did these come from?" she asked, changing the subject upon spying half a dozen cupcakes sitting near the edge of his desk.

"Tammy brought those in today to help celebrate the close of a major sale."

"Are these from Baby Cakes?"

"I think so, yes."

"How does she know your favorite bakery?"

"I think that's pretty easy to figure out, thanks to all the deliveries you've sent."

Although Jasmine's blood was starting to boil, she had to admit that he did have a point, for she had been steadily supplying him with his favorite dessert ever since they became an item. He had once shared how his mother had given him cupcakes throughout his childhood and adolescence to help soothe his aches and pains. And, he told her on their first date that she reminded him of one because of her ability to render the same effect—her presence just as comforting as the dessert. Knowing how much he loved them and the significance behind them, she therefore bought him cupcakes periodically as a sign of her love and devotion. It was a special thing between the two of them—a thing she felt no other woman had the right to share.

"Well," she began, folding her arms across her chest, "you tell *Tammy* you already have a delivery girl. Matter of fact, why don't I go tell her now."

"What?" Jackson stepped in front of her, blocking the exit. "Calm down. I don't even know what you're so upset about."

"I'm upset that she thinks she can buy you cupcakes. You know that's our thing."

Although he could see the anger and frustration all over her countenance, that didn't stop him from taunting her. And so, with a devilish grin, he looked at her and asked, "Are you saying you don't want me eating another woman's cupcake?"

Too upset to catch his double entendre, she adamantly replied, "Yes, that's exactly what I'm saying. I don't want you eating anyone else's cupcakes but mine."

"Oh, believe me," he began with one eyebrow raised, "I would love to eat your cupcake, Jasmine, and your cupcake only—"

"Jackson, I'm serious!" she shouted, pouting like a little girl after finally catching his sexual innuendo.

"Okay," he said with laughter in his voice. After retrieving his briefcase, he gave her a quick peck on the cheek then grabbed hold of her hand and said "Baby, I'll take care of this right now." She had no idea what he was planning to do, but felt her stomach drop slightly as he led her out of his office and straight over to Tammy's desk. "Tammy, I'd like to formally introduce you to my fiancée," he said before turning to Jasmine. "Baby, this is my administrative assistant, Tammy."

"Nice to meet you," said Tammy, rising from her chair. She immediately began adjusting her blouse, a move that caused Jasmine to shoot a look at Jackson, who looked back at her and smiled. "I knew he had a girlfriend but wasn't aware he was engaged," continued Tammy, who now appeared nervous. "Congratulations."

"Thanks," replied Jasmine.

"And, just so you know," said Jackson, focusing on Tammy, "she also happens to be my official cupcake provider." He glanced at Jasmine and smirked.

"Oh yes, those little boxes!" said Tammy with a smile. "He's always so happy to receive a delivery from you."

Jasmine didn't say anything and simply smiled.

"Heading out early I see."

"Yes," confirmed Jackson. "I'm taking her home to meet my family. Please forward my calls to my cell phone."

"Will do," assured Tammy. "Have a good weekend."

"You too," said Jackson, leading Jasmine away.

"I don't know if I should slap you or kiss you for that," she whispered, as the two headed for the door.

"If you do it right, I might like both," he replied with a wink.

A short while later, the two entered through the doors of the San Francisco International Airport. The very bumpy hour and a half flight to Vegas had Jasmine on edge, and Jackson unfortunately offered no solace, for he slept during most of the flight. Once the plane landed, Jasmine jumped out of her seat and anxiously headed toward the exit. She wanted nothing more than to grab a cup of coffee, and truthfully, a cigarette, although technically she had quit. Jackson noticed how jumpy she was acting, and put his arm around her to slow her pace. When he asked if she were okay, she quickly replied "Yes," although it was evident she was far from it.

After retrieving their luggage, the pair headed outside the airport, and Jackson guided Jasmine toward the luxury town car he'd reserved. Their driver opened the door for them to enter, and she couldn't help but shake her head and laugh. Here she was worried and tense, thinking they were going to be picked up by his mother or father, who she feared would be armed and ready to bombard her with a slew of questions. Yet, she should have known that a simple taxi ride or pickup from a family member couldn't satisfy his appetite for grandeur and elegance, for she had learned, ever since their first date, when he took her to Chez Panisse and ordered their entire meal in French, that everything with Jackson was top of the line, all the time.

"So, what should I call your parents?" she asked once they had taken a seat inside the vehicle. "Mr. and Mrs. Taylor, or Samuel and Evelyn?" Before he could respond, she bulldozed over him, "Or, maybe I should just let them tell me how they'd like to be addressed..."

"Relax," he said, looking at her and smiling. "My parents aren't old school, so I don't think they'll mind either way."

"I just want to make sure I don't say the wrong thing," she said, wringing her hands.

"Don't worry, everything will be fine." He reached for her hand and interlocked his fingers with hers.

Jasmine knew Jackson was doing his best to comfort her, but there were only a few surefire remedies she was aware of. *Why did I quit smoking?* she thought, as the car barreled down the highway.

About twenty-five minutes later, she noticed the car was slowing down, for it was entering the neighborhood where Jackson's parents lived. She peered out the window and was instantly drawn in by the scenery. "What city is this?" she asked, rolling the window down to take a closer look.

"Summerlin," he replied. "You've heard of Sin City—well that's reserved for the Strip. This, my dear, is *Sun City*—a retirement community with very little action, but plenty of beauty."

And beautiful it was, she thought, upon observing the gorgeous mountain peaks that outlined the horizon, and sprawling green fields. Golf courses, parks, and hiking trails surrounded the quiet yet burgeoning community that was specifically designed to provide retirees the laid back, luxurious lifestyle many dreamed.

As the car cruised along, Jasmine noticed that the homes they were driving by were quite massive, and not ones most would expect those beyond child-rearing years to occupy. *To each his own*, she thought, as she waited for the car to come to a complete stop.

Pulling up to the Taylor residence was quite a sight, as Jackson's parents owned one of the largest homes on the block. The luxury estate, Jasmine would soon discover, sat on about a quarter acre of land. Upon exiting the vehicle, Jackson reached for her hand and began leading her down the flagstone walkway toward the custom designed, mahogany wood doors that curved together at the top like an arch. Once they made it to the doorstep, she began admiring the intricacy of the door, which had iron twisted into an elaborate design, sitting atop glass cutouts in the wood. The pieces of glass provided her a glimpse inside the home, which she could tell had a large foyer, making it seem more like a hotel than someone's residence.

"I thought you said your family wasn't rich?"

"We do okay," Jackson replied with a grin before ringing the doorbell.

Jasmine felt her nerves start to unravel all over again, so she squeezed Jackson's hand tighter. She was completely in awe of her surroundings, but had no idea that the majestic scenery the outside of the home provided would prove nowhere near as exciting as what awaited her on the inside.

Chapter 8

"Mom, Dad, I'd like you to meet my fiancée, Jasmine. Jasmine, meet my parents, Samuel and Evelyn Taylor."

"Nice to meet you," said Jasmine, holding out her hand, only to have it dismissed by her soon-to-be father-in-law, who pulled her into a bear hug.

"Welcome to the family," he said, squeezing her tightly.

Jasmine felt as though her insides were getting crushed against Mr. Taylor's large frame, which emitted his personalized fragrance of tobacco intertwined with a touch of bergamot. It was a scent she found pleasant but was revolting to his wife, who despised his love of cigars. It was his tradition to smoke one whenever he closed a sale, or thought his wife wasn't looking, and had proven to be a habit that not even Jackson, who had strongly urged Jasmine to kick her nicotine habit, could get him to break.

After receiving an equally affectionate yet less overwhelming embrace from Mrs. Taylor, Jasmine stepped back and appraised her future in-laws. Mr. Taylor, who had been surpassed in height by his son, stood at about five feet nine inches tall, and had the build of a WWE wrestler. He was quite fair, and it was clear Jackson had received his chocolate complexion from his mother, who was tall, slender, and had skin as smooth as silk. Upon peering into Mrs. Taylor's dark, deep-set eyes, Jasmine was convinced it was her genes that had proven more dominant.

"It's nice to finally meet you," said Mrs. Taylor. "You're even more beautiful than Jackson described."

"Thanks," she replied, feeling her cheeks grow warm.

"Good job, Son," said Mr. Taylor, giving her the once over. His comment caused everyone to laugh.

"We're looking forward to getting to know you better," stated Mrs. Taylor once the laughter subsided. "Jackson says you're from Los Angeles?"

"Yes, born and raised."

"When he told us he was going back to school, we weren't expecting him to return with a fiancée."

"I wasn't expecting to get engaged either. It was quite a surprise," she replied, starting to feel uneasy. She glanced over at Jackson, and he looked at her and smiled. "You have a lovely home," she said, changing the subject altogether.

"Thank you," replied Mr. and Mrs. Taylor in unison.

"It's probably the largest home I've ever stepped foot in."

"I found it a bit excessive myself," began Mrs. Taylor, stealing a look at her husband. "But, Samuel convinced me it would serve us well in retirement."

"That's interesting," stated Jasmine, as she scanned the elegant yet cozy living room that provided a panoramic view of the backyard. "People usually downsize once they retire. I can only imagine what your previous home looked like."

"Actually, our last home—the one the boys grew up in—was much smaller than this."

"Yes," Jackson confirmed. "I loved that house."

"That's because we built so many precious memories there," offered his mother.

"True," he replied, looking wistful. "I can still recall the many nights Caleb and I sat on top of the roof and talked about our plans for the future—"

"And I recall how you would climb up the trellis and sneak back into your room after having stayed out all night with Xavier," interjected his mother, before shooting him an accusatory look that he neither confirmed nor denied, but simply responded to with a smile. "Samuel's original intent was to convert this home into a Bed and Breakfast," she continued, returning her focus on Jasmine. "It was his attempt at creating yet another stream of income."

"But the homeowners' association voted against it," explained Mr. Taylor, his voice low and scruffy. Jasmine attributed the rough sound to years of tobacco use. "Besides," he continued, clearing his throat, "we were denied the permits required from the city to make the renovations we needed to make, like creating separate entrances to each bedroom so that our guests could come and go as they pleased."

"Well, that just proves there are some things in life not even your persistence can conquer," stated Mrs. Taylor, glancing at her husband. Persistence was a Taylor trait Jasmine was all too familiar with, for Jackson had been nothing but steadfast in his pursuit of her. After a moment of awkward silence, Mrs. Taylor looked at her son and said, "Honey, why don't you show Jasmine to her room. We'll let you two get settled so you can rest up a bit before dinner. Your brothers should be here soon. They're both looking forward to seeing you and meeting your fiancée."

"Great," he replied, reaching for Jasmine's hand. They each took a step forward, but his mom said something that made them both stop abruptly.

"Oh, and by the way, I left a surprise for you inside the kitchen. You may want to wait until after dinner, but I doubt you'll hold out that long."

It only took but a second for he and Jasmine to figure out what that surprise was. After looking at each other and grinning, they said simultaneously, "Cupcakes."

Instead of jetting off toward the kitchen to indulge in his favorite dessert, Jackson led Jasmine toward her room as originally planned. Although she thought the butterflies she'd felt in her stomach earlier in the day would subside once she had met his parents, they still seemed to be flapping their wings as she followed him through the living room and down a hallway that had mahogany French doors at the end. Like the doors that stood at the entrance to the home, these also had an ornate design carved into the wood, but the glass windows were covered with curtains, so she couldn't see what the room looked like on the inside. She wanted to know what was behind those doors, and her curiosity intensified as Jackson led her down the hallway that stood to the right of it, passing it by altogether.

"Votre chambre à coucher mademoiselle," he said before opening the door to the guest bedroom at the end of the second hall.

Jasmine stood near the entrance and admired the décor before entering. It immediately became clear why his parents wanted to turn their home into a B&B because their guest bedroom looked like the presidential suite at the Ritz. It had a king-sized bed positioned in the center that was dressed in an ivory comforter and topped with several fluffy, decorative pillows. Positioned across from it was a fireplace, and to the left of it sat a vanity fit for a queen. To the right was the entrance to the bathroom, which had beautiful marble floors, granite countertops, and contained both a shower and Jacuzzi.

"I could get used to this!" Jasmine exclaimed before pulling the door shut. She threw herself on top of the bed and hugged one of the pillows, which she pretended was Foxy, whom she missed and couldn't wait to see once she made it back to Berkeley. She hoped she wasn't being mistreated at the pet daycare center she'd left her at for the weekend. "I'm gonna catch some z's," she told Jackson before falling back onto the pillows.

"You're kidding, right?"

"Unlike you, I didn't get any sleep on the plane, so no."

"You can't go to sleep. I haven't even finished showing you the house yet. Plus, I plan to take you out after dinner tonight."

"Close the door on your way out," she said, dismissing him with a wave.

"Don't make me come over there."

"You touch me and I'll scream."

"One…two…"

She knew that by the time he reached the count of three, he'd be tickling her relentlessly. "Okay!" she yelled, jumping out of the bed, just as he was about to attack.

"I knew that would get you up," he said, laughing. "Come on."

Jackson led Jasmine back down the hallway and began showing her around the 7,000 square foot, single story home that contained a total of six bedrooms, each with its own bathroom. The luxury estate also contained two laundry rooms, a wine cellar, den, and gourmet kitchen, where Mrs. Taylor was busy preparing their meal for that evening. He then took her out into the yard to show her the sparkling swimming pool, which was in the process of getting cleaned.

"Jackson, is that you?" asked a female voice as soon as they stepped outside.

"Vanessa?" he replied, squinting while examining the young woman who was in the midst of directing the two men who were cleaning out the pool.

"Yes, it's me."

"I almost didn't recognize you," he said, leading Jasmine by the hand as they approached the tall, skinny blonde with big boobs, which appeared to be of the manufactured kind.

"Yeah, I changed my hair," she replied, fluffing her fair tresses with her hands, inadvertently revealing dark roots that indicated she had once been a brunette. "I haven't seen you in a while. Home for a visit?"

"Yes. I came to introduce my fiancée to my parents," he said, glancing at Jasmine, who noticed the woman's cold avoidance of eye contact.

"Fiancée? Oh, okay," she said with a giggle.

"What's so funny?" Jasmine asked, frowning.

"Well, um…" Vanessa pressed her lips together firmly, as if to prevent what she really wanted to say from escaping. She then spoke slowly, as if she were carefully choosing her words. "It's just…I never pegged you the marrying type," she said finally, focusing her eyes on Jackson.

Jackson didn't say anything in response to Vanessa's remark, but Jasmine could tell by her comment and the way she was gawking at him that there had once been something between them. Before either of them could say anything, one of the pool cleaners called out to her, and she excused herself.

"I'll see you around," she said, turning to leave. Jackson, ready to head back inside the house, returned his focus on Jasmine.

"You ready to finish the tour?"

"Sure," she said, glancing back at Vanessa. "Did you two used to date?"

"No."

"Really?" she asked with an incredulous stare. "So how do you know her then?"

"Her father owns the pool cleaning company. I met her when my parents first moved here and began using their services."

"And you never dated?"

"We hung out a few times, but I don't consider that dating."

He extended his hand for her to take, but before grabbing hold, she glanced over her shoulder once more at Vanessa and noticed how she quickly turned her head, pretending as if she hadn't been looking her way as well. Deciding she wasn't going to allow such an uncomfortable encounter to ruin her trip, which had only just begun, she took hold of her fiancé's hand and followed him back inside the house, where he took her on a trip down memory lane.

Chapter 9

Lining the hallway walls that led from the kitchen to the foyer were photos of Jackson and his family. Jasmine began admiring one photo in particular, a family portrait that had been taken when Jackson was just ten years old. It was of him and his younger brother Caleb, sitting in front of their mom and dad. To the right of it was a photo of his older brother, Xavier, which had been taken when he was a teenager. For a moment, she wondered why Xavier had not been included in the family portrait, until Jackson reminded her that he was his father's son from a previous marriage, and therefore wasn't always around to participate in activities like family picture day.

"I can tell from these photos that you and your brothers have different personalities," she said, noting the different poses and expressions captured in each brother's collection.

"Yeah, we are quite different," he confirmed with a grin.

The two continued to make their way down the row of photos, and Jasmine admired the beautiful images of his parents, grandparents, nieces, and nephew. Although she enjoyed all the images, there was one photo in particular that really captured her attention. It was a 24"x36" black and white portrait of Jackson and his two brothers engaged in laughter.

"I was sixteen, Xavier, thirty-one and Caleb, twelve."

"Now this is what I call a Kodak moment," she stated, while continuing to take in the image of the three brothers.

Xavier, who was standing on the left wearing a three-piece suit and tie, had one arm draped around Jackson and the other at his chest, holding a fedora over his heart. He had been captured in the midst of telling a joke, for his lips were parted and his eyes were focused on

Jackson, who, similarly dressed, was grinning from ear to ear with his head tilted downward. Caleb was standing on the opposite side of Jackson wearing a plain dress shirt, his arm draped around his brother's shoulder. He was the only one looking directly into the camera, but was smiling just as hard as his brothers.

"It looks like you guys were having a great time."

"Yes," replied Jackson, staring at the photo intensely as if he were looking beyond it and into the past. "We were at my cousin's wedding, enjoying the festivities and libations—well, at least Xavier and I were. Caleb was too young to drink."

"Weren't you as well?" she asked, looking puzzled. "I thought you said you were sixteen?"

"I was, but according to Xavier, I was a young man, not a boy." His smile slowly began to fade, and he suddenly appeared eager to move on. "Come, I have one last room to show you." He led her back down the hall, past the foyer and through the living room, until they eventually made their way down the same hallway where the room with the mahogany French doors she had admired earlier, stood at the end. She stood back while he pulled the doors open, presenting her with the one room she had yet to enter.

"Wow," she exclaimed.

Mr. Taylor's den, or "man cave," as his wife called it, was more grand than she had imagined, for it contained a fireplace and wet bar, and had what appeared to be tons and tons of books lining the walls. Toward the back of the room was a beautiful, large oak table that had what appeared to be a worn out leather office chair behind it.

"Is this real wood?" asked Jasmine, tracing the rings around the table with her finger.

"Yes," Jackson replied. "It's solid oak. My father always said that a man's word should be this strong." He knocked on the table with his fist before pointing to the tattered chair behind it. "That chair," he explained, "has been in this family for years. It's the one item my father refuses to upgrade—"

"And that table has been around for as long as I've been alive," shared a voice from behind.

"Caleb!" exclaimed Jackson with excitement as he turned to greet his brother, who had just entered the room. Jasmine turned around also and watched as Jackson approached his younger brother, who stood at the entrance to the den wearing a pair of baggy, distressed blue jeans, a black leather moto jacket, and black highway boots. He had a motorcycle helmet tucked underneath one arm, which he moved to his hand so he could fully embrace his brother.

"How've you been?"

"Good, and you?" replied Jackson.

"I'm good," said Caleb, glancing past his brother and smiling. "But, by the looks of things, I'd say you've been great. This must be the future Mrs. Taylor," he added, nodding in Jasmine's direction.

"Yes," replied Jackson. "Jasmine, meet my little brother, Caleb."

"Nice to meet you," she replied, shaking his hand and smiling. "I've heard so much about you."

"Hopefully all good," he said, holding her gaze.

She tried her best not to stare, but the photos Jackson had shared of his "little" brother, who was actually quite substantial in size, had not done him justice, for he was more handsome than his pictures suggested. And although she could see the family resemblance, there were quite a few differences between the two. For one, Caleb wasn't fair like their father, nor was he as dark as their mother, but rather his complexion fell somewhere in the middle, and she thought that if he were a coffee drink, he'd be a warm macchiato; his father, the color of café au lait; and Mrs. Taylor and Jackson, two creamy chocolate espressos.

Caleb, who had his father's build, stood a few inches shorter than Jackson, and was much stockier. Although he also had his mother's dark, enchanting eyes, they didn't appear as intimidating against his warm, brown skin. His best feature though, Jasmine would soon discover, was his crooked smile. There was something charming yet mischievous about it, and she found it very endearing.

"I didn't mean to interrupt your tour," stated Caleb.

"No worries," said Jasmine. "This room was our last stop."

"It's great, isn't it?" he asked, his eyes scanning the room. "It's my favorite room in the house."

"I have to take this," said Jackson after his cell phone started ringing. "I'll be back in a sec." He stepped outside the room, leaving her and Caleb alone to get better acquainted.

"I love that picture of you and your brothers out in the hall. It looks like you guys were having so much fun."

"Oh, you mean the black and white one?"

"Yes," she confirmed. "I don't have any siblings, but that picture seems to capture the true essence of brotherhood."

"Yeah, we definitely had some great times together," said Caleb with a twinkle in his eye. "Jackson has always been a great older brother. He taught me a lot. I wouldn't be able to tie my shoes or tell time if it weren't for him."

"I think you give him too much credit," she said, giggling. "I'm sure you would have learned how to do those things somehow, someway."

"True," he agreed before flashing a crooked smile.

"So, if Jackson taught you all that, what did Xavier teach you?" She noticed how his smile soon faded once she started talking about his eldest brother.

"Let's just say…I've learned more of what not to do by watching him."

There was a brief moment of awkward silence, as she wasn't sure how to respond to his candid comment. Luckily, they were both relieved from having to think of a way to change the subject when they heard a knock at the door.

Chapter 10

"**K**nock, knock," said a tall, light skinned gentleman, gently rapping his fist against one side of the already open, mahogany French doors.

"Speak of the devil—" whispered Caleb, as Xavier took slow strides in their direction.

"Well, well, well, what do we have here?"

"Xavier, this is Jackson's fiancée, Jasmine. Jasmine, this is Xavier."

"You're more beautiful than the flower."

"Thank you," she replied, extending her hand for him to shake. He looked nothing like his two brothers, she thought, for not only was he the fairest and tallest of the three, but he also had emerald green eyes that set him apart, and his hair was cut so low that he was practically bald. Although tall and on the slender side, Xavier had become quite settled, his stomach slightly pudgy from the excessive alcohol consumption and late night buffet runs he'd indulged in over the years. The one thing the brothers all seemed to have in common, she thought, was a great sense of style that complemented their individuality, for he looked just as sharp in his polo shirt and khaki pants as his two brothers did in their casual attire.

"Now, is that any way to greet your future brother-in-law?" he asked, staring down at her hand. "We're family." He pulled her into a hug, and Caleb kept a steady eye on him as he pulled away slowly, planting a soft kiss on her left cheek. "So, Jackson tells me you're into marketing, is that right?" he asked before turning away and heading toward the wet bar to pour himself a drink.

"Yes," she replied. "Well, not exactly. I recently interviewed with a few advertising agencies, but haven't landed a gig yet."

"Cool. Well, I'm sure the world can benefit from your talent," he replied, tossing a few ice cubes into a lowball glass. "Care for a drink?"

"No thanks," said Jasmine, as she headed over to one of the bookcases to browse through Mr. Taylor's collection. It didn't take long for her eyes to land on one book in particular. "Zora Neale Hurston— she's one of my favorite authors!" she proclaimed while excitedly pulling a book off the shelf.

"Are you an avid reader?" asked Xavier after taking a sip of the scotch whisky he had just poured for himself.

Caleb continued to eye him as he stepped away from the wet bar and headed toward Jasmine, where he positioned himself behind her to glare over her shoulder at the book she held. Feeling his breath against the back of her neck made her feel uneasy, so she took a step forward to put some space between them, but he simply moved to the right of her and leaned against the bookcase, his body facing her side.

"I…um, I majored in English, so I had to read a lot," she said, stumbling over her words.

"Oh, I see," said Xavier, staring at her lecherously as he took the last swig of his drink. He used his free hand to grab a lock of her hair, his fingers sliding down the length of the strands. "If you have time, maybe you can read me a bedtime story," he muttered with a devilish grin. It was a look that resembled the cocky expression Jackson sometimes gave, except she found something very sinister in his.

Jasmine grabbed Xavier's wrist, and he surrendered the hold he had on her hair. Satisfied, she released him and returned the book to the shelf. "I'm going to go see if your mother needs help in the kitchen," she informed Caleb as she passed by him on her way out of the room. Xavier began heading toward the door as well, but Caleb positioned himself in front of him.

"You're lucky Jackson didn't see that."

"See what? I think you need to get your eyes checked."

"And maybe you just need to get checked," said Caleb, grabbing him by the arm.

Xavier glared down at the hold Caleb had on his arm before yanking it free. "What did I tell you about that, huh? You'd better have your bail money ready—"

"What's going on?" asked Jackson, upon re-entering the room. He noticed the tense exchange between his two brothers, who tried to play it cool once he stepped inside.

"Nothing man, how's it going?" asked Xavier, shooting Caleb an icy look.

"Good," Jackson replied, as the two embraced wholeheartedly. "It's been a minute."

"Yes, it has," said Xavier. "I still have the same number you know."

"I haven't done a very good job of keeping in touch, and for that, I'm sorry."

"It's cool, I understand. I was just about to pour myself another drink. Want one?"

"No thanks," said Jackson, as he headed toward Caleb.

"You and I haven't talked in a minute either," stated Caleb, smiling as his brother approached. "So, how are things out in Cali?"

"They're good, can't complain. You should come out sometime."

"I will. We need to plan that Hollywood trip we've been talking about."

Xavier stood behind the wet bar and found himself becoming annoyed by the camaraderie between his two brothers. He was still salty about not having been invited on their European excursion a few years back, so after pouring himself another glass of scotch, he sauntered over and rudely butted into their conversation.

"You know," he began, pausing to take a sip of his drink, "you really should take that trip out to Hollywood." Jackson and Caleb looked at him, but he appeared to be directing his conversation solely at Caleb. "I hear they're finally making a sequel to Brokeback Mountain," he continued. "You should audition."

Caleb glared at him and responded without skipping a beat. "You know what? I would, but I was told you already had the part." He and Jackson erupted with laughter, but Xavier wasn't the least bit amused.

"We're going out tonight, right?" asked Xavier, tapping Jackson, who was still laughing, lightly on the shoulder.

"I can't," he replied, noting the look of disappointment that spread across his brother's face. "I promised Jazz I'd take her to the Strip. She's never been. Rain check?"

"Breaking her in...*niiice*," said Xavier with a smirk. "Well okay, but I plan to cash that check in, soon. We haven't been out in a while. It'll be just like old times."

"Sounds good," said Jackson, glancing over at Caleb. "You're down too, right?"

"Who, church boy?" asked Xavier, before Caleb had a chance to respond. "Nah, I plan to stay out past his bedtime."

"That's funny," said Caleb, looking at Xavier with disdain. "Last time I checked, the only person who has an obligation to be home by a certain time is you. By the way, how is your wife?"

"You need to learn how to mind your own business," Xavier growled, taking a step forward. Caleb also took a step forward, and Jackson wedged himself between the two and braced a hand against each of their chests. Before either of them could say anything, the sound of Mrs. Taylor's voice pierced the air, further assisting in putting an end to the madness.

"Caleb, come here please!" she yelled from outside the room.

Xavier knew that physically, he was no match for Caleb, but when it came to sparring with words, he was all in. "Your mama's calling," he announced with a smirk. "Go on now."

Caleb kept his eyes locked on Xavier, his stance wide and shoulders squared. After hearing his mother call for him once more, he finally disengaged from their harsh stare-down and returned his focus on Jackson. "I'll be back," he said.

Jackson nodded and watched him exit the room before turning toward Xavier, who seemed to be burning a hole in the spot where Caleb once stood. "What was that all about?" he asked, glancing back at the door.

"Baby boy's been smelling his own piss for a while now," replied Xavier, as he headed back toward the bar. "You should see the way he kisses ass at work. He's somehow got it in that tiny little brain of his that he's a better salesman than me. *Please*. I was selling real estate when his ass was in diapers."

He began pouring another glass of scotch, while Jackson simply shook his head, unsure of what to make of the discord that now threatened their brotherly bonds. As the middle child, he had always served as a bridge connecting his two brothers, who had always been different as night is from day. Yet, with Xavier being the older, experienced brother he could look up to, and Caleb, the young, wise sage he could count on and confide in, he admired them both. It had always been his desire for the three of them to remain close, but apparently, in the interim of having lived apart from them for a while, the gap that had always existed between them had widened, making it more difficult for the three to stay united.

"How are things at work?" asked Jackson, hoping to gain better insight as to what had gone down in his absence.

"They're alright...I guess. They'd be much better if the old man gave me more responsibilities though."

"How so?"

"No disrespect, but I think he's becoming more and more incapable of making sound decisions."

"And what makes you say that?"

"Look around you," said Xavier, throwing his hands into the air. "I'd say buying this house is indication enough. Who in their right mind would buy a house this big—that requires this much upkeep during retirement?"

"His original plan was—"

"His original plan failed," interrupted Xavier, cutting him off. "Ah, I don't even want to talk about it anymore," he said with a dismissive wave. "I want to learn more about what's been going on with you. What you riding around in out there in Cali?"

"I still have the Mercedes."

"That old thing?"

"Old?" Jackson laughed. "I've only had it a little over three years."

"Well, it's time you traded it in. Here," said Xavier, tossing him a set of keys.

"A Lambo, wow," replied Jackson after observing the logo on the keychain.

"I call it the pussy wagon. You ride around in one of them, and you'll hear the kitties purr."

"Thanks," began Jackson, tossing the keys back, "but I'll stick with what I've got."

"Suit yourself," Xavier replied, shrugging.

Jackson couldn't help but notice how his brother, who was still very much married the last time he checked, hadn't mentioned anything about his wife or children, and was now talking as if he were a single man in his twenties again.

"I'm surprised Sheila let you get a ride like that," he said, trying to read his brother, who appeared indifferent. "How is she doing by the way?"

"She's good, I guess," he said, shrugging.

"What's that supposed to mean?"

"You know how women are. One minute they're up and the next, down. I can't figure it out."

"So, I assume things are down at the moment?"

"Oh, we're working on it," he said before taking another sip of his drink.

Seeing that he wasn't going to get much information regarding their current marital status, Jackson decided to drop the subject altogether and began to inquire about his nieces and nephew, who he hadn't seen in a while. "How are the kids?"

"Those little crumb snatchers? They're good."

"That's good to hear," said Jackson, smiling. "Tell them Uncle J misses them."

"Will do," said Xavier, staring into his half empty glass. "You sure you don't want a drink?"

"Yeah, I'm good."

"I hate drinking alone. It makes me feel like…"

"An alcoholic?"

"Now, here you go…"

Just as the two brothers were wrapping up their conversation, Jasmine re-entered the den to announce that dinner was finally ready.

"Have you met Xavier?" asked Jackson as she made her way over to join them.

"Yes, we've met," she replied, glaring at Xavier, who looked at her and winked.

"Oh okay. Well then, I guess it's time we head on over to the dining room. Xavier, you coming?"

"Nah," he replied, setting his empty glass down onto the wet bar. "I'm gonna head home. Will catch you later though—to cash in that check."

"Sounds good," said Jackson, wrapping his arm around Jasmine's waist. The couple saw Xavier to the door before heading toward the dining room, where they enjoyed a nice home-cooked meal with the rest of the family. After they were both fully satiated, they each retreated to their separate bedrooms to change clothes and prepare for their night out on the Strip.

Chapter 11

Jackson took Jasmine to the Bellagio, for he thought it the perfect spot to take her on her first night out in Vegas. For one, the famous water show that took place in front of the hotel and casino, paired with its whimsical lights and music, provided a very romantic setting. She found herself getting lost in the performance, while he became lost in her. He enjoyed watching her expressions of awe and excitement, and was hoping to make the night truly memorable.

"What?" she asked, once she finally peeled her eyes away from the fountain to find him staring at her, his dark eyes smoldering.

"Nothing," he replied, although his expression said otherwise. "Come on. I want to take you inside."

He took her by the hand and led her through the doors of the hotel and casino, which was bustling with patrons. She thought he was guiding her to the casino floor, where she was raring to go, but instead, he stopped at the registration desk.

"Long time no see," said the middle-aged gentleman positioned behind the counter. He and Jackson bumped fists before he glanced over at Jasmine, his eyes now wide. "When you told me you were in town and bringing your fiancée, I almost had a heart attack."

"Very funny," replied Jackson before turning to Jasmine. "Babe, I'd like you to meet my friend, Julian."

"Hello," she said, extending her hand.

"Hello," he replied. "Jackson always could pull the dimes."

"Thanks…I think," she said before stepping away to take in the opulence of the lobby.

"You ready?" asked Jackson, once he and Julian ended their conversation.

"Yes," she replied, taking his hand. It wasn't until they stopped in front of a row of elevators that she asked, "Where are we going?"

"You'll see."

Once inside, Jasmine watched as Jackson removed a room key from the pocket of his suit jacket. She hadn't seen his friend at the counter hand it to him, because she was too busy eyeing the lobby.

"Are we going to the presidential suite?" she asked, once he inserted it inside the designated slot and pressed the button with the number thirty on it.

"You ask a lot of questions, you know that? I told you; you'll see where we're going soon enough. It's a surprise."

"Whatever you say," she said, growing antsier by the minute. Once the elevator finally stopped on their floor, Jackson positioned himself behind her and placed his hands over her eyes. "What are you doing?" she asked, giggling while trying to walk without sight.

"I told you, it's a surprise. I'll let you see where we're going in a minute." He guided her steps down the hall, and once they made it to the door of the room he had reserved, he spun her around so that she was facing him. Without breaking eye contact, he inserted the key into the lock. "Take a look," he said, nodding toward the room once he opened the door.

Jasmine turned around and was instantly amazed by the luxurious suite, which had a living room fully equipped for relaxation and entertainment. There was a large, flat screen television positioned on the wall in front of the couch, and an electric fireplace beneath it. The suite also included a small dining area, sleeping area, and his and her bathrooms.

"Wow," she said, taking a tour of the room, which looked more like a one-bedroom apartment considering it was just as, if not more spacious than the one she lived in. After glancing around the bedroom with the plush, king-sized bed, she then headed back into the living room and stood in front of the floor-to-ceiling window to take a peek at the view, which included The Eiffel Tower of Paris Las Vegas amidst the backdrop of fully lit hotels and casinos. "This view is amazing."

"It is," agreed Jackson, approaching her slowly from behind. "But, I'm not talking about that," he said, pointing toward the window. "I'm talking about the one right in front of me." He slid a hand down the sheer sleeve of her black cocktail dress and said, "I don't think I told you how beautiful you look tonight."

She stared at their reflections in the window and could see that he had removed his suit jacket, and his eyes were now fixated on her neck. "Thank you," she replied, watching as he swept away the soft curls she had crafted with a curling wand off her shoulders. "Why do we need a room if we're staying with your parents?" she asked, feeling butterflies fluttering inside her stomach.

"I figured if we stay out too late, we might just want to crash here," he said. There was a brief moment of silence before he raised his hand again. This time, he used his index finger to trace a line from the back of her ear and down her neck, the tingling sensation causing her to pull away. When she turned to face him, their eyes met. Instantly, she became hypnotized by the spectacular show of lights that exploded in a miraculous display, as the images she had just seen of the city, shone vibrantly against his dark, lustrous irises. "I love you, Jasmine," he said, staring down at her. He expected her to tell him she loved him, too, but instead she remained silent, for he had no idea she was caught in a daze. "Jasmine," he said, bringing her back into the moment.

"Um, sorry," she said, trying to regain control of her senses. Enchanted by his beautiful eyes, the lavish room, and the magic of the city, Jasmine felt herself falling head first into the moment and knew that if they didn't leave the room soon, there was no telling what she might do. "Let's head to the casino now," she said, unable to hide her jitters.

Jackson stared at her for a moment, a look of disappointment briefly washing over him. "Okay," he replied, following her to the door.

He took her on a tour of the casino, where she gambled for the first time. "All this smoke in here is making me nostalgic," she said, eagerly inhaling the second-hand smoke of the patrons.

"Don't even think about it," Jackson warned, for he hadn't missed her nicotine-filled kisses one bit.

After deciding she had lost all she was willing to lose for the night, Jackson took her beyond the bright lights of Las Vegas Boulevard to an area downtown known as the Arts District. He parked in front of a row of houses that had been tagged with art and for a moment, she thought he had taken her to the hood.

"These houses are designated for taggers," he explained. "The police figured the best way to put a stop to all the graffiti cropping up around the city would be to give the artists a legitimate place and space to display their talent."

Jasmine thought it was cool that the city provided these unconventional artists an opportunity to express their creativity and suddenly found the whole vibe oddly familiar. "This sort of reminds me of Berkeley," she said. "A place where you're free to be who you are."

"I figured you'd think that," he replied, smiling. "Come, there's one last place I want to take you."

After a short drive, the two ended up at what used to be one of his favorite hangouts: the Center Bar inside the Hard Rock Hotel. It was situated a few blocks East of the Strip, but despite its location, it was still considered an epicenter of action and entertainment for those wishing to experience all that Vegas had to offer. The place was brimming with locals and tourists, some of who were there to party while others merely considered it a pit stop before venturing to their next destination.

As the couple strolled down the hall that led from the parking garage elevators to the hotel and casino, they took time to admire all the rock n' roll memorabilia lining the walls, not to mention some of the interesting shops that stood along the way. They even peered inside the Hart and Huntington Tattoo shop, where they spied brave souls, both young and old, getting fresh ink. Before they knew it, they were on the casino floor where the Center Bar stood, smack dab in the center of it, just as its name suggested.

Jackson led Jasmine by the hand as they made their way toward an open area of the bar. They took seats in a section where a female bartender was already busy serving other customers, so they had to wait a bit. Her back was to them when they approached, but she eventually turned around and was apparently startled, for she ceased shaking the mixer she held in her hands and stared at them both with eyes wide and mouth agape. Taken aback by her expression, Jasmine glanced at Jackson, who, to her surprise, appeared stunned as well.

"Jackson Taylor," murmured the bartender, slowly regaining her composure. She resumed the up and down motion with the shaker then said, "Long time no see."

"Hello Charmaine," he replied after a long pause. The two stared at each other for a moment—a long moment, and Jasmine felt like she was dealing with the pool cleaner's daughter all over again.

"So, what can I get you?" asked the bartender, trying to remain professional despite her apparent discomfort.

"I'll take a Sidecar, and you?" asked Jackson, turning toward Jasmine.

"I'll just have a Sprite," she replied, remembering the hangover she had suffered after graduation.

"Coming right up."

"I'm going to go powder my nose," said Jasmine, excusing herself from the bar.

A few moments later, Charmaine returned with their drinks. "Here you go," she said, setting two glasses down onto the counter. "Where's your friend?"

"The bathroom," Jackson replied, peering into her eyes. Although he hadn't seen her in about four years, she was as he remembered her— slender yet curvy with exotic features. "You look good."

"So do you," she said, and for a moment he thought all had been forgiven. "Although, I'm sure that deal you made with the devil is what's keeping you fine."

"Charmaine—"

"Save it. I've already heard everything you have to say," she snapped, fighting the urge to throw his drink at him. He was able to stay dry thanks to Jasmine, who she spotted heading back from her trip to the restroom. "So, is that your latest victim?"

Jackson glanced over his shoulder at Jasmine, who was steadily approaching. "Actually," he began, unsure of whether he should feed her curiosity or not, "that's my fiancée."

"Fiancée?" she asked with a laugh laced with skepticism. Shaking her head, she pursed her lips together then said, "Poor thing has no idea what she's getting into."

"People can change, Charmaine. I have."

"Bullshit."

Jasmine returned to the bar just as Charmaine began making her way over to another area where new customers awaited. "I guess they're taking this whole 'sex, drugs, and rock n' roll' theme seriously," she said, resuming her seat next to him. "Did you know they have containers in the bathroom where you can safely dispose of hypodermic needles? There can't be that many diabetics in here…" Her voice trailed off once she noticed he wasn't listening. His silence prompted her to follow his gaze, and she saw that he was staring off into space, his pensive look very telling. "So, I take it that's another woman you never dated?"

Jackson took a swig of his drink and remained silent for a moment. "We dated," he said finally, throwing a tip onto the counter. "You ready?"

He turned to leave, and Jasmine stared down at her Sprite. "I haven't even taken a sip yet," she said, although it was clear he wasn't going to wait for her to drink it. After taking a quick sip, she followed him out of the bar and wondered why he was suddenly so desperate to leave.

Chapter 12

Jasmine spent her second day in Vegas with Mrs. Taylor, who wanted to become better acquainted with her future daughter-in-law. After indulging in a few relaxing treatments at Spa Mandalay, the two headed out for what would prove to be one of the greatest shopping extravaganzas Jasmine had ever experienced. Sure, she had done some great shopping in L.A. and the Bay, thanks to the Westfield centers and of course the Garment District, which she frequented whenever she paid a visit to her hometown. Yet, Vegas had a plethora of malls and outlets, and she particularly enjoyed hitting up her favorite stores Bebe and Caché while touring the Grand Canal Shoppes at the Venetian. The massive Forever 21 inside the Fashion Show Mall could rival the three-story version on Powell Street in San Francisco, and the Prada store inside the Bellagio was a fashion snob's dream. There was no way she and Mrs. Taylor could cover all the shopping there was to be had, and she was careful not to wear Mrs. Taylor out. If shopping were an Olympic sport, Jasmine would be a gold medalist, and she figured if heaven truly consists of all the things one loves, then she had found hers, in Sin City no less.

"What's in here?" she asked Mrs. Taylor, who led her through the doors of A Hollywood Bridal and Tux, a wedding gown superstore on the Strip.

"Wedding gowns silly. Wouldn't you like to look at some?"

Suddenly, Jasmine felt her chest tighten, and her breathing grew shallow. "Uh…wedding gowns? Don't you think it's a bit premature to be doing this?"

"How so?" asked Mrs. Taylor, puzzled. "You are getting married, aren't you?"

"Yeah—yes, but—"

"But what? You'll need a gown, dear. The dress is one of the greatest parts of your special day. When is the wedding by the way?"

Jasmine took a deep breath, as she tried to gather her thoughts. Mrs. Taylor obviously had no clue that as a recovering commitment phobe, making plans for happily ever after wasn't necessarily at the top of her to-do list. She and Jackson hadn't even talked about a wedding let alone what their life would be like post ceremony, so all this was quite new to her. She was trying to take things a step at a time, but was now feeling pressured to move several steps further than she had planned.

"Um…we haven't set a date yet."

"Oh, okay," said Mrs. Taylor, watching lines of stress suddenly appear across Jasmine's forehead. "Well, we can do this some other time then?"

"Sure," she said, as the two headed out the door.

*****

Jackson and Caleb played mercy in the middle of the Nevada desert while their father retrieved some items from the trunk of his car. "Ha!" Caleb shouted, holding his arms victoriously high above his head after granting Jackson's wish to be relieved of the pain he inflicted upon him during the few minutes they'd been outside. "I knew you'd break before me, just like old times."

"Please," said Jackson, dusting dirt off his trousers. "I let you win."

"Yeah right—"

"Here," interrupted Mr. Taylor, approaching his grown sons, who had spent most of the morning laughing and joking around as though they were teenagers again. He handed Jackson a long cardboard tube with a white plastic cap on the end, then watched as he opened it and pulled out the rolled up piece of paper inside. Jackson handed the empty container to Caleb, who threw it over his shoulder and then under his arm as if it were a pair of nunchucks.

"The two of you quit horsing around," commanded their father. "You're acting like two-year-olds."

"Ahem, sorry," said Jackson, choking back laughter as he glanced over at Caleb, who was also struggling to conceal his amusement.

"I'm sure you're both wondering why I brought you out here. This…" began their father, pausing to point toward the horizon, "…is your future." The three stood side-by-side and stared at the barren field that lay before them. Then, after a brief moment of silence, the senior Mr. Taylor turned toward his sons and asked, "So, what do you think?"

"Um…I think my future had better include some water, because it's hot and dusty out here—wherever *here* is," said Jackson, turning around to take in the great expanse.

"You always were a smart ass," proclaimed his father, as he headed toward his parked Maybach. "Perhaps you'll understand things better once I finish explaining. Come."

Jackson and Caleb followed Mr. Taylor to the trunk of his car, upon which he instructed them to spread out the rolled up piece of paper Jackson was holding. The three of them examined it closely, and Jackson wasn't quite sure what he was looking at, although he'd soon discover it was a blueprint for something grand.

"I recently purchased this land with the money I earned after selling those high rises at the top of the market. I had the same impression as you at first, because I wasn't quite sure this was the place I wanted to carry out my vision. But, given the current market, once I saw the price tag, I knew it was too good to pass up. What you're looking at is the new location of Taylor & Sons Realty. As you know, we currently have twelve staff members that work remotely, but I think it's time I gave them an office."

Jackson surveyed the blueprints, which contained plans for a building much larger than what would be required to house a twelve member staff, and wondered what his father was getting into. "I can understand you needing more room than what the den at the house provides, but is all this space necessary?"

"This will house more than just a real estate agency," informed Mr. Taylor, who had yet to fully describe the details of his master plan. "Sure, the main focus will be our business, and I plan to designate a space for our commercial division, and another for our residential. But, considering we often partner with top tier businesses that need help locating real estate suitable for their operations, as well as many individuals in search of their dream home, I figured we need to offer our clients something that will set us apart from our competitors. Something that will keep them coming back and sending more clients our way."

"And that is?"

"A one-stop shop. A place where one can find the new office or home of their dreams, grab a bite to eat, and take care of whatever errands they need to run—all in the same place."

"What?" inquired Jackson, who had yet to see the connection between his father's real estate business and proposed strip mall.

"Let me show you," said his father, pointing toward the blueprint. "Here is where we'll build the dining hall that will serve breakfast and lunch. It'll have Wi-Fi stations for those wanting to check their email or surf the web. And here," he continued, pointing at a different location, "…is where we'll put a convenience store so that our clients can pick up whatever knick-knacks they might need; and here is where the dry cleaners will be. I'm even thinking about putting in a nail and hair salon for your mother and that pretty little lady of yours," he said with a wink.

Mr. Taylor then pointed toward a large rectangular shaped area on the map, "Here is where our training academy will be. Although this family has always valued education, a college degree isn't always desirable or feasible for some. That is why I intend to build a training academy for those wishing to learn the ins and outs of the real estate industry. Although any and all are welcome, our program will cater to high school students, as this may provide hope for those unsure of what path to take upon graduating. Since a four-year institution may not be in their plans, this will provide them an opportunity to get the ball rolling on a career before they get their diplomas. We'll provide internships and help them ace their broker's exam. I also hope to provide scholarships to those wishing to further their education as you two have."

"Wow," stated Jackson, taking a step back. "This all sounds great, Dad, but don't you think it's a little ambitious?"

"What do you mean?"

"With all due respect, I don't see how building an epicenter as the one you just described is conducive to your retirement. I thought you cashed out your investments so that you could reduce your schedule; no more property management—"

"What good is it to sit on top of money like that?" asked Mr. Taylor, frowning at his middle son. "There are only so many nice dinners, fancy cars, and holes of golf to enjoy. I'd much rather invest my money and know it's being put to good use."

"I understand," Jackson replied, "but, you promised mom you'd slow down—"

"He doesn't know the meaning of the term," whispered Caleb.

"My ears aren't in retirement yet either," countered the senior Mr. Taylor, shooting Caleb a sharp glance. "I plan to keep my promise," he assured. "And, I'll be better able to do so with your help."

Jackson stared at his father, dreading what he was about to say next. *This is why he wanted me to come out here*, he thought.

"I want you and Caleb to head up this new venture," he said, confirming Jackson's suspicion. "I'll be involved, but on a consulting basis only. It's going to take young blood like yours to get this going."

"Dad—"

"Just think about it," interrupted Mr. Taylor, sensing but ignoring his son's hesitation.

"You knew about all this?" asked Jackson, turning toward Caleb.

"Yeah, but I was waiting for Dad to tell you. I think it's a great idea. And, you and I have always made a great team..."

"Shouldn't Xavier be included in this conversation?" asked Jackson, his eyes darting back and forth between his father and Caleb, who stared at each other as though they were sharing a secret neither was ready to reveal.

"Um, look—" began Caleb before his father cut him off.

"Xavier forfeited his share in this endeavor the moment he decided to make Jack Daniel's his best friend."

"What?!" exclaimed Jackson, belting out a laugh at their overly serious tones. "Xavier has always been known to have a good time, but he can certainly hold his own. Besides, he's worked for you a long time, Dad—longer than I did. That's got to count for something."

"Your brother needs help."

"Yeah, he does," confirmed Caleb. "Things have really gotten out of hand these last few months. He's been coming to work late and almost walked into a meeting drunk. I had to restrain him, and he threatened to have me arrested for assault."

"You're kidding."

"I wish I was. It's like he's slowly coming apart at the seams."

"Your brother's right; Xavier is out of control. I can't trust him with something as important as this—not now. Hell, if Sheila, who he vowed before God to honor and cherish can't get him to act right, what makes you think we can? It's a wonder she's put up with his philandering for as long as she has."

Caleb nodded in agreement, and although Jackson wasn't yet sold on the assertion that his brother was an alcoholic, he knew they were right about his sister-in-law putting up with a lot. After all, it was common knowledge that infidelity had always plagued their relationship, for Xavier had never been discreet about his numerous affairs. Hoping that things would get back on track for his big brother, and wanting to believe what he'd said about things being fine, Jackson tried to offer his father and brother a little reassurance.

"He told me they were working things out."

"Hogwash," sputtered his father, immediately dismissing his claim. "Sheila kicked him out six months ago. He's been staying in one of our corporate rentals for free, although I'm about to start deducting the rent from his paycheck."

Jackson rubbed his beard and gazed up at the clear blue sky. He didn't want to believe the accusations Caleb and his father were making against Xavier, and was certain this was all just some sort of big misunderstanding that could be cleared up with the right amount of communication. After all, the Taylors were known for their persuasive powers, so Jackson was confident he could get to the bottom of things.

"Let me talk to him."

"You think we haven't tried that?" asked Caleb.

"We practically gave your brother an intervention, and he dismissed everything we said to him as if we were blowing things out of proportion."

Although Jackson didn't say it, he too felt they were blowing things out of proportion. "Just let me talk to him," he said before rolling up the blueprint. "And as for this, I'll have to get back to you."

"Take your time," said his father, giving him a pat on the back. "I'm sure you'll make the right decision."

"Speak of the devil," said Jackson, who held up his ringing cell phone to see Xavier's name flash across the screen. He engaged his brother in a brief phone conversation, then turned toward Caleb to fill him in. "Xavier wants us to hit up the Strip tonight. You down?"

"I guess," he replied with slight hesitation in his voice. Given their tense encounter the day before, he found it difficult to be excited about spending time with his eldest brother, but figured he'd do so for Jackson's sake. "I'm going to stop by my place to shower and change," he said, placing his motorcycle helmet on his head as he made his way over to his bike. "I'll meet you back at the house."

"Okay," said Jackson. "Don't forget to use deodorant. I almost passed out when you had me in that headlock."

"Shut up," Caleb retorted before revving up the engine.

Jackson watched Caleb take off on his bike, then headed toward the front of his father's car, where he found him leaning against the driver's side door, puffing on a cigar. He watched as he drew in a deep breath before blowing out a plume of smoke.

"Don't tell your mother about this," he begged, holding up his cigar.

"Right, as if she's not going to smell it on you. You really should quit, Dad," stated Jackson, frowning.

"Now Son, what have I always told you?" asked Mr. Taylor with a stern look. "Nobody likes a quitter." His harsh expression melted into a smile, as he erupted with laughter.

"Ha, ha. Very funny."

"Hey, you kids aren't the only ones that got jokes," replied Mr. Taylor before resuming his post at the driver's seat. He headed for home, and Jackson spent the entire car ride thinking about Xavier, and his father's proposal.

Chapter 13

Exhausted from a day of indulgence, Jasmine returned to the Taylor residence with Mrs. Taylor, hoping to get some rest before dinner, but soon discovered that the spa treatment she enjoyed a few hours earlier would be the only peaceful experience the day would bring. While heading down the hall toward her room with her hands full of shopping bags, she became startled upon bumping into an unexpected visitor—another ghost from Jackson's past.

"I'm so sorry!" said the young woman who almost knocked her down after making an abrupt exit from Mr. Taylor's den.

"It's okay. Here, let me help you," said Jasmine, setting down her shopping bags so she could assist the young woman with collecting the papers she had been carrying, which were now scattered all over the floor.

"Thanks," replied the young lady, kneeling down beside her. "I'm so sorry about this. I was in a hurry. I didn't mean to frighten you."

"Don't worry about it."

"Are you Mrs. Taylor's personal shopper?" she inquired, eyeing the many shopping bags that sat next to them on the floor.

"Um, no," replied Jasmine with a giggle. "Those are mine. I'm just visiting for the weekend. My name's Jasmine, and yours?"

"I'm Bianca," replied the twenty-something dimpled beauty, flashing her pearly whites. She appeared to be of similar height, build and complexion as Jasmine, except her hair was shoulder length with auburn highlights. "I just stopped by to pick up some documents for one of Mr. Taylor's clients."

"Oh, so you're in real estate, too?"

"Yes. I'm his office manager. Are you the niece he's always talking about?"

"No. I'm engaged to his son."

"Congratulations!" she exclaimed, her eyes sparkling with excitement. "I had no idea Caleb even had a girlfriend."

"Caleb? No, I'm Jackson's fiancée," Jasmine corrected. Suddenly, the light she had just witnessed catch fire in Bianca's eyes dimmed.

"Jackson? Oh—okay. So that's what he meant about things going according to plan," she muttered, suddenly recalling the comment he had made during their brief phone conversation a few weeks prior.

"What?"

"Oh, nothing," said Bianca before adding with a smirk, "well, I wouldn't let him out of my sight for too long if I were you."

"Excuse me?"

"You look young, so take it from me: he's easily distracted. And, if he's anything like how I remember, it's going to take a lot to keep him interested…" Her voice trailed off as she began eyeing Jasmine from head to toe.

Noting Bianca's obvious and acute examination, Jasmine shook her head then thrust the papers she was holding into her hands. "Don't worry about me. You handle your business and I'll handle mine." With that, she collected her bags and proceeded down the hall toward her bedroom without giving Bianca another thought.

*****

Around the same time that afternoon, Jackson and Caleb met with Xavier, who had arranged for the three of them to get properly groomed for their night out on the Strip. Their first stop was at his favorite barbershop, where they each got precision haircuts and a shave. Then it was off to the tailor, where they planned to get their newly purchased suits altered. Their father had taught them early on that a man wearing a nice suit and tie could enter through more doors than one sporting a T-shirt and jeans. And, what would prove more important than the designer name on the label, or price on the tag, was the fit.

"Your suits should be ready in about an hour," informed the tailor, who would be performing the alterations.

"Thanks," Xavier replied, taking the receipt.

"Let's go get something to eat while we wait," proposed Caleb. "I'm starving."

"You're always hungry, He-Man," said Xavier, rolling his eyes. He then threw his arm around Jackson's shoulder and said, "Check this out."

"What?"

Xavier reached inside one of the shopping bags he was carrying, pulled out a bottle of cologne and handed it to him.

"Code," said Jackson, reading the label aloud. He couldn't help but chuckle after reading the ad copy on the back of the box, which made some ridiculous claims about how the fragrance had the power to transform a frog into a prince, and contained the sweat of a giant, or something corny to that affect.

"The old man wears this," explained Xavier. "It has somewhat of an orangey scent to it, and I thought it was kind of fruity at first, until I started noticing how the ladies respond to it."

"Really?" asked Jackson, smiling.

"Yeah man. You start rocking this, and I swear the ladies will come flocking to you like a fly on sh—"

"No thanks," interrupted Jackson, after eyeing the $160.00 price tag. "I can get the same effect, but for half the price."

"Whatever," said Xavier, tossing the pricey cologne back inside the shopping bag.

A few hours later, the three brothers entered the lounge at Tao Nightclub, decked to the nines. Just like old times, Xavier led the way, with his younger brothers in tow. Although he had been there many times, the extravagance of the décor never ceased to wow him, as he reveled in its beauty and splendor. The entrance alone, lined with beautiful models wading inside small tubs of water, was enough to rouse the senses, and Xavier practically salivated over the women whose taut bodies, draped in barely-there bikini bottoms and rose petal nipple covers, emerged from the water as they approached.

The women undulated as if they had been awaiting the arrival of their personal snake charmers, each possessing the power to release them from bondage. Xavier's eyes locked on one performer in particular, whose ample bosom, he thought, begged to be caressed. He reached out to cup her left breast, the one closest to him, but Caleb slapped his hand down, avoiding contact.

"You trying to get us kicked out?" he asked, glaring at his eldest brother, who simply belted out a laugh as they continued their trek toward the interior of the lounge.

Boasted as one of the best restaurants and nightclubs in town, Tao was the embodiment of a Southeast Asian getaway, from the Asian fusion cuisine served up by its top chefs, to its rich gold and maroon décor, full of Buddhist monk sculptures and lavish silk tapestries. It had always been one of Xavier's favorite hangouts because it was the one place he knew he'd find the quality he was looking for in terms of liquor and women. The fact that celebrities often frequented it made it the go-to spot of Vegas, and also one of the most expensive. Having been around the Strip a few times, the Taylor men knew how to get inside places where access may at times proven difficult. Being fine didn't hurt either, for each brother was handsome in his own right.

"What's so funny?" asked Caleb, upon noticing Jackson's amused look once he removed his suit jacket and threw it over his shoulder.

"I could tell you were just itching to get up out of that suit the moment you changed into it, and what's the first thing you do once we make it inside? You take your jacket off."

"Is it that obvious?" asked Caleb, smiling.

Before taking a seat on one of the lounge's plush couches, Xavier whipped out his cell phone and quickly typed away at the keys before sliding it back inside his pants pocket.

"Who have you been texting all night?" Jackson wondered, after spotting his brother send the last of several text messages he had sent throughout their outing.

"Oh, I'm just calling in a little entertainment, that's all," he replied with a grin. Jackson knew all too well what his brother's idea of entertainment was, and slightly dreaded what the night might bring.

Shortly thereafter, a waitress providing bar and bottle service took their order, and returned promptly with drinks in hand. Xavier removed the straw from the highball glass she had set down in front of him and tilted his head back, taking a large swig of the Long Island Iced Tea he'd ordered.

"I'm really glad you're back, even if it's only for a little while," said Caleb, raising his glass toward Jackson.

"Thanks," he replied, smiling. "I'm glad to be back."

"Jasmine seems really cool," Caleb continued. "I can tell she's a firecracker. I think you finally met your match."

Jackson couldn't help but laugh, for it had been Jasmine's fiery nature that had attracted him to her, and it was therefore no surprise that his little brother had taken notice of one of her most prominent attributes.

"So, you really think she's the one?" interjected Xavier, who had just finished ordering his second round.

"Yes, I do," stated Jackson without hesitation. "I wouldn't have proposed to her if I didn't."

"And how can you be so sure?"

"I'm sure because I've never felt this way about any woman, ever."

Xavier shook his head and smirked before taking another swig of his drink. "Really? If you would be so kind, please enlighten us about what it is that makes her so special."

"Xavier—"

"It's cool," said Jackson, laying a hand on Caleb's shoulder after he attempted to put a stop to questions he felt were inappropriate. Jackson could sense the tension between his brothers resurfacing, but wanted to squash it before it ruined their time together. Resuming eye contact, he firmly replied, "I love her, and that's all you or anyone else needs to know."

"Right," said Xavier, chuckling. "I loved Sharon on Monday and Monica on Tuesday…"

"What's that supposed to mean?"

Caleb took a sip of his drink and rolled his eyes. This time, he chose to remain silent, for he figured it time Jackson saw what he and his father had tried to warn him about.

"All I'm saying is, you can love anybody, but that doesn't mean you have to marry them. I mean, she's fine and all, but there's plenty more where that came from. I'm just curious as to what it is that sets her apart from all these other hoes."

"Well for one," began Jackson, his patience waning, "she's not a hoe, and secondly, you and I both know that sex and love are two different things."

"Wow, she must have really put it on you for you to say some mess like that. Please, do tell—and spare no detail. I'm dying to know what she did that was so fascinating." Xavier kept his eyes locked on Jackson's, as he eagerly awaited his response, but instead of replying, he simply adjusted his tie then took a long sip of his drink. "Wait a minute," said, Xavier, leaning forward in his seat, his keen senses homing in on something. "Do you mean to tell me that you and her have never—"

"Cool it," said Jackson, trying to remain calm, although inside, he could feel his blood starting to boil.

"Ha!" shouted Xavier, throwing his head back and laughing. "So, there lies the fascination! I was wondering why you hadn't spilled the beans about your recent sexcapades." He continued to laugh, for Jackson's silence confirmed his suspicion. Sharing graphic tales of their intimate encounters had always been a major part of their bond, so tight lips said it all. "Perhaps that's why my phone hasn't rang."

"Whatever, man," Jackson replied, shaking his head. "My wild oats are sown, brother. This time is different. I've finally met someone who makes me want to be better. Do better."

"Now you sound like a Hallmark card," replied Xavier with a skeptical look. "Don't worry, I get it. You're afraid that once you've popped that cherry, you'll lose all interest, and believe me, you will. This just means you'll enjoy what I have planned all the more…"

Jackson didn't give much thought to his brother's remark, but soon discovered what he meant when just a few minutes later, two scantily-clad women arrived at their table.

"I guess this is his entertainment," whispered Caleb, as they watched the two young ladies, who had each come teetering in on five-inch stilettos, approach. One immediately parked herself in Xavier's lap without so much as a hello. And, with no hesitation, she grabbed his face and drew his mouth toward hers, kissing him hard.

Jackson and Caleb glanced at each other, their eyes saying what their mouths didn't. It was apparent that their brother's latest mistress, or rather, flavor of the week had arrived.

"These are my brothers," stated Xavier, formally introducing them to his friend once she finally peeled her mouth off of his.

The woman ran a finger across her upper lip to wipe away the saliva then said, "Oh, hi," as if she had just noticed the two of them sitting there.

"Hey," they replied in unison.

"Don't forget my friend," she said, nodding toward her girlfriend, who had yet to take a seat. Jackson and Caleb scooted toward the end of the couch to allow her room to sit, but she plopped down so close to Jackson that they may as well have stayed put.

"Hey," she said, her thigh pressed firmly against his. She leaned forward, glancing first at Jackson then at Caleb and said to her friend, "They're cute."

"Did you hear that?" asked Xavier, grinning. "She thinks you're cute," he said to Jackson, despite the fact she had referred to both of his brothers.

"Is this the engaged one?" the still unidentified lady asked, pointing at Jackson, her finger lightly tapping his chest. She sat so close he could smell the peppermint breath mint she had just consumed.

"Yes, it is," Xavier confirmed. "And, he's here to celebrate," he added with a sly grin.

"Good, because I'm ready to have some fun."

"Great, he could use a release," said Xavier, laughing.

The young woman bit her bottom lip and stared at Jackson with her bedroom eyes. Although not his type, he considered her attractive and knew had they met a few years ago, he would have gone to bed with her and not thought twice. Yet, the warmth of her body, which she was deliberately pressing against his, did nothing but make him think about Jasmine, and how he longed to be with her. Unfortunately for him however, she seemed pretty firm in denying him the one part of her he still desired most, despite his many attempts at seducing her. He knew based on her own admission that she was holding out because she didn't want to become another notch on his bedpost. And although he tried his best to convince her that sex between them would be different because he loved her, she insisted on taking things slow...*extra slow*, he thought.

He had once thought himself incapable of celibacy, but that was before he met her. To him, she was an enigma: tough yet soft at the same time. She had succeeded, rather unwittingly, at capturing his heart—a feat no other woman had ever accomplished. Before her, feeding his carnal desires had been his number one priority, but she was the first woman he had actually taken the time to get to know. After all, she had given him no choice, considering she had resisted all his advances. He could still clearly recall how guarded she was when they first met, and it perplexed him to see someone so impervious to his charms. He could coax the panties off a nun, so the more she rejected him, the more he became intrigued by her, until fighting his way into her heart became more important than fighting his way into her bed. He believed that she would eventually give herself to him completely, and although it was taking longer than he would have liked, he surprisingly found himself enjoying the journey.

While in the midst of thinking about his baby, whom he hadn't seen all day, his couch buddy grew increasingly frisky. He felt her place a hand on his left knee, which he promptly removed.

"You're engaged, not married. We can take this party back to our room," she proposed, gazing into his eyes, which were now locked on hers. They were so dark and mesmerizing, like two cosmic, black holes, she thought. It was almost impossible to not fall into them...

"I know what I am, sweetheart," said Jackson, snapping the minx out of her trance. "Have a good night," he added before rising out of his seat.

"Oh, come on!" shouted Xavier, but Jackson ignored him and began fishing inside the pocket of his trousers for his wallet.

His brother had proven, yet again, that he had no boundaries, and Jackson almost felt silly for having expected him to show some respect for him and his relationship. Hell, he didn't respect his own. At that point, he couldn't help but feel pity for Xavier and his poor wife, their marriage now in shambles. She had been left with the difficult task of raising their children alone while he gallivanted around town with one woman after the other. *Jasmine would kill me if I ever tried to have something on the side*, he thought.

"Don't be a party pooper," said Xavier, as if he were ten years old.

After throwing a twenty-dollar bill down onto the table in front of them, Jackson said, "I guess some things never change," then proceeded toward the exit.

"Where are you going?!" shouted Xavier, as he watched him depart. "The night is young, and we're just getting started—"

"That's enough," said Caleb, glaring at his eldest brother in disgust.

"What? I'm just looking out for him, that's all. You and I both know that Jackson has run through a lot of women, and he ain't been serious about none of 'em."

"You heard him. This is different. He's different. Perhaps he, I don't know, grew up. What a concept. People can change."

"Bullshit."

Xavier took a sip of the third drink that had been placed in front of him that evening while his mistress whispered something in his ear. Caleb watched as he dismissed whatever she said with a wave. "Don't you think you've had enough?" he asked.

Instead of responding in regards to his alcohol consumption, Xavier continued his anti-monogamy tirade. "I haven't heard from Jackson in a minute, and suddenly he comes home with a fiancée? Like I'm really supposed to believe that the tin man finally found his heart."

"Well," began Caleb, throwing a bunch of ones down onto the table, "it's clear the scarecrow has yet to find his brain."

"Watch it," snapped Xavier, as his two female companions giggled at his brother's remark. Deciding he too had had enough, Caleb turned to head for the exit, but Xavier stopped him. "Aren't you forgetting something?"

"What?"

Xavier nodded toward his brother's suit jacket, which was draped across the back of the couch. Caleb rolled his eyes and snatched it up, then proceeded toward the exit of the lounge, leaving the party of three behind.

Not wanting to give any credence to what his brothers had to say, Xavier leaned back and enjoyed the company of his two female companions, while indulging in yet another round of drinks. It wasn't too long before the trio headed up the stairs toward the club, where they spent the rest of the evening dancing in a drunken stupor. And, when he thought his girlfriend wasn't looking, he fondled a few go-go dancers while scouring the scene in search of the next ex-Mrs. Taylor.

Chapter 14

"You're home early," said Jasmine upon opening the door to Mr. and Mrs. Taylor's guest bedroom after Jackson asked to enter. "I thought you and your brothers were staying out all night?"

Jackson didn't say anything, and instead walked over to the foot of the bed, where he took a seat on the one section that was available, as it was covered with new clothes, the tags still attached. His eyes scanned the bed before moving to the vanity and certain parts of the floor, where a few shopping bags stood. "I see you had a busy day."

"Yes!" she replied enthusiastically. "Your mom took me on one of the greatest shopping adventures of all time! We even got manis and pedis," she said, holding out her hands so he could examine the hot pink polish on her nails, but instead of commenting on the design, he grabbed her hand and pulled her down on top of him.

Jackson kissed Jasmine like she were a full course meal, and he hadn't eaten in months. He had left the club on fire, his brother's friend having been the one to light the match, but the only person he wanted to extinguish the flames was Jasmine.

Oblivious to the yearning with which he had approached her, she wriggled herself free from his embrace, stood up and said, "Oh, and I have great news!"

Damn, he thought, for she never ceased to dampen the mood…

Ignoring his pained expression, she continued with excitement, "I got a call from Infinity today, the company I interviewed with last week…I got the job!"

"That's great," he replied, his response lacking the enthusiasm she had hoped.

"What's wrong?"

"Nothing," he said, still trying to shake off the unpleasant outing he had just had with his brothers. "That's great. I'm really happy for you."

"I'm so excited!" said Jasmine, traipsing toward the vanity. Jackson rose from the bed and followed as she took a seat on the stool. He stood behind her and watched as she gathered her hair into a ponytail. "I start next Monday," she announced, staring at his reflection in the mirror.

"And you've already spent your first paycheck," he noted after peering inside one of the shopping bags sitting atop the vanity. She continued to ramble on about her new job and what her position would be, and he listened, for a little while, but soon decided to change the subject by kissing the back of her neck.

"...Isn't that great?" she asked, as he continued to plant soft kisses along the nape of her neck. The sweet smell of her skin tickled his nose, and he inhaled it eagerly. Desiring more, he wrapped one arm around her waist, his thumb grazing the underside of her breast. He then used his other hand to pull away the strap of her tank top so his lips could touch the flesh on her shoulder.

"Are you even listening to me?"

"Yeah...yes," he said, pausing to respond. "You know you don't have to work though," he added, whispering softly in her ear.

"You're kidding, right?" she asked, turning to look at him. She placed her hand on top of his and felt his grip loosen slightly.

"It was an option, not a command," he said, backing away.

"And what do you propose I do?" she asked, staring up at him. "I mean, you do realize I didn't endure four years of college, writing term paper after paper, reading books I didn't like and staying up all night studying just so I could sit on my butt and do nothing, don't you?"

"Yes, I do," he said, trying to choose his words carefully to prevent an argument from erupting, although he could already feel the tension between them mounting. *The mood is officially ruined*, he thought. "All I was saying is that you don't have to work if you don't want to. Besides, by the time we have children, you may see things differently."

"Children?!" she cried out, jumping up from her seat. Here she was trying to cope with the fact that she had just graduated from college and was about to enter the workforce, and now he was pushing her into a life of domesticity.

"Yes, children!" he replied, mimicking her impassioned response. "That's usually what couples do; they get married and have children. It's a natural progression of life."

"We never talked about this," she said, shaking her head and frowning.

"What do you think we're doing now?"

"You know what?" she asked, incensed by his sarcasm. "I can't deal with this right now."

"That's the problem," he said, loosening his tie. "You never want to deal with anything, but guess what? You can't avoid everything forever, Jasmine. When are you going to grow up?"

"Grow up?!" she shouted, her anger intensifying. "So now I'm immature because I don't want to talk to you about all the ridiculous plans you've made for me and my life?!"

"Stop yelling. You want to wake my parents?"

"Maybe I should. Maybe I should let them know that their son is an overbearing lunatic who always wants things to go his way!"

"What? That's ridiculous. I think things have been going more your way than they have mine," he said, turning his back to her as he headed toward the door.

"And what's that supposed to mean?" she asked, following him.

"I think we both know what it means," he replied, turning to face her. The two stared at one another, neither saying a word, for each knew what the underlying issue was without it being mentioned.

With her arms folded across her chest, Jasmine glared at Jackson for a moment then finally broke the awkward silence that had suddenly filled the room. "What was all that talk about you wanting to be 'different' than your former self? 'Turn over a new leaf?'" she asked, her eyes never leaving his. "Were those just lies?"

"No."

"Well then, why throw that in my face as if I'm somehow depriving you of something? I mean, it's not like I haven't given up anything for you!"

"Oh really?"

"Yes, really!"

"And just what exactly have you given up for me, Jasmine? Huh? Please, do tell."

"Um, let me think," she said, scratching her temple as if she were truly searching for an answer. "When I met you I was a smoker, remember?"

"And?"

"*And*, I quit smoking for you."

Jackson clapped his hands together loudly. "Thank you. Thank you for forfeiting lung cancer on my behalf."

"You know what smart ass? You can get out of my room. I was having a great day until you came along and messed it all up!"

"Yeah, well I was having a crappy day, and I came here hoping you'd make it better. You know what, I don't have to put up with this," he said, heading for the door.

"Good, leave!" she yelled, throwing her arms up into the air. "Why don't you go back to wherever it is you just came from? You reek of liquor and cheap perfume anyway. I smelled it the moment you walked in!"

"Yeah, maybe I will," he said, turning to face her once more. "At least I could finally get some action." He squeezed his eyes shut and cursed under his breath, knowing he'd gone too far. "Baby, I'm sorry. I didn't mean—"

"Leave," she said in a whisper.

"Jazz—" he reached out to grab hold of her arm, but she yanked it away. Although she was hurt, she couldn't help but notice the look of sincere regret now plastered all over his face.

Seeing that she wasn't going to allow him to console her, Jackson said, "Goodnight Jasmine," then headed out the door. Not wanting the night to end on a sour note, he turned to rush back inside, but stopped abruptly upon spotting a female figure, lurking in the shadows of the hall.

"Trouble in paradise?"

"What are you doing here so late?"

"Working," said Bianca, staring up at him as she approached. "Well, at least I was until I heard all that yelling you were doing with your—wait, what did she say she was again? Oh yeah, your *fiancée*."

"Listen," said Jackson, approaching her with anger in his eyes. "You had no business eavesdropping on a private conversation. Perhaps I should tell my father that instead of handling his business you were all up in mine."

"Or, I can go in there and tell your fiancée how you were *'all up in mine'* once," she said, emphasizing her words so that their meaning wasn't lost on him. "From what I heard, you haven't been up in anyone's business lately—"

"That's it," he said, grabbing hold of her arm and forcefully leading her back down the hall. "You need to leave."

"I'll leave when I'm ready," she said, wrenching her arm free from his embrace. "I know you're used to women caving in to your every command, but that's not going to fly with me."

"If I recall correctly, you caved in pretty easily."

Now seething with anger, she said through clenched teeth, "Too bad that fiancée of yours doesn't know you're a man whore. At least she has sense enough to not put out because Lord knows you can't keep it in your pants."

"I haven't seen you in years and yet you think you know me."

"You haven't changed. Guys like you never do. Maybe I'll do her a favor and let her know not to waste her life on you."

"As if she would be interested in hearing anything you have to say."

"She might once I tell her how we've been sleeping together."

"What? You're crazy."

"Maybe. But, you're not the only one who can make threats, so don't tempt me."

"I just want you to leave me alone."

"And I want you to pay."

"Pay for what?"

"For thinking you can use women as your personal trash receptacle."

"I never forced you to do anything you didn't want to do. I'm just sorry you couldn't accept things for what they were." Jackson noticed a glimmer in Bianca's eyes, as if what he said finally resonated, but it vanished as quickly as it appeared.

"You'll get yours," she said before hurriedly strutting down the hall.

Stunned, Jackson remained still for a moment, watching as Bianca headed down the hall until she disappeared from his sight. Rubbing his goatee, he glanced up at the ceiling in disbelief. The night had quickly gone from bad to worse, and he suddenly feared what might happen if she were to deliver on her promises.

Chapter 15

The next morning, Jasmine arose with the events of the previous two days weighing heavily on her mind. A part of her wanted to confront Jackson about everything she had seen and heard, and particularly about what he had said to her the previous night, yet another part of her feared what he would possibly reveal. *Had their relationship been a lie? Was he seeing other women on the side because she wasn't giving him the sex she knew he could so easily get?* Perhaps she had been a fool to think that a man with that much experience—and such a large sexual appetite—could hold out as long as she was making him wait.

Her mind was running wild, concocting the worse scenarios possible, but there was one thing that provided her with an ounce of comfort: the look she saw in his eyes when he attempted to apologize. She couldn't deny the pain she saw in them, and sensed there was something deeper than their tiff that was bothering him. She just needed to know what it was.

She began searching the house for him early in the morning, but couldn't find him or anyone else for that matter. She checked his room and the living room, but he was nowhere to be found. She even knocked on a few bedroom doors with no luck. She then headed toward the kitchen, where she found a note attached to the refrigerator that read: **Out buying groceries. Help yourself to some breakfast. Be back soon.** Hearing the rumble in her tummy, she decided to heed the suggestion on the note, and began pouring herself a bowl of cereal.

After chomping on some Cheerios, she headed back down the hall and entered the foyer, where her nose picked up a very strong yet familiar scent: bergamot combined with the distinct aroma of cigar smoke. That smoky, orange-laced scent was unmistakable, and she instantly recalled having taken it in the moment Mr. Taylor swept her into a bear hug.

"Knock, knock," she said as she approached the den, the doors to which were wide open. She was certain she would find Jackson's father inside after having followed his scent throughout the halls. "Oh, excuse me," she said upon discovering that it was Xavier and not Mr. Taylor occupying the den.

"Don't mind me," he called out from behind the wet bar. "I just dropped by for a visit, but everyone seems to have disappeared."

She watched him step away from the wet bar and head toward the large oak table with a bottle of whisky in one hand and a glass full of ice in the other. A burning cigar sat in an ashtray on the counter, and it had been the aroma of the cigar combined with his cologne—the same fragrance his father wore—that had thrown her off track. "According to the note I found on the refrigerator, they're out shopping."

"Well," he began, as he took a seat on the edge of the table, "it seems we've been left alone to get better acquainted. Care for a drink?"

"No thanks," she said, noting his disheveled appearance as he poured some of the liquor into his glass. It appeared as though he had slept in his clothes, for his suit was wrinkled and tie undone. "I have this rule about not drinking in the A.M.," *or ever*, she thought, still traumatized by the effects of her first hangover.

"Oh, okay," he said while peering at her over the rim of his glass, which he had raised to his lips. "I hear that's not the only thing you don't do."

"Excuse me?"

"Why don't you come sit down next to me," he said, rubbing the spot on the table next to him. "I'd like to get to know my future sister-in-law better." He cocked his head to the side and smiled while his green eyes undressed her. His entire expression made her skin crawl.

"Thanks, but I'm fine where I am," she said, folding her arms across her chest. She made sure to stay as close to the door as possible. There was a moment of awkward silence, and he looked at her and smiled. "I'm going to head back to my room now," she said before turning to leave. "It was good talking to you," she lied.

"You know, I think it's really great you and Jackson have been hanging in there," he said, causing her to turn around.

"Come again?"

"Relationships are tough. Hell, my wife and I don't see eye to eye on much of anything anymore."

Jasmine didn't know what to think of Xavier's sudden interest in discussing private details about his marriage, and wasn't sure what to say other than to offer her regrets. "I'm sorry to hear that," she said, inching her way closer toward the door.

"The fact that you're able to accept my brother and his storied past is…well, it's commendable."

"I'm not sure I understand what you mean," she said, now interested in what he had to say.

"Come on," he said, laughing. "It's no secret he's been with a lot of women. You should feel proud to know you're the one he's chosen to settle down with."

"I guess…" she replied, irritated by his callousness.

"A lot of women get tripped up by a man's past, but the fact that you're able to overlook it is awesome. And, if it makes you feel any better, I can attest to the fact that my brother is a changed man," he said, raising his glass up high, which was now empty. He lowered it and began to refill it.

"Yeah…I mean, yes…he has changed," she said, stumbling over her words.

"I first noticed a change in him when he discovered he was going to become a father. I remember his fiancée, Charmaine, was so thrilled until…well, it was all sort of tragic now that I think about it…"

Jasmine could feel her heart sink into her stomach. She wasn't sure if what Xavier was saying was true, or if the alcohol had gotten the better of him, causing him to lose all control of his senses. Yet, having remembered the tense encounter she witnessed between Jackson and

Charmaine—the bartender that had served them the night he took her to the Hard Rock Hotel, she couldn't help but believe that what he said was true.

"I'm going to head back to my room now," she said, suddenly feeling the need to lie down. "I'll see you later."

"You sure you don't want a drink?" he asked, chuckling. "Looks like you could use one."

Jasmine could still hear Xavier laughing as she made her way back to her room. Once inside, she made sure to lock the door behind her before collapsing onto the bed. She then buried her head inside one of the pillows and waited for Jackson to return.

Chapter 16

About half an hour later, Jasmine heard a knock at her bedroom door. Dragging herself out of bed, she headed toward the door and opened it. "Hey, I've been waiting for you."

"I was hoping you'd find my note," said Jackson, searching her face to see if she was still upset about the previous night.

"I did," she replied.

"My mom wanted to pick up some things for lunch. She'd like for us to share one last meal together before we leave."

"That's cool," she said, taking a step back to allow him room to enter.

He noticed that her cheeks were slightly stained from the tears she had released prior to his arrival. "Sweetheart, listen," he said, reaching for her hand, "I want to apologize for what I said last night. I didn't mean it."

"Yeah, I'm sorry too," she said with anger in her voice as she yanked her hand away and began heading toward the vanity.

"What does that mean?" he asked, frowning.

"I've decided to take a little detour on the way back. Since I'm not that far from home, I figured I'd drop in on my father and pay him a visit—"

"Why do you do that?"

"Do what?"

"Pretend like you don't hear me."

"I don't know what you mean," she said, nervously fiddling with some items that sat on top of the table.

"You can be the queen of avoidance, you know that?"

"Yeah, and maybe you're the king of deceit," she fired back, glaring at his reflection in the mirror.

"What—"

"Do you have a child, Jackson?" she asked, whipping her body around to face his. She instantly noticed the stunned and confused look on his face.

"What?" he asked with a frown. "Why would you ask me that?"

"Xavier said you and Charmaine were engaged and had a baby."

"Xavi—what? Why would he…" He began pacing the floor, and she watched his confusion transform into anger. "I can't believe he told you—"

"So, it's true?"

He stopped pacing once he noticed the horrified look that swept across her face then took a few steps toward her, but she backed away, bumping into the vanity. "Oh my gosh," she said as he reached out to her. "It is true."

"Yes, but—"

"Let go of me!"

"It's not what you think!"

"I feel sick," she said, pushing him out of the way as she raced toward the bathroom, where she was reunited with her breakfast.

"Jasmine, baby, please come out," Jackson begged through the door. "Just let me talk to you."

Jasmine felt tears well up in her eyes as she tried to control the anger that raged inside her. Upset didn't begin to describe how she felt, for she was embarrassed and angry, all at the same time. He had told her she was the only woman he had ever loved, the only woman he had really gotten to know, and now she had discovered that he had proposed to someone else and started a family! The betrayal was too much to handle, the situation too reminiscent of Demetri: another liar and more deceit. She had always figured, based on his reputation, that he had a colorful past, but had no idea it included something as dramatic as this.

I knew I couldn't trust him! she thought, as she stared at her reflection in the mirror.

Jackson continued to speak to her through the bathroom door, pleading for her to come out. Knowing that she couldn't stay holed up inside the bathroom forever, she eventually emerged, her eyes swollen and red.

"Please, let me explain," he said, gesturing for her to take a seat on the bed, but she was too fired up to sit.

"There's nothing for you to say. You lied to me!" she shouted, frantically slapping him across the chest. "You told me I was the only woman you ever loved—the only woman you ever allowed yourself the chance to get to know, but now I find out you were engaged?! Where's this child?!" she screamed, pushing him toward the bed. She wanted him to be gone, the mere sight of him making her already emptied out stomach feel even sicker.

"Stop it, Jazz," he commanded, grabbing hold of her wrists so she could no longer pummel him with her fists. "Get a hold of yourself!"

"Don't tell me what to do!" she yelled, struggling to wrench her arms free, but his strength was overpowering. "Let go of me!"

"Not until you stop fighting," he said, staring down at her. "Even criminals are entitled to a fair trial."

"Fine," she said, ceasing her ambush. He kept a firm grasp on her forearms until he was certain she was done. After releasing her, she dropped her arms at her sides, and he watched as she took a seat on the bed and grabbed hold of one of the pillows, clutching it to her chest.

"I don't know where to start—"

"From the beginning," she snapped.

"Okay," he said, taking a seat next to her. "The bartender that served us at the Hard Rock…that was my ex, Charmaine. She and I met six years ago, and we dated off and on for about two years." He paused, as he couldn't stand to see the pain and anger he saw in her eyes. He hated to think that he was the cause of it, especially since it had taken them so long to arrive at the point they were now at in their relationship. He knew she had trust issues that stemmed from her past, for he had already overcome the many obstacles she had laid out before him. It were as if she had built a tiny fortress around her heart, and just when he thought he had finally succeeded at busting through its walls, there she was building them back up again.

"Continue," she said, sensing his hesitation.

"About a year or so into our relationship, she told me she was pregnant. I told her I would support her and the child, but honestly, I wasn't ready for that type of commitment. I felt blindsided by the whole thing—"

"Nobody gets blindsided by a baby, Jackson. Pregnancy is always a possibility—"

"I understand that," he said, rising from the bed. "It's just that this all happened during a time when I wasn't thinking about anyone or anything but myself. To find out I was going to become a father was scary enough, but finding out I was going to have a child with a woman I didn't love was very sobering to say the least."

"What happened to the baby?"

"She had a miscarriage," he said, staring down at the floor. "I think deep down she knew I wasn't ready to give her what she wanted. She knew I was unfaithful, but was secretly hoping that I'd come around someday. I think she thought the baby would change things…bring us closer together, so when she lost it, she was devastated."

"And you proposed to her?" she asked, her voice quivering uncontrollably. All this time she had thought, based on what he had told her, that she was the only woman he had ever loved, so to think he almost married someone else was driving her bananas.

He let out a deep sigh then said, "Yes. I felt it was the right thing to do, but honestly, my heart wasn't in it. Luckily, she and I never took it any further. Our engagement was brief. She called everything off after she found out I was still seeing other women."

"Oh my gosh," said Jasmine, shaking her head in disgust. "You've probably seduced Lord knows how many women, playing with their hearts by sleeping with them then tossing them to the side—"

"I'm not perfect, Jasmine, and neither are you. You may not have slept around, but you've toyed with people's hearts too."

"What?!" she asked, springing up off the bed.

"You heard me," he said, not backing down. "Before we got together, I saw how you flirted with other guys, toying with them to get what you wanted—free access to parties, drinks, you name it. You didn't care about them. You may not have slept with them, but you still used them to serve your own ends."

"You'll say anything to avoid blame, won't you?"

"Trust me when I say I take full responsibility for my actions. I'm not trying to judge you. I'm just trying to get you to see that we've both done things that aren't right. At least I'm willing to admit my mistakes. And, I regret them."

"Really?" she asked with a skeptical glare. "Why should I believe you? I mean, you've kept all of this a secret until now!"

"Because it's true!" he exclaimed, his gaze now focused and intense. And just when she thought she had heard the worst of his story, he dropped another bombshell. "She tried to take her own life, Jasmine."

His words caused her to sink back down on the bed, for his revelation was too much for her to take standing.

"She downed an entire bottle of anti-depressants and was rushed to the hospital to have her stomach pumped," he continued. "I tried to visit, but they wouldn't let me inside the room. He sat back down on the bed and glanced up at the ceiling. "I had never thought about how my actions were impacting others until then. To say that I lacked sensitivity for her and her feelings would be an understatement. I know it sounds crazy, and to someone like you, it probably seems like common sense, but I honestly never thought that my actions could affect someone else so deeply."

Jasmine listened intently to Jackson's story and could hear the sincere regret in his voice. Having experienced heartache of her own, she could only imagine how Charmaine must have felt, getting her heart stomped on like that. And all this time she thought her dreadful experience with her ex, Demetri, had been bad, him pretending to love her, only to betray her by bragging about having taken her virginity. Then to add insult to injury, her so-called friends turned against her, spreading vicious rumors about how she had slept with most of the guys in their class, falsely depicting her as promiscuous. Jackson's experience, however, was much worse than she had imagined, and yet the more she thought about it, the more it made sense. She recalled how he had talked about wanting to give up his player lifestyle while on their first date, having spoken as if he had simply grown tired of the fast life and was looking for something more challenging. Yet, it was now clear that there existed a much more compelling reason behind his transformation.

"Why didn't you tell me?" she asked, her heart pounding inside her chest.

"I didn't think it mattered."

"You didn't think it mattered?!"

"I didn't see how any of this had anything to do with us…with today. You knew about my past and said you didn't want to know any details—"

"I know, but—"

"But what?" he asked, grabbing hold of her arms. He gazed deep into her eyes and could see her retreating. "I didn't tell you because I didn't want you to look at me the way you're looking at me now."

"Have you been sleeping with other women, Jackson? I mean, since we've been together?"

"What? No!" he immediately replied, genuinely shocked by her accusation. "Look, baby, I love you," he said, pulling her toward him so she could sit closer to him. "I have never loved any woman before—I've told you this. All that stuff in my past…it doesn't matter anymore. I would have told you had I thought it would somehow affect you, but it doesn't."

"I feel sick," she said, her stomach churning in knots.

"Don't let the past ruin our future. Don't let it destroy what we've worked so hard to build!"

"This...this is a lot to swallow, Jackson. I just wish you had told me—I just wish I didn't have to hear about it from—"

"Xavier had no right to tell you."

"It's not his fault," she said, still struggling to fight the negative thoughts that were swirling around inside her head. She didn't know what to think, but wanted to believe that he had been faithful, that he truly had changed. Yet, this shocking revelation had her questioning how true he really was. And, after running into his friend and a few of his exes and seeing how they had responded to him—Vanessa, skeptical that he could ever settle down; Julian, surprised that he was engaged after seeing him run with a steady stream of "dimes"; Charmaine, disgusted by the mere sight of him; and then Bianca, who warned her about his wandering ways—it all made her wonder if she was making a terrible mistake.

Considering she had never tried to dig deep into his past, a part of her felt slightly to blame for how things were currently unfolding. She already knew, based on his reputation and what little insight he had shared, that she'd uncover enough skeletons to fill a graveyard. She never even dared ask the infamous question—how many women he'd slept with—for she knew that no number would prove satisfying. Plus, she didn't want to judge him for his past, for she herself was no saint. After all, he was right; she had toyed with men's hearts, allowing them to fall for her while she remained non-committal. Yet, she hadn't considered her actions a crime until now, because she had only learned how to use her feminine wiles as a defense mechanism and at times, a pre-emptive strike.

"Baby, say something."

"I...I just need some time, that's all," she said finally.

"Okay," said Jackson, rising from the bed. "Lunch will be ready soon. Our driver will be here around five."

"Okay," she replied, watching as he headed toward the door. After placing his hand on the knob, he turned back suddenly as if he had forgotten something.

"I love you," he said, planting a kiss on her forehead.

Chapter 17

Jasmine didn't say much during the ride to the airport, and even though Jackson was very apologetic for not having shared certain details about his past, a part of her was still unsure about her feelings concerning their relationship. She didn't understand why he had kept something so big a secret, although finding out about it hadn't made her feel any better. Once they finally made it to the McCarran International Airport, he offered to walk her to her gate, and she had every intention of letting him do so, that is, until they ran into yet another one of his former flames—an attractive ticket agent.

"Hey, how've you been?" asked the woman behind the counter as Jackson and Jasmine approached.

"Good, and you?" he inquired, while Jasmine checked her luggage.

"Great. How long have you been in town?"

"Got in on Thursday."

"Aww," said the woman, twirling a lock of hair around her finger while batting her lashes at him. "Too bad I'm catching you on your way out. Had I known you were in town, we could have hung out, just like old times—"

"Um Susan, I'd like for you to meet my fiancée, Jasmine."

"Hi," said Jasmine, flashing a phony smile. She had observed their entire exchange, and couldn't help but notice how Susan immediately dropped the flirtatious act and tried her best to straighten up once Jackson introduced them.

"Oh, hey," replied Susan, quickly averting her eyes from Jasmine's so she could stare at the computer screen in front of her.

Jasmine watched as the woman smiled awkwardly and fidgeted anxiously while updating Jackson on his frequent flyer miles. Suddenly, she began to feel nauseous.

"Where are you going?" he called out, as he watched her storm off toward the security checkpoint.

"To catch my flight," she retorted.

"Wait a minute," he said, struggling to catch up to her. He grabbed her by the arm, causing her to turn around and face him. "You're not upset about that, are you?" he asked, pointing toward the ticket counter, but instead of responding, she rolled her eyes, yanked her arm free and proceeded to head toward security. Frustrated, he stayed behind and threw his arms down at his sides. "You're going to leave, like this?"

Turning around slowly, Jasmine stood still and glared at him.

"I can't help that I have a past, Jasmine. Remember, you have one too."

"Yeah, well at least mine allows me to walk around town without bumping into every single one of my exes. Geez, isn't there a woman in this state you haven't slept with?!"

Jasmine watched as Jackson clenched his jaw tight, his expression reminding her of how Stacey once looked when she slapped him hard across the face after he rejected and insulted her. The difference, however, was that she had slapped Stacey with her hand, whereas Jackson felt slapped by her words.

"Look," she said, slowly inching her way over to him. "I'm sorry, okay? It's just...I just want to go home, that's all. We can...I dunno, talk about all this later." She stood on the tips of her toes to give him a kiss on the chin, and couldn't help but notice the longing in his eyes as she pulled back and prepared to walk away.

"I love you," he said, watching her turn away. When she didn't respond, he called out to her. "Wait."

"What?" she asked, turning around to face him.

"I said, I love you," he repeated, taking a few steps forward to close the gap between them. She remained still and quiet while he stared down at her, his dark eyes steady and penetrating. "You can't say it, can you?"

Jasmine averted her eyes from his for a moment, so he grabbed hold of her chin and turned her face toward his. He was right: she couldn't say it. Not as often or as easily as he could at least. They were only three little words, yet they held so much meaning, and she feared that the more she said them, the more power he would have over her. Unlike so many other guys she had dated, Jackson had the ability to make her come completely undone, and a part of her hated him for it.

"You already know how I feel about you," she said, trying hard to not get lost in his eyes.

He stroked the side of her face with his hand then leaned in close, his mouth grazing her ear. "I want to hear you say it," he whispered, the warmth of his breath sending a shiver down her spine.

Jasmine glanced to her left and noticed a few other travelers were staring at them, but Jackson didn't seem to mind one bit as he held her close. She tried pulling away from him but couldn't, his grip firm and unyielding.

"I love you," she whispered finally, hoping he'd let her go.

He pulled away slightly so he could look her in the eyes again, and before she could say anything else, he kissed her. She resisted for a moment, not wanting their affection to be put on display, but soon her body relaxed, as her lips melted into his.

Jackson refused to let Jasmine leave on bad terms, and wanted to make sure she walked away with him on her mind. His efforts proved successful, as she spent the duration of her short flight to Los Angeles thinking about him and everything that had transpired during her trip to Vegas.

She couldn't stop thinking about his past, and whether or not he truly was a changed man. Both of them had been forced to contend with unflattering reputations that somehow managed to follow them wherever they went. The difference, however, was that the negative reputation that had followed her around since high school had been primarily built on lies, whereas his more closely resembled the truth. And it seemed the more time passed, the more remnants of his player lifestyle invaded their happy union. Although meeting his family was a crucial part of learning more about who he was as a person, a part of her wished they had never gone to Vegas, for the trip had seemingly driven a wedge between them…a small one, but an apparent one no less.

Once she made it to the Los Angeles International Airport, she hopped inside a cab and thanked the taxi driver when he pulled up in front her father's house. Mr. Fairchild lived in the same three-bed, two-bath, Spanish style home she had grown up in. He didn't have the heart to move out of it once his wife passed away, for it had been the place they called home, and was the only home Jasmine knew. She hadn't been home in a year and therefore thought her dad would appreciate a surprise visit considering they hadn't spent much time together following her graduation ceremony. And although she didn't necessarily miss her hometown, she was happy to be home, for her recent trip to Vegas had her feeling more uncertain about the future than she had before, and she wanted nothing more than to go some place familiar, somewhere she could rest and gather her thoughts.

"Hey…Jasmine…what are you doing here?"

"I thought I'd surprise you," she said to her father once he opened the door. She could tell he was surprised to see her, but wasn't quite sure if he was happy. "Is something wrong?"

"No, no," he replied, although his expression said otherwise. "Come in."

"I know I didn't call or anything, but I didn't think it would be a problem…where are your glasses?" she asked, suddenly noticing that he wasn't sporting the spectacles she was used to seeing him wear. "Are you wearing contacts?"

"I um—"

"I couldn't find the wine glasses," interrupted a voice from behind. "Oh, is this your daughter?"

Jasmine glanced over to her left and saw a woman, who appeared to be around her father's age, wearing a floral print summer dress and holding a bottle of Merlot.

"Who is this?" she asked, turning toward her father, who appeared flustered.

"This...uh...this is Angela. Angela, this is my beautiful daughter I've been telling you about."

"Hello," said Angela, extending her hand to Jasmine, who was too stunned to return the gesture. "It's so good to finally meet you," she continued, allowing her hand to fall at her side. "Your father has told me so much about you."

"That's funny, because he's told me absolutely nothing about you—"

"Jasmine!" scolded her father.

"It's okay, really," said Angela, inching her way closer to Mr. Fairchild, who wrapped his arm around her waist.

Jasmine noticed how the two glanced at each other, as if they shared a secret she wasn't privy to. Then, after taking a deep breath, her father turned his gaze back on her and said, "Honey, I was going to tell you this soon, but since you're here, I guess there's no better time than the present." Angela looked at him and smiled while he took another deep breath then said, "Angela and I have been seeing each other for a while now, and I've asked her to marry me."

Jasmine could feel her heart plunge deep into her stomach. It was similar to the feeling she felt after finding out Jackson had been engaged once and almost had a child. Her father had never mentioned anything to her about having so much as a girlfriend, and now she was supposed to accept the idea of him having a wife!

"I'm on *Punk'd*, right?" she asked, her eyes searching the room for hidden cameras.

"I'll leave you two alone to talk," said Angela before retreating inside the kitchen.

Jasmine watched Angela exit the room, while her father remained still and quiet. It wasn't until after a long period of silence that he finally spoke. "You should have told me you were coming."

"What?" asked Jasmine, feeling sick all over again. "I thought you'd be happy to see me?"

"I am. I just wasn't expecting you, that's all."

"I see," she said, now extremely agitated.

Again there was silence until her father asked, "How was your trip?"

Jasmine shook her head in disbelief. Her father had just dropped a nuclear bomb on her, and was now trying to shoot the breeze as if this new piece of information was no big deal. Yet, a part of her wasn't too surprised considering he had always been incapable of intimacy, evidenced by how he struggled to console her following her mother's death. Perhaps the apple didn't fall too far from the tree…

"The trip was great," she finally replied, although she knew it was a lie.

"That's good," said her father.

Seeing that her head was now spinning, thanks to all the revelations that were unfolding before her, she decided to call it a night. Besides, she knew it would prove impossible to engage in a serious conversation with her father with his fiancée standing just a few short feet away.

"I'm going to head to my room now. I'm tired and really just want to lie down."

"Um, about that…"

"What?" she asked, noting the strained look on his face.

"I had to move my office to your room, considering that it is the second largest room in the house—"

"What?!" Jasmine threw down her belongings, raced up the stairs and headed straight to her bedroom, the one with the queen-sized bed, oak chest of drawers and posters of The Pussycat Dolls plastered all over the walls. She hadn't changed anything in it since high school—hence the posters of The Pussycat Dolls. Yet, once she finally made it to the door, she opened it and gasped, for nothing was as she had left it.

There was no queen-sized bed, oak chest of drawers or posters of The Pussycat Dolls. Instead, there was an L-shaped glass desk with a filing cabinet to the left of it, an office chair behind it, and a laptop and desktop computer on top.

"Where's my stuff?!" she demanded after spinning around frantically to question her father, who was standing in the doorway.

"Your stuff is safe," he said. "I put it out in the garage—"

"The garage!"

"Yes, the garage. I needed more work space. You can sleep in the other room—the guest bedroom."

"The guest bedroom? So now I'm a guest?!"

"That's not what I meant—"

"I can't believe you changed my room without even asking me! I can't believe you just hauled all my stuff out of here!"

"I told you: I stored your things in the garage. I figured you took all the important things with you to Berkeley anyway. You haven't lived here in *four years*, Jasmine."

Deep down, she knew he was right. He had every right to do as he pleased with the room because, after all, it was his home. Besides, she hadn't lived there in four years and when she did come home to visit, all the room did was remind her of her horrific senior year of high school, when she stayed holed up in it to avoid all the nasty rumors that were circulating about her around campus.

"That's fine," she said, finally relenting. "I'll see you in the morning." Storming out of the room and past her father, she headed toward the guest bedroom, where she spent the rest of the night lying in bed, listening to him and his fiancée laugh and giggle as though they were having the time of their lives. Although she had often wondered what it would be like for him to date again, actually seeing him with someone made her feel lonely. And, to know he was marrying someone she didn't even know existed made her feel deceived. The fact that he had transformed her bedroom into his personal domain, having removed all traces of her presence, made her feel even more betrayed.

She tried to clear her mind and get some rest, but images of her father and his fiancée invaded her thoughts, as did her visit with Jackson's family. Her mind seemed to drift back and forth between the two subjects, until she became exhausted. Finally resolving to get some rest, she shut her eyes and figured tomorrow would provide yet another opportunity for her to deal with the issues that were boggling her mind. She only hoped, however, that the new day wouldn't bring any new surprises.

Chapter 18

The next morning, Jasmine awoke to the enticing aroma of pancakes and bacon. The familiar and comforting scent wafted through the house, causing her to break out of the funk she had been in the previous night. She was still upset that her father had kept his new relationship a secret—that and the fact he had converted her bedroom into his home office. Yet, she didn't want to start the day off on the wrong foot, and figured she'd at least enjoy breakfast before allowing anything to ruin it.

"Good morning," she said upon taking a seat at the breakfast table.

"Good morning," replied her father. "I got your favorite."

"I see," she said, her eyes scanning the disposable containers and empty IHOP bag that sat on top of the counter.

"Did you sleep well?"

"Not at all," she replied, expressing her true feelings for once. "I can't believe you've been lying to me all this time." *So much for not starting the day off angry.*

"I haven't lied to you, Jasmine."

"Oh, right. You just omitted the truth."

"Who is the parent here?" questioned her father, incensed by her tone.

"I'm not a child, Dad. You could have told me you were seeing someone."

"Right, because you're taking this so well," he said with sarcasm in his voice. Jasmine didn't say anything in response to her father's remark. Instead, she just sat quietly at the table and watched as he pushed his glasses, which were sliding down the bridge of his nose, back into position. She couldn't help but notice how differently he had appeared the previous night when he had chosen to wear contacts, undoubtedly to impress his new mate. It was as if she had been looking at an entirely different person, one she knew nothing about.

"So…" began Jasmine, after several minutes of awkward silence, "if I hadn't shown up last night, when were you going to tell me about your engagement?"

Mr. Fairchild took a few bites of his food then said, "When I felt it necessary, like once our plans were more firm."

Jasmine was angered by his response, for it reminded her of how Jackson had also felt it "unnecessary" to share intimate details about his past—details that ended up slapping her in the face. Having stumbled upon new and shocking information about the two men she loved most, she couldn't help but wonder what else they may have been keeping secret from her.

"Don't you want me to be happy?" asked Mr. Fairchild, interrupting her thoughts.

Suddenly feeling guilty, Jasmine peered across the table at her father and replied, "Of course."

"Good," he said. "I want you to be happy, too."

Neither of them spoke after that, and Mr. Fairchild finished the last few bites of his meal while Jasmine pushed her food around her plate with a fork. Distracted by her own thoughts, she didn't even notice when her father stood up and cleared his place at the table. Now alone, she took a few moments to play with the remaining portion of her meal before discarding it. Despite having been thrown for a loop, she was glad she had stopped by for a visit, but was now ready to head back to her apartment in Berkeley, which was starting to feel more like home than any place else.

Chapter 19

After Jasmine's plane touched down at the Oakland International Airport, she hopped inside a cab and asked the driver to take her to the pet daycare center so she could pick up Foxy before heading home. Jackson had offered to be her chauffer, but considering the two had barely spoken to each other after saying goodbye at the airport in Las Vegas a few days prior, she figured it best she make other arrangements. Her trip back home had been just as unsettling as her trip to meet her future in-laws, and all she wanted was to spend some time alone to gather her thoughts. Yet, once the cab pulled up in front of her place, she immediately spotted a familiar face waiting at her doorstep.

"Let me get that for you," said Jackson, as he headed toward the back of the cab. He removed her luggage from the trunk while she paid the fare.

"I told you I'd call when I made it in."

"I know, but I wanted to see you."

Although a part of her felt frustrated by his inability to respect her desire for space, another part of her wanted to see him, too. "You look nice," she said, admiring his dark blue jeans and graphic T-shirt. Although she thought he looked sharp in his suits, seeing him dressed down—as rare as it was, was refreshing. "Come on," she said, beckoning for him to follow her inside.

As soon as they made it over the threshold, she freed Foxy from her carrier, wrapped her in her arms and said, "It's good to be home, isn't it girl?"

"I wish I could get that kind of affection," said Jackson, awaiting his hug.

"Animals don't keep secrets, so they deserve it," she replied, shooting him an accusatory look.

"Jazz, we've been over this already."

"I know," she said, releasing Foxy from her embrace. She watched as the cat scurried toward the back of the apartment where the bedroom was located.

"How was your trip home?" he asked, changing the subject.

"It was good," she lied, heading toward the kitchen. "Want something to drink?"

"Sure," he replied, following her lead.

"All I have is water and lemonade."

"Lemonade sounds good." They each took a seat at the kitchen table, and after enjoying a few sips of the refreshing beverage, he looked at her and said, "My mom had a lot of fun hanging out with you."

"That's good," she replied. "I enjoyed hanging out with her, too."

"My whole family is looking forward to getting to know you better," he added, staring into her eyes. She stared back for a moment then looked away. "Jazz," he began, reaching across the table to grab hold of her hand, "I'm really sorry about how the weekend ended. I didn't mean for you to find out like that."

"It's cool," she said, staring down at her glass. He squeezed her hand tighter, causing her to look up at him.

"Look, if there's anything you want to know, anything at all, just ask. I don't want to keep any secrets from you. That was never my intent." He watched closely, awaiting her response, but she remained silent and slowly nodded. "And," he continued, "I want to apologize for how our first night in Vegas went. I should have never booked that room. I don't want you to feel any pressure, and I realize how juvenile it was of me to have put you in that position. I'd be lying if I said this no-sex rule of yours has been easy for me, but I'm willing to wait…for however long you need."

Jasmine hesitated for a moment, somewhat stunned by his apology. "I appreciate that," she said finally.

"By the way," he began, changing the subject, "There's something I've been wanting to share with you, but because of how things ended, I didn't get a chance to."

"What is it?"

"You know how I used to work for my father, right?"

"Yeah, you told me."

"Well, it seems he wants me to work for him again."

"Oh," she said, slightly confused. "So…he wants you to move back to Nevada?"

"Well, that's part of the equation."

"For some reason, you don't seem too thrilled," she said, sensing his lack of enthusiasm.

"I just never wanted my father, or anyone, to hand me a job. I want to know that I have something because I've truly earned it."

"I see," she replied, "but it's not like you have anything to prove. I mean, your parents didn't hand you your degrees. If my father owned a company in my field, I would work for him in a heartbeat. It sure would have saved me the hassle of going through all those dreadful interviews."

"I know, but it's a little more complicated than that," he stated. "Don't get me wrong, owning something that your whole family can benefit from is wonderful. I know my father considers it—the business and us kids—all a part of his legacy. It's just that working for him has always been Xavier's dream. After all, he is the oldest and has worked for him the longest."

"What's the matter?" asked Jasmine, confused. "Isn't he working for your father now? I thought the only person he was trying to get on board was you."

Jackson rose from the table and shoved his hands inside his jean pockets. Jasmine watched as he began pacing the floor. She could tell that he was stressed, but didn't understand why.

"My father is planning to expand his business, but those plans only include myself and Caleb. He's cutting Xavier out."

"What? Why?"

"According to them, Xavier is…well, he's going through a rough patch—he and his wife have separated, and I think the stress is starting to get to him."

"That's too bad," she replied with sincerity. "I did notice that he seemed to have a thing for your father's liquor cabinet—"

"What are you saying?" asked Jackson sharply, the harshness of his tone causing her to stare up at him.

"I just noticed he had a few drinks, that's all," she replied, attempting to clarify her comment. "I mean, people tend to drink a lot when they're stressed—"

"Yeah, or they smoke," he said, shooting her a look.

"I wasn't trying to say anything," she stated, still somewhat alarmed by his defensive tone. "It was just an observation, that's all." There was a long moment of silence, as the two were both somewhat baffled by how quickly the conversation had turned left. Then, after rising from her chair she said, "I need to unpack."

"I'm sorry for snapping at you," he said, trying to stall her attempt at kicking him out. "I have a lot on my mind, that's all. I shouldn't have taken it out on you."

"It's okay. I have a lot on my mind, too. It seems my father is also making plans for expansion, except his are personal, not business. But," she continued, placing her empty cup inside the sink, "unlike your father, his plans don't include me."

"What do you mean?"

"Well, I showed up at his doorstep thinking I'd surprise him, but instead, I ended up being the one surprised. He and his fiancée were in the middle of dinner."

"Fiancée?! Whoa," said Jackson, his eyes now wide. "That's big. I didn't even know he was dating."

"That makes two of us."

"Well, good for him."

"What?"

"You said yourself you wanted him to meet someone."

"Yeah, meet and date, like go out for coffee or something, not get married!"

"Your dad's been alone for a long time, Jasmine. I'm sure things have gotten even lonelier for him since you moved out—"

"I didn't abandon him!"

"I didn't say you did," he replied with a frown.

"You know what, maybe we should just call it a night."

"What's wrong?" asked Jackson, wrapping his arms around her waist. "We were just getting to a good place again—"

"I know," she said, averting her eyes from his. "I'm just tired, that's all."

He kept one hand at her waist and used the other to stroke the side of her face. "Listen, I understand how you feel. A lot of change is taking place right now, and it probably feels like a lot. But, you have to know that your father loves you—I love you."

"I know."

"Everything will work out just fine, you'll see," he affirmed, giving her a quick peck on the lips. "Get some rest."

"I'll call you tomorrow," she said, as he headed toward the door.

Chapter 20

"Hi. It's Jasmine, right?"

"Yes, and you're Lisa."

"Welcome," said the thirty-something Filipina as the two shook hands. "I didn't notice that before…Congratulations," she added, staring down at the fat rock that sat on top of Jasmine's ring finger.

"Thank you," she replied, smiling.

Lisa was one of the senior-level copywriters on staff at the advertising agency Jasmine now worked for, the same one who had helped settle her nerves each time she glanced at her during the two panel interviews she had participated in during the hiring process. With beautiful, doe-shaped eyes and full lips that stood out against an oval face, Lisa seemed doll like, and appeared to be much younger than her actual age. She was warm, friendly, and eager to take the newbie under her wing, unlike some of the other staff members she encountered, who feared that a new face somehow meant their positions were in jeopardy.

"Come, I'll show you around."

Jasmine followed Lisa around the mid-size office the company occupied on the fifteenth floor of the twenty-story, high-level security building in downtown Oakland. Her new colleague pointed out the conference rooms, kitchen, and break room before directing her to her cubicle, which didn't provide nearly as much privacy as she had hoped.

"Is this a welcome gift from the staff?" she asked upon spying the beautiful vase full of purple and orange calla lilies that sat on top of her desk.

"Not that I'm aware of," Lisa replied, shrugging.

Jasmine removed the note embedded inside the bouquet and read it silently:

Congratulations on your first day at work. Love, J

After taking a quick whiff of the freshly bloomed flowers and putting away her belongings, she continued to follow Lisa, who proceeded with the tour. In addition to showing her the layout, Lisa made it a point to immediately warn her about some of the madness and cliques that existed inside the office.

"Those are the 'reps,'" she said, gesturing toward an area of the office where the account director, management supervisor, and account executives sat. "They basically keep us employed."

"How so?"

"They're responsible for helping the agency maintain strong client relationships by making sure we deliver what the client wants." The two then headed toward another area of the office where Lisa pointed out the "-ologists."

"The account planners, who have a background in psychology, sociology, anthropology, or some other form of 'ology,' perform most of the research we use to structure our ads. They study human behavior and help us determine the best way to appeal to the average consumer."

Jasmine nodded to show that she was following along, as the two headed toward a small, transparent conference room, where a meeting was taking place.

"Those," Lisa explained, "Are the 'creatives.' Technically, you and I belong to that group because we're the ones that produce the content—images and text—for the client."

Jasmine peered through the glass window of the conference room and observed the intense discussion a few co-workers were currently engaged in. "Who is that?" she asked upon noticing an attractive young woman with striking red hair, who appeared to be in charge of the situation.

"That's Morgan," Lisa replied after following Jasmine's eyes to see whom she had suddenly become fixated on. "You'll get to know her, soon enough."

Jasmine took in the scene for a few more moments before finally peeling her eyes away. "It's funny how you talk about these various positions like they're high school cliques," she noted, as they headed back to their workstations. "I mean, aren't we all on the same team?"

Lisa turned to face Jasmine, who in her mind was as green as a fresh dollar bill. "You'd be surprised," she said, shaking her head. "I'd do my best to avoid all the nonsense that takes place around here if I were you, but believe me when I say, there is more drama in this office than in ten seasons of ER."

It didn't take long for Jasmine to learn that what Lisa said was true because just a few weeks later, while attending her very first staff meeting, she was formally introduced to one of the biggest instigators at the agency.

"Our last client wasn't very pleased with the comps we submitted," stated Carl, the beady-eyed account supervisor who was overseeing the team's latest project. "I know it's frustrating to put your heart and soul into something just to have someone else come along and criticize it," he continued, "but, we must maintain a certain level of professionalism at all times."

Morgan, the redheaded, take-charge, senior-level art director who had caught Jasmine's eye on her first day of work, attempted to defend the recent encounter she had with one of the agency's long-standing clients. "With all due respect," she began, her eyes steadied on Carl's, "I've worked with Mr. Baker on several campaigns, and he has the tendency to want the sun, moon and stars delivered to him on a shoestring budget." Some of the meeting's attendees laughed as she continued to justify her actions. "His criticism of our work is unjustified," she explained. "As far as I'm concerned, we should be complaining about his unreasonable expectations."

"Now, now," said Carl, trying to quell the laughter in the room. "What we need to focus on are better ways to serve the client. Our personal opinions of them serve no purpose in the matter. I was hoping that together we could brainstorm ways to give Mr. Baker and his company the type of campaign they're looking for."

Only two senior-level staff members offered suggestions, while everyone else remained tight lipped. Although Jasmine had only been on board with the agency for two weeks, she could already see, based on some of the info Lisa had shared about how the creative team worked, ways in which their creative process could be improved upon. "I have a suggestion," she offered, raising her hand. Suddenly, every eye in the room was on her.

"We're always happy to receive feedback from staff, including a fresh face like yours. Please, proceed," stated Carl, giving her the floor.

"Well," she began, feeling a slight twinge of nervousness as she spoke, "as I understand, only the account executive meets with the client initially to discuss the project, after which he or she then communicates the client's needs to the rest of the team."

"That's correct."

"Well, I was thinking it might help if a few of us from the creative team were also present so that we can hear the client's vision firsthand. It just seems some important details may be getting lost in the communication process—details that can help us get a better feel for what it is the client wants."

"I think you have an excellent point," stated Carl with a smile.

"We've suggested that before and got shot down," interjected Morgan, glancing over at him. "You said management felt that sitting in on meetings took away from time that could be spent working on existing projects."

"I know we've shot this down before," replied Carl, who now appeared agitated. "However, I feel that we should revisit this idea, especially now that we've received valuable feedback from one of our clients."

Morgan glanced down at the table, mortified, for she knew it had been the negative feedback the agency received regarding her unpleasant interaction with a long-standing client that was causing them to consider revamping the creative process.

"I'll talk to management and get back to you on this," stated Carl, glancing at Jasmine before moving on to a different topic.

The meeting continued for another half hour, as the team discussed other pressing issues. Once adjourned, Jasmine gathered her belongings and began heading toward the exit of the conference room when suddenly, a tornado blew by her. All she saw was a mass of red hair, followed by a pair of brown eyes that sliced through her.

"Who pissed in her coffee?" she asked Lisa, who had witnessed the entire exchange.

"You," she replied, placing a hand on her shoulder. "You may want to bring a catcher's mitt to the next meeting, because you are now on her hit list."

Jasmine didn't know what she had done to get on Morgan's bad side, other than speak her mind, something she felt she had every right to do.

"I'll catch up with you later," said Lisa, dispersing with the rest of the crowd.

"Okay," said Jasmine, as she began making her way back to her workstation. She found her cell phone ringing on top of her desk when she arrived, Jackson's picture flashing across the screen.

"Hey, how's work?" he asked once she answered the phone.

"It's cool…" *More like freezing,* she thought, suddenly recalling Morgan's icy stare. "I just attended my first staff meeting."

"How was it?"

"Okay I guess. I made a suggestion and my supervisor said he will talk to management about it and get back to me."

"That's great," said Jackson, smiling. "If you're anything like you are outside the office when you're in it, then I know your voice is bound to be heard."

"Thank you. I'll take that as a compliment."

"I meant it no other way," he said, chuckling.

"Yeah right," she replied, knowing he meant something more.

"Well, I'll let you get back to work. Dinner tonight?"

"I can't. Lisa and I are going to have a brainstorming session for a new project we're working on at happy hour tonight."

"You've been spending a lot of time with her. I want to come visit you so I can make sure Lisa isn't Larry."

"Very funny," said Jasmine, rolling her eyes. "But yes, you should come and visit me, soon."

"Soon?" asked Jackson, clutching the phone to his ear. "How soon?"

"Hmm, I dunno. Maybe sometime next week."

"How about right now?"

"Right now?" she asked with laughter in her voice. "I just told you, I'm busy."

"I can't tell," said Jackson, scoffing. "You've been twirling that pen in your hand for the past five minutes, and your golden brown legs are stretched out so far to the side that you're in no position to type."

Jasmine felt her heart skip a beat. "How do you know that?" she asked, dropping the pen she had been twirling onto the desk.

"Turn around."

"Oh my gosh!" she exclaimed, jumping to her feet. "What are you doing here?"

"I thought I'd surprise you."

"Yeah, well, it worked," she said, her heart now racing. She took a few steps forward and wrapped her arms around his neck.

"You missed me?" he asked, holding onto her tightly.

"A little bit," she said, biting her lower lip.

"Well, I missed you…a lot. And, I got you something."

"Really? What?"

"Here," he said, handing her a medium sized rectangular box.

"An iPad?" she asked, slightly confused. "What's this for?"

"Now you can download all your reference materials onto one, sleek device," said Jackson, eyeing the many books that sat on the shelf above her cubicle. "Aren't you tired of lugging around all those clunky books? How many dictionaries do you need?"

"They're not all dictionaries," she said with a laugh. "That's a style guide, that's a grammar book, and that's a thesaurus."

"Well, either way, they're fossils."

"Whatever," she said, shaking her head. "I like my fossils, but thank you. This is very sweet of you."

"You're welcome," he said, leaning in for a kiss. They were however interrupted by Lisa, who suddenly approached.

"Ahem," she said, clearing her throat. "I hope I'm not interrupting anything."

"Oh, hey," said Jasmine, happy her new friend and co-worker had arrived so she could introduce her to Jackson. "Lisa, this is Jackson, my fiancé. Jackson, this is Lisa."

"Hello," said Jackson, turning to greet her. He shook her hand and said, "I've heard so much about you."

"Likewise," stated Lisa, grinning from ear to ear. "I was wondering why there was a sudden surge of estrogen in the building. Now I see why," she said, eyeing him from head to toe.

"What are you talking about?" asked Jasmine, frowning.

"I guess you didn't notice," she began, glancing over her shoulder, "but most of the female staff have been whispering and pointing in this direction for the past five minutes or so. That's why I came over, to see what all the fuss was about."

Jackson felt flattered by the admiration, while Jasmine felt annoyed. "Well, you tell them to get back to work and mind their own business," she said, setting her gift down on the desk. "Come on," she said to Jackson, grabbing hold of his hand, "I'll walk you out."

"Okay," he said.

The two headed for the elevators, and once it arrived, she pushed him inside and said, "Thanks for almost giving me a heart attack."

"You're welcome," he replied, pulling her inside.

"I have to get back to work," she said, staring up at him.

"I know," he replied, staring down at her.

She closed her eyes and kissed him, then sent him on his way.

Chapter 21

Work made Jasmine feel empowered. Writing had become her passion, so her new job was in many ways a dream fulfilled. And although there was a lot of competition in her field—both internally and externally—it helped that she had made a strong ally in the business. She and Lisa were becoming fast friends, as the two ate lunch together on most days and met up for happy hour several evenings throughout the week. Although some of their after-work meetings were job related, others weren't, as the two enjoyed talking about a variety of topics—things that were going on in their lives that were just as, if not more important. Because of their friendship, the two became quite the dynamic duo on the job, often creating powerful and effective ad copy, while building on and proofing each other's work. Their camaraderie and teamwork was so apparent that management soon began placing them on joint assignments.

Three months into her new position, she and Lisa were asked to work on a pivotal project together. Management had approved the creative team's request to participate in client meetings, so the two were given the chance to speak directly with the owner of a new online shoe store that specialized in limited edition sneakers for which they were asked to create a banner ad.

"It was nice meeting you," said Lisa, extending her hand to the client, who sat across the table from her and Jasmine inside one of the agency's small conference rooms.

"Likewise," stated the client before turning his attention to Jasmine. "It was a pleasure meeting you as well," he said, shaking her hand.

With the meeting now adjourned, Jasmine gathered her belongings and quickly headed back to her cubicle to get started on her new assignment, but the ringing of her cell phone stalled her efforts.

"Hello?"

"Hey Beautiful."

"Oh, hey babe. What's up?"

"I was calling to see if you wanted to meet up for dinner tonight."

"I can't," she replied, staring at her computer screen. "I have a ton of work to do, so I'll probably be here late." She heard a heavy sigh on the other end. "What?"

"It seems all you have time for these days is work. Why don't you try focusing on *our* business for once."

"And what business is that?"

"You don't even know, do you?" asked Jackson, sounding exasperated. "We've been engaged for what, four months now, and we have yet to discuss any wedding plans. Hell, you won't even set a date. I've tried my best to not put any pressure on you, but am now starting to wonder if you've even given it any thought."

"How can I think about a wedding when I barely have time for myself these days?"

"Yeah, or me."

"Jackson, don't start this, okay?"

"Start what?"

"This," she said, feeling heat rising to her temples. "I'm at work."

"Really? I think we already established that."

Letting out a deep sigh, she remained silent for a moment then said, "Look, I don't want to argue with you, okay? You know how competitive things are around here. I was just given a new assignment and need to do a good job so I can prove I have what it takes."

"I understand that," he replied, "but there are other things that are just as, if not more important. I didn't want to talk about this over the phone, but since you insist on working all day and night, I guess I have no choice."

"What is it?" she asked, feeling her stomach starting to wrap around her spine.

"I think I'm going to take my father up on his offer. I haven't made any commitments yet, because I wanted to talk to you about it first, but I think it would be a fresh start, for both of us."

There was silence for a moment as Jasmine contemplated the implication of his statement. "So, you expect me to just up and move to Vegas? Give up my life—my career?"

"I can support us if need be, but you don't have to give up your career. There are other ad agencies—"

"And there are other real estate agencies!"

"You know it's not the same. You can't compare the two."

Frustrated, Jasmine let out another deep breath and laid her head down on her desk, the phone still at her ear.

"You know, I don't get you," said Jackson, breaking the silence.

"What don't you get?" she asked, her voice coming out muffled against the table.

"Most women I know get excited about marriage and the prospect of planning their wedding. I've even had some tell me it's something they've dreamt about since childhood. I know plenty of women who would jump at the chance to be sitting where you're sitting."

"And there are plenty of guys who would love to be sitting where you're sitting!" she snapped, lifting her head up. His comment incited more anger than he thought possible, for it sparked memories of all his exes and fans she'd bumped into as of late.

Confused by her sudden outburst, Jackson said, "I didn't mean it like that. I don't know what it is with you, but you've been acting, I don't know…different. I know this whole job thing is new to you, and I realize work requires a certain amount of your time and attention, but so do I."

"I think you get more than enough attention," she argued.

"What are you talking about?"

"Nothing. I have to go," she said, ending the call. As soon as she pressed End, the sudden sound of a masculine voice broke through her thoughts.

"How long have you been working here?"

"Oh!" she said, spinning around in her chair with her hand clasped to her chest to find the client she had bid farewell to moments ago, standing in front of her. "You startled me."

"Sorry, didn't mean to," said Richard Lawson, the handsome, blue-eyed, shoe store owner the agency had entrusted her and Lisa to work with. The two were going to help take his company's sales "to the next level," as he put it.

"I um, I've been here a few months," she replied, finally responding to his question.

"Okay, great. Well, I look forward to working with your agency," he said, pulling a business card out of his pocket, "and seeing more of you," he added, handing her his card. She noticed how his eyes sparkled and smiled just as much as his mouth, and wondered if he was still talking business. "My cell number is at the bottom. I hope you use it sometime," he said, removing all suspicion.

Having been in a steady relationship for over a year, Jasmine didn't give much thought to other men, either ignoring or remaining oblivious to their advances. Plus, she had grown accustomed to being the aggressor, and hadn't had her sights set on anyone since she and Jackson got together, and she'd relinquished her pursuit of Stacey. Although she had never been one to shy away from a little innocent flirtation, she didn't think an office hook up is what management had in mind when they coined the term, "courting your client."

"Married?" he asked, glancing down at the sparkling diamond ring on her finger.

"No, engaged," she corrected.

"Oh, okay. I can work with that."

"Excuse me?"

"I was engaged once, so I know anything can happen…not that I'm wishing failure upon you, but, at least I know I have a chance."

Shockingly, Jasmine was at a loss for words. She hadn't picked up on Richard's attraction to her during their meeting, and definitely hadn't expected him to be so forward. Considering he was a client, and they were at work, she didn't know what to say, but knew she needed to remain professional.

"Look Mr. Lawson, I—"

"I hope to hear from you," he said, cutting her off. "After all, we could all use a friend every now and then."

Jasmine sat with eyes wide and mouth agape as Richard pivoted on his heels and began heading toward the elevators. As soon as she saw him disappear behind the sliding doors, Lisa, who had been standing close by and heard everything, rushed to her side.

"Oh my gosh, he was so into you!"

"What?" Jasmine asked, confused. She had no idea Lisa had been eavesdropping.

"Blue eyes. He was totally flirting with you!"

"Yeah, I see," she said, glancing down at the business card she held in her hand.

"I swear, life just isn't fair…"

"What are you talking about?"

"Here I am, single and ready to settle down, with no prospects on the table, while you on the other hand are engaged, and now have another great catch vying for your attention. Life isn't fair."

"Yeah well, I just hope this…" stated Jasmine, holding up Richard's card, "…doesn't interfere with the work we're doing for his company. I could really use more samples in my portfolio."

"I'm sure you can handle it," Lisa assured with a smile before heading back to her desk.

Chapter 22

Jasmine spent the next few days working closely with Lisa on Richard Lawson's account. Meanwhile, the company announced its most recent account acquisition and Jasmine, along with other members of the creative team, expressed interest in working with the new client. Lisa had prepped her early on for the fierce competition present in the field, but what she had yet to master, however, was ways to combat some of the divisiveness and backbiting that plagued their otherwise pleasant work environment.

"I was assigned to this account yesterday," replied Morgan, after Jasmine inquired about the possibility of working with the new client. She kept her eyes fixed on the papers in front of her, not once looking up to meet Jasmine's hopeful, expressive gaze. "I already have a copywriter working on it," she added quickly, dismissing her with a wave.

Jasmine was livid, the proof evident in the hot steam now pouring out of her ears. She stormed out of the small conference room, leaving Morgan behind as she made her way back to her desk. Once there, she plopped down in her chair and began rubbing her temples. Not wanting to give anyone the satisfaction of seeing her lose it, she bolted through the office, ran inside one of the vacant conference rooms, and slammed the door shut behind her.

"I hate this stupid place!" she yelled while fumbling around inside the dark in search of the light switch. Once she found it, she flipped it on and saw Lisa lounging on one of the chairs.

"It took you long enough. I felt the same way after just a few weeks here."

"Oh my gosh, I'm so sorry," said Jasmine, now extremely embarrassed. "I thought this room was empty." *I really need to reserve my outbursts for the privacy of my own home*, she thought.

"I come in here to meditate whenever I find myself feeling stressed."

"You too?"

"I know things haven't been easy for you," began Lisa, rising from her chair. "But, I tried to warn you about some of the people around here. I had hoped none of their ridiculousness would affect you."

"Yes, you did," said Jasmine. "I just didn't think things were as bad as you claimed."

"Yeah, well, I'm a little older than you, and I've worked here longer, so I've grown accustomed to the company culture. Don't worry though, in a few weeks, whatever's bothering you today will feel like nothing compared to the issues tomorrow will bring."

"Great," replied Jasmine, frowning.

"What is it this time?"

"Morgan cut me out of the General Motors account. She knew how much I wanted to work with them. I could have really used a company like that in my portfolio, not to mention the bonus that comes along with it."

"I know how you feel," Lisa assured, "but you have to learn how to pick your battles around here. GM may be a great account, but there'll be plenty more. It's rare for the reps to allow any copywriters or graphic designers on the junior level to work on large accounts like that anyway. Don't worry, your time will come."

"I guess," said Jasmine, feeling disappointed. Yet, Lisa was right: her time would come sooner than she expected, for it was the following week when the two received word from management that Mr. Lawson was extremely pleased with the slogan they crafted for the banner ad he had requested. He was so pleased in fact that he hired the agency to build an entire campaign around it.

Jasmine and Lisa received accolades from their fellow staff members for helping the agency acquire a new account, and even Morgan said a few congratulatory words, although the sincerity behind them seemed questionable.

"Congratulations," she said to both Lisa and Jasmine upon hearing the news.

"Thanks," replied Jasmine enthusiastically.

"Enjoy your victory," she added before strutting away.

"She means, enjoy it while it lasts," Lisa whispered, shaking her head.

"You think?" asked Jasmine, who was so happy about her and Lisa's latest accomplishment that she had completely forgotten about how upset she'd been with Morgan a week prior.

"I'm positive," said Lisa with absolute certainty. "Come on, let's go."

*****

Later that evening, Jasmine headed to Jackson's condo to extend the celebration she had with her co-workers earlier in the day because she wanted to share her recent accomplishment with him. With her new job demanding more of her time, the two were finding it increasingly difficult to connect. Considering how sour their last in-depth conversation had been and how upset he was about the lack of time and attention he felt he was getting from her, she figured it high time she made it up to him. She therefore decided to surprise him with takeout, and had just stepped out of the taxi she had reserved for the ride over, when she suddenly saw the door to his condo swing open, and a female figure emerge. Ducking behind the bushes nearby, she watched him and the unidentified lady who stood at his doorstep share an affectionate embrace before seeing her off.

Emerging from the bushes, Jasmine rushed over to the woman as she headed toward the lot where her car was parked. She wanted to see whom Jackson had been spending his time with unbeknownst to her, and felt it best to get the woman's side of things first. True, what she saw might have been innocent, but knowing Jackson and his past, it probably wasn't.

"Excuse me," she said, approaching the young lady who had just made it to her vehicle. She hadn't been able to make out the woman's identity from the bushes, but immediately recognized her face and body once she got in close range: it was Carmen, the curvy Latina she had met at the barbershop a few months prior.

"Oh, hey…Jasmine, right?" stated Carmen, smiling.

"Yeah…yes," she replied, a little surprised Carmen remembered her name, although she definitely remembered hers. "What are you doing here?"

"Oh, I just stopped by to see my friend."

"Jackson, you mean?"

"Yes," she confirmed, tossing some of her long, dark locks over her shoulder. "Jackson and I go way back."

"Oh you do, do you?" asked Jasmine in a rhetorical rather than inquisitive tone.

"Yes, we do," stated Carmen, smiling brightly. "I just love what he's done with the place. Glad he took my advice to lighten the décor a bit, you know, give it a more feminine touch."

Jasmine was incensed not only by Carmen's presence, but also by the way she intimated her relationship with Jackson was more personal than business. And here she thought she was just someone he bumped into from time to time at his friend's barbershop.

"Well," she began, straightening her posture, as she stood in front of Carmen, who was a good four or five inches taller, "I can assure you he won't be needing anymore of your help."

"Oh really?" she replied upon stepping inside her vehicle. "I think he can speak for himself."

Enraged, Jasmine had one mind to kick Carmen's fender in, and another mind to dump the food she was carrying, all over her windshield. Yet, before she could do either resentful act, the car sped off, leaving her standing alone in the parking lot, a little dazed and very pissed. It took everything in her to keep from exploding as she rushed to Jackson's door, banging on it frantically.

"Hey…what are you doing here?" he asked, stepping out of the way as she barged past him.

"You would wonder that, wouldn't you?"

"What are you talking about?"

"I came over to surprise you with dinner and instead got a surprise of my own after running into that bitch from the barbershop in the parking lot. What the hell was she doing here?!"

"Calm down—"

Calm down? Calm down! What Jackson failed to realize, she thought, was that uttering those two words when she was already at her boiling point would do nothing but incite the opposite reaction. "I'm not going to calm down until you tell me what's going on!"

"She just stopped by to drop off the signed documents I need to close on the new location for the barbershop. I told you; Rob is looking to relocate—"

"Yeah, and she's not Rob."

"She's his assistant."

"I bet," said Jasmine with an incredulous stare. "And just what has she been assisting *you* with? According to her, she helped you decorate your place."

"What?"

"We had a little chat out in the parking lot. She sure didn't look like she was here on business with those tight fitting jeans she had on. And, why are you two conducting business so late? Couldn't you have found a neutral place to meet at, or better yet, why didn't you just stop by the shop in the morning?"

"Because she was in the neighborhood, and I need to send these off first thing tomorrow," he said, pointing at the papers that sat on his coffee table. "And as for her attire, you've seen how the women dress at the shop, so why are you surprised?"

Jasmine kept a firm grip on the handle of the takeout bag she was still holding, and tried her best not to hurl it at him. She could feel heat rising to her temples as he stood in front of her, attempting to defend the activity that appeared highly suspicious. His story may have been true, but before she could make up her mind to believe it, she noticed a smile slowly creep across his face, and that's when she lost it.

"Hey!" he yelled, catching the bag full of food she tossed his way with all her might. Luckily for him, he had quick reflexes.

"I don't see anything funny!"

"Neither do I. Sit down!" he barked, his voice filled with enough bass to cause the hairs on the back of her neck to stand up.

Like a child getting scolded for bad behavior, Jasmine took a seat on Jackson's couch and stared up into his eyes, the darkness of which was more spellbinding than frightening.

"I don't have anything to hide, Jasmine, and I'm telling you the truth. Carmen and I are friendly, but that's it."

"You never slept with her?"

"No," he declared, noting the skeptical look on her face. "And, contrary to what you may think about me, I do remember who I've been with, and I've always used precaution—"

"Yeah, except for when you got Charmaine pregnant, right?"

Jackson didn't respond and instead glared at her, the intensity of his eyes forcing her to look away. There was no doubt he was pissed. The two remained silent until finally he said, "The only reason why you saw me smiling earlier is because I do find your anger toward me a bit comical. I mean, if it weren't for these random fits of jealousy, I wouldn't think you cared much about me considering how consumed you've been with work."

"Oh, so you find security in my discomfort, is that it?" she asked, springing up off the couch. "Believe me, now is not the time to have your ego stroked—"

"I've missed you, Jazz," he said, cutting her off as he grabbed hold of her. She tried wriggling free from his embrace, but his grip was firm. "We barely spend time together anymore, and I'm sorry you let your imagination get the best of you."

"My imagination?" she asked, growing incensed all over again. "I just saw—"

"What you saw was a business transaction, nothing more, nothing less."

"Do you always hug your clients? If I recall correctly, you shook hands with Rob after meeting with him at the barbershop."

"It's different between men, you know that."

"Oh, okay, so you won't mind me hugging my male co-workers and friends?"

"You're free to do whatever you want because I trust you. I realize I messed up by not telling you about Charmaine, but aside from that, I've been nothing but transparent with you. I've introduced you to my family and friends; I've given you the keys to my car; I even gave you a key to my place, yet you rarely come over and when you do, you insist on knocking on the door."

She stared up into his eyes, speechless, for he was telling an undisputable truth. Aside from choosing to not disclose his previous engagement and pregnancy scare, he had been very open with her, sharing his life and feelings freely while she remained guarded in certain aspects. Just telling him she loved him still proved challenging, and now that they were engaged, a slight case of cold feet was slowly becoming an issue.

He tilted his head down toward hers so that they were almost eye-to-eye with each other and said, "You know I wouldn't hurt you, Jasmine. Not intentionally at least." She remained silent, but he could tell by how her frown lines had softened that she was no longer as angry as she had been when she first stormed into his place. He brushed her cheek softly with the back of his hand and she leaned into it slightly. He took that as a green light, moving in for a kiss.

She didn't do anything to stop the kiss, which was filled with as much passion and heat as their argument had been. Jackson had been driving her crazy from the moment they met, but she never once thought she'd be crazy in love with him. It was a truth she hated to admit, but he had an exceptional ability to get under her skin...in more ways than one. He could upset her like no other, and yet possessed a level of irresistibility not even a cynic of her magnitude could ignore.

"Damn," he said, once their tongues had disengaged.

She hadn't even realized how aggressive she had been until she glanced down at her hand and saw the bulk of his tie wrapped around her fist, having used it as leverage to pull him to her. Prior to that, her hands had taken on a life of their own, first wandering all over his chest, then dipping down to his waist before roaming all over his backside. He responded in kind by lifting her up by her thighs and wrapping her legs around his waist. She allowed herself to get lost in the moment, but then suddenly pulled away in an attempt to regain control, for she enjoyed every minute of their physical contact—contact the two hadn't shared much of as of late.

"In the future," she began, struggling to control her breathing as she slowly unwound his tie from around her hand, "out of respect for me...us, can you please have clients that look like Carmen meet with you in the daytime, and at a public place?"

Laughing, Jackson lowered her back down to the ground and said, "Yes, I can do that." He brushed a few strands of hair out of her face before cupping her cheek with his palm. "Look," he began, his breathing now heavy, as he too was trying to regain his composure. How the same woman could push his buttons, inciting anger in one second and then his arousal the next was beyond him. "The only woman I want to be with is you," he stated, his forehead pressed firmly against hers.

"Really?" she asked, desiring nothing more than for his words to ring true.

"Yes, really," he replied, taking a deep breath. "Just promise me I won't have to wait too long for you to kiss me like that again," he said, glancing down at his now wrinkled shirt.

"Whatever," she said, rolling her eyes as she adjusted her clothes, which were also disheveled, as his hands had been all over her, too.

Although she had forgiven him, she wasn't quite ready to dismiss her encounter with Carmen. "Carmen said you and her go way back, and that she even helped you decorate your place," she stated, trying to gauge his response, yet he appeared unfazed by the claim.

"I met her the same time I met Rob, and the two of them did come over shortly after I moved here. She may have made a few suggestions, some of which you don't seem to mind. You've told me several times how much you like the décor and the fact that it isn't all black, because believe me, had she not given me some female advice, this place would look a lot more drab."

Jasmine believed what he said to be true, but a part of her was still irked by the fact that another woman was taking pride in having helped decorate his pad. She was starting to feel more and more displaced, as if the women from his past and present held a special place in his life that she had yet to occupy.

"You know me better than anyone, Jazz," he said, as if having read her mind. "You have me in ways no one else has. I want you to trust that."

She gazed into his eyes and couldn't believe her ears. Somehow he knew exactly what to say, what she needed to hear in order to feel safe with him again.

"If you're upset that Carmen helped me decide the color scheme for the living room," he continued, "then perhaps you'll find comfort in knowing that I still need help decorating the bedroom. I could really use your ideas." He slid his hands down the length of her arms until their fingers interlocked. "Come," he said, pulling her toward the stairs.

"You've been here for over three years," she said, now grinning from ear-to-ear. Surely he didn't think she would fall for a line like that. "Last time I checked, your room looked just fine," and with that, they both burst into laughter.

"Hey, it was worth a shot," he said, still laughing.

With their squabble now squashed, the two decided to eat some of the Thai food Jasmine had brought over, some of which had spilled out of the containers and into the bag, thanks to her having hurled it across the room at him. Yet, despite the fact it had been jostled around, they were hungry enough to give it a go, and she stood back and watched as he spread a blanket out on his living room floor so they could enjoy an indoor picnic.

"Lisa and I helped the agency land a new account," she said, finally able to share the reason behind her surprise visit.

"Congratulations," said Jackson, in between bites. "I'm proud of you, babe."

"Thanks," she replied, giving his chin a light squeeze.

"By the way, do you always dress like this at work?"

"Like what?" she asked, glancing down at the sheer, cinched-waist blouse she was wearing with a solid camisole underneath. She had paired it with a flared pleated skirt that fell right above her knees, along with a pair of three-inch pumps. Jackson looked her up and down and raised a brow, an expression that made her ask, "What's wrong with this?"

"Absolutely nothing," he said. "I just think I need to visit your job again and let all the men know you're taken."

"You're silly," she said, shaking her head and laughing. "Oh, I almost forgot!" she exclaimed, suddenly leaping up from the floor. She ran toward the kitchen counter where she grabbed an item from the takeout bag. "Close your eyes," she said, approaching him with her hands hidden behind her back. She knelt down in front of him and said, "Now, open."

His forehead creased as his eyes scanned the once intact cupcake she held out in front of him. Like the Thai food, it too had been victimized by her act of fury. Had he not recognized the logo of his favorite bakery on the outside of the container, he would have thought she was offering him a lump of cream pie.

"Um, thanks," he said. "I wonder what it looked like before."

"Oh, shut up," she said, opening the container so that he could take a bite. "I know it looks crazy, but I'm sure it still tastes good. I'll just go ahead and sample it first to make sure it's okay," she teased, playfully drawing it toward her mouth.

Knowing how serious he was about his favorite dessert, she wasn't the least bit surprised when he steadied his eyes on hers like a lion on the prowl and said, "Jazz, you know I love you, but don't make me tackle you to the floor."

Instead of responding, she raised the cupcake to her nose and inhaled deeply. "Mmmm," she purred.

"Jazz…"

"Okay!" she shouted, once he positioned his body as though he were preparing to pounce. "Here, take it," she said, pushing it toward him.

"Smart girl," he declared with a wink.

Although Jackson was happy to hear that Jasmine was handling her transition from full-time student to full-time employee well, he wanted to make sure that she was also taking her new title as fiancée, just as serious. So, after washing down the last few bites of his cupcake with a can of soda, he glanced at her and asked, "Have you thought about a date for the wedding?"

"Not yet," she said, her body shifting slightly, as she was starting to feel uncomfortable about the new direction of their conversation. It seemed that ever since they had gotten engaged, things had started happening…things that made her feel less confident about their relationship in general, let alone their intent on becoming husband and wife. Her unpleasant encounter with Carmen earlier that evening being case in point.

Sitting quietly while his eyes scanned her face, she couldn't help but feel that he was searching for some sign, some confirmation that they were still on the same page. She hated how he seemingly had the ability to pierce through her with a single look, as if he were capable of examining her very soul. She therefore knew there was nothing she could say that could mask the uneasiness he already sensed, so she just offered a faint smile.

With his dark eyes steadied on hers, he said, "Well, I think you should think about it more."

She could tell by the way he was looking at her that he was disappointed she hadn't made any firm commitments concerning their future together. She still needed time to figure things out and was just starting to get her legs at work, and therefore hadn't yet mastered the art of balancing her career with her social life. Yet, despite all that, she loved him and wanted to give him the reassurance he seemed to be so desperately craving, so she scooted closer to him and said, "I will."

A satisfied smile spread across his face, and she could feel all the hostility that had been present between them earlier evaporate. He showed her he was indeed pleased with her response by giving her a quick peck on the lips before sucking on her bottom lip. Her tongue grazed his mouth, and she could taste the cream cheese flavored icing he had just devoured, tickling her taste buds. The sensation of their mouths taking in each other's essence intensified with each passing moment, and Jasmine soon felt herself falling down that rabbit hole again, as his body stiffened against hers.

"I think...I should go," she whispered softly, slowly pulling away.

He gripped a chunk of her hair as he held on tightly to the back of her head. "You sure you don't want to go upstairs and decorate my room?" he asked, peering deep into her eyes.

"Goodnight Jackson," she replied, landing a soft kiss on the tip of his nose.

"You really know how to torture a guy, you know that?"

Chapter 23

"I need to talk to you," said Lisa, appearing anxious as she stood outside Jasmine's cubicle early one winter morning.

Without hesitation, she followed her friend down the hall and inside one of the conference rooms. "What's up?"

"You remember that ad campaign we worked on a few months back—the one for that cosmetics company Carl liked?"

"Of course," replied Jasmine, smiling. "What about it?"

"Morgan is trying to take credit for it. She's claiming the concept was all hers and that you and I stole it. She's had management in her back pocket for some time now, so you and I are in serious trouble unless we can prove it was our baby from start to finish."

The proud smile plastered across Jasmine's face faded. "That's it—" she began, heading toward the door.

"Calm down," said Lisa, cutting her off. "Believe me, I almost lost it too at first, but we have to stay focused so we can win this."

Jasmine felt heat rising from her feet and found herself having to say a silent prayer as Lisa continued to speak. Encouragement from the Lord was the only thing keeping her from marching straight over to Morgan's desk and dragging her across the office by her fiery red hair.

"...Just give me some time to think of something," said Lisa, unaware that Jasmine had tuned her out. "I'll get back to you by end of day today."

The two dispersed, and Jasmine headed back to her cubicle and laid her head down at her desk. Getting anything accomplished after hearing Lisa's news proved extremely difficult, for she couldn't take her mind off of Morgan and how low she had finally sunk. She was so angry she couldn't think straight, and even got off on the wrong floor upon returning to the office after lunch.

Once she made it back to her cubicle to finish up the second half of the workday, she noticed a vase full of long-stemmed roses, sitting on top of her desk. Smiling, she pulled one rose out of the bunch, raised it to her nose, and inhaled deeply. Jackson's gift was right on time, she thought, for it reminded her that there were bigger issues outside of work she needed to focus on, like him and their impending nuptials.

Taking a seat, she returned the rose to the vase then jumped slightly at the sound of her office phone, which had started to ring. "Hello?"

"Hi. Can I speak to Jasmine please?"

"Speaking."

"Hey…it's Richard."

"Oh, hey," she replied, surprised to be hearing from her former client. "How can I help you Mr. Lawson?"

"Please, call me Richard."

"Okay…Richard. How can I help you?"

"I was just wondering if you received the flowers I sent."

Stunned, Jasmine's eyes shot over to the corner of her desk where the vase full of flowers stood. "Yeah—yes, I got them," she stuttered.

"You never called, so I wanted to send you something to let you know I haven't forgotten about you."

"Oh, I see," she said, staring down at her engagement ring. "I didn't think it was a good idea."

"So, you're still engaged?"

"You sound surprised."

"Not at all," stated Richard, clearing his throat. "If I were him, I'd do my best to hold on to you too."

"Thanks," she said, smiling.

"Well, I hope you enjoy the flowers. Hopefully they'll add some light to your day. How is work by the way?"

"It's good," she replied, although lately there hadn't been anything good about it other than the regular paychecks she was receiving. "But, things can get complicated at times," she added, hoping to infuse some truth into her statement.

"How so?"

"Well, there's a lot of competition in my field. And, it's not just with other agencies, but internal as well."

"I see," said Richard. "External competition can be great, but internal, not so much. The last thing you want to do is fight with co-workers on a regular basis. That redhead—what's her name? Mo—"

"Morgan," replied Jasmine, finishing his sentence.

"Yes. She strikes me as someone you might have difficulty with."

"Really?"

"Yeah. She wasn't very friendly with me and some of my staff, so I can only imagine how she is at the office."

Wow, she thought. *This man is very perceptive.* "Well," she continued, trying not to smile too hard, "she is definitely a handful."

"You seem to be a pretty tough cookie though," Richard admitted. "And, you're sharp, so I'm sure you can hold your own."

"Well thanks," Jasmine replied, happy to receive much-needed affirmation. True, Jackson had been supportive as well, but he had no idea what types of obstacles she was dealing with as of late considering he had practically deemed any work-related topics off limits in hopes that she would focus more on him and their plans for the future.

After sharing some of his shoe store's recent successes, which he attributed in part to the advertisements she helped create, Richard asked, "Can I call you again sometime?"

"I don't think so Richard…" she replied, her voice trailing off as she glanced over at the bouquet of roses he had sent.

"Come on," he pleaded. "You're allowed to have friends, aren't you?"

Jasmine knew from experience that most men were incapable of engaging in platonic relationships, especially if they felt any sort of attraction to the woman in question. She already knew Richard was attracted to her, and he wasn't too hard on the eyes either. Thus, deep down she knew she should have declined his request, but considering Jackson had a few female friends he seemed to believe were harmless, she didn't see any reason why she couldn't have a few male friends of her own. "Okay," she said finally, providing him the number to her cell. After ending the call, she tried to resume working, but soon her cell phone started ringing.

"Hey, you busy?" asked Jackson once she answered the phone.

"I'm getting there. What's up?"

"I just got off the phone with my mom. She wants us to come home for Christmas. She would like to celebrate by throwing us an engagement party...Hello? You still there?"

"Yeah...yes," she replied, her mind now racing.

"Well, what do you think? I haven't confirmed yet because I figured you may want to spend Christmas at home with your dad."

"No, that's not it," she replied, suddenly recalling her disastrous surprise visit. "I'll check my calendar and get back to you before the week is out."

"Okay. Just let me know. My mom is really excited, so I'd hate to disappoint her."

He just had to throw that in there, she thought. Now his mother's happiness was her responsibility, too!

After ending the call, Jasmine leaned back in her chair and rubbed her temples. She was struggling to stay focused on the few tasks that lay before her, for she couldn't stop thinking about Morgan or Richard, and now Jackson's desire to take her back home to Vegas. Then, just when she was about to shut down her computer and call it a day, Lisa returned to her cubicle as promised.

"Hey, I've got a plan, but I'll need your help," she said, taking a seat on the edge of Jasmine's desk. She leaned in close to keep prying ears from hearing their conversation. "I have some print orders to track that can be used as a date stamp," she continued. "Morgan claims to have come up with the concept right before she left for vacation. She told Carl we must have come across some notes she left on her desk—notes that she of course, can't find. We had already sent a few comps out well before then. Now I just have to prove it."

"What should I do?" asked Jasmine, eager to help.

"I need you to start digging through old emails. You and I were bouncing concepts back and forth for weeks before finally settling on the one we submitted. If we can find some of those emails, that'll help."

"Got it," she said, although not the least bit confident Lisa's plan would work. She had already seen during her short stint at the agency just what a dog-eat-dog environment they were working in, and was starting to question whether or not she had the energy or desire to compete.

"Hey," began Lisa, upon noticing the distressed look and tiny frown lines etched across her forehead. "Are you okay?"

"Yeah…" she began, although she knew that answer was far from the truth. "Actually, no, I'm not."

"Why do I have the feeling this isn't just about Morgan?"

"It isn't," she confirmed.

"Uh oh. What's up?"

"Jackson wants me to spend Christmas in Vegas with his family."

"And that's a good thing, right?"

"Yes it is, but we still have a lot of things to figure out as far as our relationship goes, so that on top of this is starting to feel a bit much."

"Yes, I'm sure deciding which designer wedding gown to wear is quite stressful," said Lisa, rolling her eyes.

"Ha ha," said Jasmine, unamused by her lack of sympathy. "It's a little more complicated than that. For one, he's thinking about moving back to Vegas to work for his father. He says I should look for work out there or just quit working altogether. Says he can support us."

"Wow," said Lisa, surprised. "I'd love for a man to take care of me. This day and age, you can barely get a guy to pay for dinner."

"I hear you," began Jasmine, frowning, "but I'm used to being on my own. In the past it was just my father and me, then later it was just me. Now he has Angela and I have Jackson. Don't get me wrong, it's great having a partner, but sometimes it feels like a lot. Trust isn't something that comes easily for me. I mean, I trust Jackson…I do, but sometimes I feel like he's asking for more than I can give."

"Hmmm," said Lisa, glancing down at her feet, her legs dangling off the desk. "I do see how it would be difficult to give someone your trust like that. For one, you'll be giving up your independence. Marriage alone will do that, but now you'll be putting yourself in a position where you'll be financially dependent on him, which means you'll have even less freedom. I think it depends on the type of guy you're with though, because some men use money as a tool for manipulation, whereas others, I believe, genuinely want to support their wives and still allow them the freedom to make decisions and spend money as they see fit. The question is, which type of man is he?"

Jasmine remained silent for a moment, as she had yet to contemplate all the implications surrounding the possibility of her quitting her job and moving. She loved Jackson dearly, and didn't want to believe he would prove himself to be the type of man who would use money as a tool for manipulation. "I believe he really loves me and just wants me to be happy," she said finally.

"I hear you," said Lisa, smiling. "I'm sure you two will figure things out soon enough, but my vote is for you to stay here. All this drama wouldn't be the same without you."

"I bet," Jasmine replied, shaking her head

Lisa stood up and prepared to leave, but paused to offer a few encouraging words. "Good luck with Jackson; I'm rooting for you guys. And as for Morgan," she added, her eyes now sharp, "you and I are going to take that heffa down."

"Heffa?" asked Jasmine, now smiling. "You have officially been hanging around me for too long."

Lisa giggled, then headed back to her workstation while Jasmine gathered her belongings and prepared for the trip home.

Chapter 24

Jasmine agreed to spend Christmas in Vegas with Jackson's family considering the alternatives didn't seem very appealing: spend the holiday with her father and his new fiancée; or stay home with Foxy and ponder all the foolishness at work. Yes, an engagement party sounded stressful, but it was definitely her best option. Jackson planned to head out a few days before she did so he could assist his mother with the party arrangements and discuss business with his father.

The plan was for her to fly in on a Wednesday in the morning, but she made the mistake of going to work, thinking she could put in a few hours and leave. Instead, she got tied up and ended up arriving at the airport late, which meant she got bumped to a later flight. Jackson told her to call him once she made it to the airport, so after retrieving her luggage, she took a seat on a bench and dialed his number.

Meanwhile, Jackson was out running errands for his mother, who was putting a lot of time and energy into planning his and Jasmine's engagement party. Mrs. Taylor was in the kitchen going over her to-do list when she spotted his cell phone sitting on top of the counter. Since she was about to head out to the dry cleaners to pick up her outfit for the party, she decided to give the phone to her husband, who was conducting business inside the den.

"Excuse me," said Mrs. Taylor, upon entering through the French doors.

"Yes dear?" replied Mr. Taylor, looking up from the paper he held in his hands.

"Sorry to interrupt," she said, glancing over at her husband's office manager, who was sitting across from him at the large oak table. "I'm about to head out, but I should be back soon," she continued, returning her focus on her husband. "Please give Jackson his phone when he gets in. He left in a hurry and forgot it in the kitchen."

"Will do," replied Mr. Taylor, placing the phone on the table next to him.

Mrs. Taylor prepared to exit, and Mr. Taylor excused himself. "I'm going to see my wife out," he told Bianca, who was helping him close another sale. "Help yourself to a drink at the bar. I'll be back, soon."

"Okay," she replied, her eyes following the couple as they exited the room. She started to make her way over to the wet bar to fix herself a drink when she heard Jackson's cell phone begin to vibrate against the table. Curious, she walked over to the table and glanced down at the phone. Upon seeing Jasmine's picture flash across the screen, she was instantly struck with a devious scheme.

After allowing the call to go to voicemail, Bianca picked up the phone and raced toward the French doors of the den. She peered out into the hall to make sure the coast was clear before closing them. Quickly, she unfastened the buttons on her blouse and used the camera on Jackson's cell phone to take a few very indecent snapshots of herself—ones that did not include her face. Once she felt she had planted enough incriminating evidence, she returned the phone to the large oak table and succeeded at putting her clothes back in place before Mr. Taylor returned to the den, completely unaware of the misconduct that had taken place at his son's expense.

*****

After attempting to reach Jackson several times by phone with no luck, Jasmine finally hopped inside a cab and provided the driver with the address to Jackson's parents' house. It didn't take long for her to arrive, and once she made it to their doorstep, she was surprised to find him standing in the entryway with a wide grin on his face.

"Hey," he said, sweeping her into a hug. "I thought you were going to call."

"I did," she said once she pulled away. "You never answered your phone."

"Really?" he asked, patting his pockets. "That's strange. Well, anyway, I'm glad you're here. Let me get that for you," he said, taking her bags.

The two headed past the living room and down the hall toward the den, and right as they were about to turn the corner to enter the second hall that led to the guest bedroom, the door to the den flew open, and Bianca emerged.

"Oh, hi," she said, appearing surprised.

"Hello," said Jasmine, glancing at her and then back at Jackson, who appeared unfazed by her presence. Before he could say anything in response to her greeting, his father suddenly approached.

"Thanks again for all your help, Bianca," said Mr. Taylor, leaning against one side of the French doors.

"Anytime," she replied with a smile. "You two have a good evening," she said to Jackson and Jasmine as she passed by them on her way out.

"Jasmine," said Mr. Taylor, turning his focus on his son and his fiancée. "It's so good to see you again. Glad you decided to return and celebrate the holiday with us."

"Thanks," she said before quickly glancing over her shoulder at Bianca. "I'm happy to be here," she added, giving her future father-in-law a hug.

"I'm going to show her to her room," said Jackson, smiling as he watched the two embrace. "We'll see you and mom later for dinner," he said, grabbing hold of her hand.

"I'm sure she can find the room on her own," said Mr. Taylor, giving his son a sly grin. "But okay, I'll see you two later...oh, by the way," he said, suddenly remembering what his wife had asked of him earlier. "You left your cell phone here. Your mother wanted me to give it to you."

"Oh…okay," said Jackson, suddenly realizing why he had missed Jasmine's call. After retrieving the phone from his father, he led her down the hall toward the room she had stayed in a few months prior, and as soon as they made it inside, he dropped her luggage on the floor and pulled her into a tight embrace.

"Hello again," she said with a slight giggle once he had removed his mouth from hers.

"I'm so glad you're here."

"You seem surprised."

"Maybe I am," he said with a serious expression.

"Why?"

"Well, things have been kind of up and down with us lately. I wasn't sure if you wanted to spend the holiday with my family, let alone allow my mother to throw us an engagement party."

"I know," said Jasmine, taking a deep breath as she took a seat on the edge of the bed. Jackson sat down next to her and took her hand in his.

"I just want us to get back to a place of normalcy," he said, peering deep into her eyes.

"I feel like nothing has been normal since I graduated," she replied, staring back at him. "Work has been crazy, my father's engaged, and you and I spend less time together than we did before. I never thought I'd say it, but college life seemed so much easier."

"I understand how you feel," he said with a slight chuckle. "You do have a lot going on right now, but that's life. Despite how hectic things may get, you just have to center yourself and find peace in the midst of the chaos."

"I hear you," she replied, glancing down at his hand as it embraced hers. "So, Bianca was working here today?"

Jackson hesitated for a moment as he tried to decipher her expression. "Yes. She does a lot of work for my father in his den."

"Oh, okay," she said, glancing down at the floor.

"Why do you ask?"

"Well," she began, looking up at him, "I bumped into her during my first visit here. She tried to warn me about you—about your 'wandering' ways."

"What?" A look of shock and anger suddenly appeared across his face.

"What exactly happened between you two?"

He let out a deep sigh then asked, "Off the record?"

"Off the record" was a code they used to denote information one needed to share with the other that may prove difficult to handle. It basically meant that in that moment, each was allowed to say whatever was on his or her mind without any judgment or backlash from the other, and he knew, based on how upset she had been with him as of late that what he was about to share needed to be "off the record."

"Yeah...yes," she replied, the hesitancy in her voice contradicting her response. He shot her a look, so she said, "Okay, okay, off the record...I promise."

"Well, a few years ago, before you and I ever met," he began, making sure to stress the fact that he was speaking of the past, not the present, "Bianca and I had a one-night stand. I learned the hard way that not too many women can handle that sort of arrangement, regardless of how much they claim they can. Anyway, she's hated me ever since, so I wouldn't put anything past her. I even asked my father to let her go once, but instead, he scolded me for not using discretion, said I had no business scr—I mean, sleeping with the employees."

"Well, that definitely explains a lot," she said, shaking her head. "I could tell right away that she's not a big fan of yours, and believe me, that's rare."

"Yeah, well, I can assure you she's not the only one," he said, looking away. It only took a second for him to change the subject. "Anyway, enough about her," he said, stroking the top of her head with his hand. "I just want to focus on us. Speaking of which, I reconnected with my pastor and he's looking forward to meeting you on Sunday. He said he'd love to meet with us, if you're willing."

"For what?"

"Just to talk. He counsels couples all the time and thought he might be able to help us iron out our issues, you know, communicate better. Don't you think we've been arguing a lot lately?"

"No," said Jasmine, noticing his incredulous stare. "Okay, well, maybe just a little."

Jackson nudged her playfully then said, "He might be able to help with your trust issues too."

"I don't have trust issues," she argued with a frown.

"Okay, maybe he can work on your denial then." He smiled and she rolled her eyes at him, but soon began smiling too.

It was two days before Christmas, and their engagement party was scheduled for the day after. Jasmine was happy to see that she and Jackson were on good terms again, and that he was determined to work on their relationship. She wanted to be just as devoted, but couldn't help but think about all the stuff she needed to do concerning work. She had already found a few emails that could help prove the authenticity of her and Lisa's work to management, who was starting to believe Morgan just as Lisa suspected. She hoped to find more evidence and needed time to look for it; but she knew, based on how upset Jackson was about all the time and attention she was directing toward work, that it would have to wait until she returned home. She therefore resolved to enjoy both the holiday and their party, considering Mrs. Taylor had worked so hard to pull everything together. She didn't want the issues plaguing her relationship or the trouble at work to interfere with the festivities, and sincerely hoped she and Jackson could continue to maintain the peace, if not for themselves then for everyone else.

Chapter 25

The Taylor household was a sight to behold the night of Jackson and Jasmine's engagement party. Mrs. Taylor had the house decked out in red, green and gold to fall in line with Christmas, and although the holiday had already passed, everyone could feel the warmth and spirit of the season as soon as they stepped inside. "Wow," said Jasmine, admiring the decorations for the first time. "You've really outdone yourself."

"Thanks," said Mrs. Taylor. "Glad you like it."

"Like it? I love it!" she declared, feeling like a kid again as she headed over to one of the tables Mrs. Taylor had the caterer set up inside the foyer. It was covered in hors d'oeuvres and had a chocolate fountain in the center. Mrs. Taylor laughed as Jasmine took a huge bite out of a strawberry after dipping it inside the chocolate. "Where's Jackson?" she asked with her mouth full.

"I thought you knew. Perhaps he's still getting ready."

Mrs. Taylor was partially right, for Jackson was inside his father's den with Caleb, but instead of getting dressed, he was trying to mentally prepare himself for the night ahead. Although things between he and Jasmine appeared to be back on solid ground, deep down he knew there were still quite a few unresolved issues they needed to tackle.

"I still can't believe you're getting married," said Caleb, who stood a few feet away from Jackson as he sat on the edge of the large oak table, nursing a vodka tonic.

"Yeah," he replied, staring into his glass. "A part of me can't believe it either."

"Have you thought more about dad's proposal?"

"I have…" he began, pausing to take a sip of his drink. "But," he continued, "I haven't made any decisions yet."

"I should have known," said Caleb, flashing a crooked smile. "Always the rebel, this one."

"I'm not trying to rebel; I just have some things I need to figure out, that's all."

"It's cool, I get it. You're getting married—you probably want to run things by wifey first."

"She's not sold on the idea. It would be a big move for her—us. Plus, this whole thing with Xavier still bothers me," he said, rubbing his goatee. "I just wish he was included in all of this. He's worked so hard for dad, longer than you or I have. I'd hate for him to think I'm taking over."

"You don't owe him anything, Jackson," stated Caleb, who was quite aware of the long-standing rivalry that existed between his two brothers—the same one Jackson conveniently tried to ignore. "Xavier has to take responsibility for his role in all of this. Trust, his issues far surpass anything we've got going on at work."

"I hear you," Jackson replied, although not completely convinced.

"Have you spoken with him since our night out at Tao?"

"No. I've thought about calling him, but just haven't gotten around to it. I still can't believe he told Jasmine all that stuff about me and Charmaine."

"Xavier's a jerk—always has been. Nothing he says or does should surprise you."

Jackson didn't say anything in response to Caleb's comment. Perhaps because deep down, he knew it was true.

"Look, I love him too," added Caleb, sensing Jackson needed to hear it. "But," he continued, "I just can't get down with a lot of the things he says and does."

"I know," said Jackson, who had more on his mind than he was letting on. He stared off into the distance for a moment then said, "You know that stuff we were talking about at Tao?"

"You mean about you and Jasmine?"

"Yeah." Although neither of them stated what it was, they both knew exactly what he was referring to. Jackson felt slightly embarrassed to talk about his celibacy with his baby brother, but considering how Xavier had yanked the cat out of the bag, he figured he might as well get his opinion on it. "You don't think I'm a fool, do you?"

Caleb looked at his brother and smiled. "Look, if she's happy and you're happy, that's all that matters. Besides, I wouldn't take any relationship advice from Xavier if I were you."

"Thanks," he replied before downing the last bit of his drink.

"No problem," said Caleb, glancing down at his watch. "I'm going to go see if mom needs any help out there." He headed toward the door, but suddenly turned back around as if he had forgotten something. "Oh, and go easy on that, will you?" he asked, pointing toward the empty highball glass that sat on the table next to his brother.

"Don't worry," said Jackson, noting his concerned look. "I'll be out in a minute."

When he finally emerged from the den, he was wowed, just as much as Jasmine had been, by all the work his mother had put into planning the event. "This is really great, Mom," he said as he entered the living room where the deejay was setting up. He gave her a kiss on the cheek then glanced over at Jasmine, who was helping herself to more hors d'oeuvres inside the foyer. Their eyes locked and they smiled at each other. "Excuse me," he said, as he stepped away from his mother and began heading toward his fiancée.

Jasmine had just taken another big bite out of a strawberry, but had to pause in order to catch her breath once Jackson came into full view. "Wow," she said, admiring him as he approached. "You look...great."

"Thanks," he replied, smiling.

She thought he looked exceptionally handsome in the ocean blue, pure wool suit he had purchased specifically for the occasion. Its classic fit, which had been cut to allow for extra room throughout the chest, made him look like a black James Bond. She knew, having shopped with him several times, that even his plain white dress shirt had been chosen with great consideration, for she recalled how she had once offered to take him to Macy's to purchase a new dress shirt and tie, but he insisted on purchasing them from Thomas Pink, a place she soon discovered specialized in designing well crafted shirts and accessories for men. From its luxurious silk ties, high quality knitwear and designer cufflinks, Thomas Pink was to menswear what Victoria's secret was to lingerie. Seeing him decked out in an outfit only he could piece together made her realize just how consumed with work she had become, for she had the tendency to forget just how lucky she was to have someone like him in her life. Jackson wasn't just some pretty boy who liked to flash his latest toys, for he put just as much time and energy into caring for her as he did in his appearance. Although she had gotten angry when he said it, truth was, there were plenty of women who would love to be sitting where she was sitting…and she knew it.

"You look beautiful, as always," he remarked before slowly eyeing her from head to toe. He was just as enamored by her appearance as she was with his, and took a moment to relish in her semi-formal ensemble: a black mini dress with a wide scoop neckline and three-quarter length sleeves. It had sparkling red, silver, and gold sequins throughout, making it appear trendy and festive. She topped it off with a pair of shiny gold stilettos that showed off her curvy yet toned legs, and his reaction proved she had made the right choice.

"Thanks," she said, blushing.

"Apparently I've been a good boy because Santa has definitely been good to me."

"You have been good, and that's why I bought you a gift," she said, handing him the rectangular gift box she had placed on the serving table before his arrival.

"What's this?"

"Another Christmas gift. Open it."

He opened the box, and she watched as his eyebrows rose high onto his forehead. "Whoa, this is nice," he said, holding up his brand new watch. "How much did this set you back?"

"Don't worry about it. It's the least I could do after you gave me this," she said, holding up her ring finger, "and this," she continued, tugging at the crystal heart pendant draped around her neck, the one he had gifted her the night before for Christmas.

"This was a gift," he said, pointing at her necklace, "but this," he continued, holding up her hand, "is not. It's a promise of what's yet to come."

She examined the ring and took a moment to contemplate what he said before helping him put on his latest accessory. She watched as he admired it on his wrist and could tell by the excited look in his eyes that he was quite pleased with it. She was glad because she had put a lot of effort into finding it. When she walked into Tourneau and asked the salesman to help her pick out a gift for a "special person," she wasn't sure he would actually succeed at helping her find a gift that would suit her style conscious beau, because he seemed to have everything. Yet, seeing the stainless steel, dual time zone watch with a black dial wrapped around his wrist made her feel grateful for having heeded the salesman's advice. It was contemporary, sophisticated and sleek, just like him. And, with a face constructed of sapphire crystal—one of the strongest substances on earth next to diamond, she thought it the perfect engagement gift, for it symbolized how strong she desired their bond to be.

"You ready?" he asked, once they heard the doorbell ring.

"As ready as I'll ever be," she replied, smiling. Although not quite sure what to expect, Jasmine knew that the party was more for Jackson's benefit than her own, as the guest list was primarily comprised of his family and friends. Soon, the house was brimming with guests, as one person after another arrived, and before she knew it, she found herself smack dab in the center of his world.

Chapter 26

"Jasmine, I'd like you to meet my boss, Mr. Decker."
"Nice to finally meet you," said the seasoned gentleman, reaching for her hand. "Now I see why Jackson sneaks off to take personal calls while he's at work—you are stunning."

"Thank you," she replied, feeling her cheeks grow warm.

"Jackson is one of our top employees, so I'd hate to lose him. I hope you two aren't planning on settling down out here."

"We'll see," said Jasmine, glancing over at Jackson, who grabbed her hand and interlocked his fingers with hers. He and his boss continued to talk while she scanned the room full of partygoers. She couldn't get over the number of people in attendance, and it made her wonder what their wedding would be like. Suddenly, her palms grew sweaty.

Once Mr. Decker excused himself to accompany his wife near the hors d'oeuvres, Jasmine soon became bombarded by a slew of introductions, as she came face to face with Jackson's co-workers, neighbors, and friends until finally, she got a chance to make a few introductions of her own. "Thanks so much for coming, Dad," she said upon seeing him enter the Taylor residence. She gave him a warm embrace before turning to greet his fiancée, whom she was still a little perturbed by. "I'm glad you could make it too…"

"Angela. Angela Dennis," said her father's bride-to-be, as she assisted her in recovering her suspiciously failing memory.

"Angela, right. Well, Angela, this is Jackson. Jackson, this is my father's fiancée."

"Nice to meet you," said Angela, shaking his hand. "You two make a handsome couple."

"Thank you," he replied. "May I get you two a drink?"

"No thank you. We're good."

Jasmine watched as Angela clung to her father's arm, a sight which, combined with hearing her refer to the two of them as a "we," made her cringe. "Excuse us," she said, tugging on Jackson's arm. "Let's go say hi to Lisa." She led him over to the other side of the room where she found her good friend and co-worker, sipping on a cocktail.

"Hey," said Lisa, her eyes growing wide as the couple approached. "This is quite a turnout."

"I'll say," said Jasmine, glancing around the room.

"It's good to see you again," said Jackson, giving Lisa a hug. "So glad you could make it."

"You know I had to support my girl," she replied, smiling.

He wanted to stay and chat some more, but got distracted upon spotting Xavier enter the room. "I'll be back," he told Jasmine before planting a kiss on her cheek.

"Okay," she said, although she had no idea why he was leaving her side.

Once he had made it out of earshot, Lisa leaned toward her and said, "Okay, is it just me, or is he even more handsome than he was the day I met him?"

"It's just you," said Jasmine, rolling her eyes. Although, she had to admit, Jackson had taken her breath away when she first spotted him in his latest ensemble. She glanced over in his direction and witnessed the brief yet awkward exchange he appeared to be having with his brother. It was then that she realized she had failed to ask him how things were between the two of them after discovering that Xavier had exposed some of his dirty secrets.

"So, they say weddings are the best place to meet people, but they need to add engagement parties to the list because there are some good-looking guys here."

"Really?" asked Jasmine, returning her focus on Lisa. "Like who?"

"Well, there's the tall, green-eyed one over there."

"That's Jackson's brother," said Jasmine, catching Xavier's eye. He looked at her and nodded. "But," she continued before looking away, "He's taken...at least I think he still is."

"Oh okay," said Lisa, choosing to leave well enough alone. "Well then, what about him?" she asked, gesturing toward Caleb, who was standing in one corner of the room, cupping his cell phone to his ear. "He's hot."

"That's their younger brother, Caleb. He is a cutie, but he's only twenty-four."

"What are you trying to say?" asked Lisa, cocking her head to the side. "I may be older than you, but I'm not a cougar yet."

"Excuse me," said Jasmine, laughing as Lisa flexed her fingers like a cat on the prowl. Suddenly, she felt her throat grow dry. "I'm going to get a drink. You stay put," she ordered, shooting a look at her friend. "Don't do anymore hunting until I get back."

"Okay, I won't," she promised with a smile.

Jasmine headed toward the punch bowl, grabbed a cup and began filling it when a soft tap landed on her shoulder. "Ahem," said a voice from behind. She turned and saw a young man she had yet to identify, standing before her. "Remember me?"

Jasmine's eyes scanned up and down the young man's person, and it wasn't until she took note of his thick, dark eyebrows and dark eyes...eyes that were very reminiscent of Jackson's, that she figured out who it was. "Jamal?"

"Yes."

"Wow, you look...different," she said, her eyes now falling on the newfound biceps and pecs that protruded from beneath his white dress shirt. She noticed how he made sure to keep a few buttons undone to best show off his hard work. "You've filled out quite a bit."

"Yeah," he said, smiling. "I needed to bulk up for football season."

"And that you have," she confirmed, still needing a moment to fully comprehend his drastic transformation. "What a difference two years make."

Jasmine could still clearly recall how scrawny and uncoordinated Jamal had been two years prior, and found it funny how Jackson had asked him to serve as her bodyguard during the Big Game between Cal and Stanford, although he himself needed one. When disgruntled fans tore up the stadium, causing an all out riot, the two became separated. It wasn't until Jackson came to their rescue that they were finally reunited, and she found him disheveled, banged up and bruised. With twenty extra pounds of muscle added to his frame, he now appeared better able to hold his own.

"You can now give Jackson a run for his money—"

"Let's not get carried away," interrupted Jackson, who had caught the tail end of their conversation. He draped an arm around Jamal's chest, drew him into a chokehold, then kindly reminded him, "You still are and always will be, my *little* cousin."

Jasmine had always thought, based on how much they resembled each other, that Jackson and Jamal could have been brothers. Seeing them side-by-side again and now having met his real brothers only confirmed that. After watching the two exchange playful jabs, she excused herself and began heading back over to where Lisa stood, but decided to take a detour once she discovered her in the midst of chatting with one of Jackson's male business associates. As her eyes began scanning the room, she soon spotted her father, and decided to chat with him for a bit, but chose to cut the conversation short after spotting his fiancée re-emerge from her trip to the bathroom. Deciding it time to refill her glass, she headed back toward the punch bowl, and that's when she spotted someone familiar helping themselves to a drink.

"Hello again," said Jasmine, positioning herself next to Bianca.

"Oh, hi, so nice to see you again," said Bianca, glancing over at her. "Mr. Taylor added me to the guest list. Hope you don't mind."

"Not at all."

"Well, it's good you're so secure in your relationship. If my fiancée paraded his exes around in front of me, I'd be livid."

"Exes?" asked Jasmine, now completely tired of Bianca's snarky remarks. "I don't see any exes here, and from what I hear, you weren't exactly an ex."

"Is that right?" asked Bianca with a smirk. "And how do you know what we were?"

"Because he told me," replied Jasmine with irritation in her voice. "You spent one night together, big deal," she said, trying to sound unaffected by it all, although deep down, the thought of Jackson being with any woman other than herself—past or present, made her feel sick.

"How do you know it was just one night?" asked Bianca, cocking her head to the side. "How do you know he wasn't with me a few days before you came into town? Oh, that's right," she continued, snickering. "You know because he told you. Sweetie, you have a lot to learn," she said, fixing her mouth into a phony pout. "Men like that don't settle down, and they're full of secrets. By the way, have you gone through the photo gallery on his cell phone lately? He has a thing for keeping naughty mementos on there."

"You're lying," said Jasmine, her heart now racing.

"Really? Ask him," said Bianca, brushing past her.

Stumbling slightly, Jasmine instantly saw red and was prepared to dig her claws into Bianca when suddenly, she caught a glimpse of Jackson amidst the crowd talking to a pretty young woman with cocoa brown skin. She watched as the two shared a laugh, his female companion tossing her head back and flashing a toothy smile before flirtatiously placing a hand on his arm.

"Enjoying yourself?" asked Caleb, who suddenly approached.

"Yeah…yes," she replied, keeping a steady eye on Jackson and his female companion. "Who is that?"

Caleb followed the path her eyes had taken and said, "That's um…an old family friend." She shot him a look, and he could tell she wasn't buying it, so he begrudgingly added, "and…one of his exes."

"That's what I thought," she said, becoming incensed all over again. Scanning the room full of partygoers, her gaze first landed on her father and his fiancée, then on Lisa, then back to Jackson, and suddenly, all the issues and underlying stress she had tried to suppress came rushing back, and she just couldn't take it anymore. "Excuse me," she said, stepping away from Caleb, who watched as she exited the foyer and made a beeline for the den. Once inside, she closed the door behind her, and it wasn't until she made it over to the large oak table that she noticed Xavier, sitting on the leather couch across from the wet bar, smoking a cigar.

"Leaving the party so soon?"

"I um…I just needed to take a break," she said, averting her eyes from his.

"Me too," he said, holding up his cigar. "Want a hit?"

"No thanks."

She turned to head back out to the party, but Xavier had risen from the couch and was now standing in front of the French doors, blocking the exit.

"Excuse me," she said, trying to step around him.

"Not so fast," he said, stepping in front of her.

She wanted nothing more than to exit through the French doors and head back out to the party, but Xavier seemed determined to stand in her way. And to think she had tried to escape her troubles by retreating inside the den, when all she did was run into some new ones.

Chapter 27

Startled, Jasmine peered into Xavier's bloodshot eyes and took a step back. "I need to get back out there," she said.

"What's the rush?" he asked before taking a few steps towards her. "You came in here for a reason, and I could use the company."

"Had I known you were in here, I would have gone elsewhere."

"And what's that supposed to mean?"

"Nothing," she said, noting the wild look in his eyes. Suddenly, she felt her heart rate increase. "I…I just want to be alone, that's all."

"That's funny," he said, inching his way closer. "This is supposed to be an engagement party for you and your fiancé, and yet you want to be alone? As fate would have it, you're in here with me."

Backing away, Jasmine bumped up against the table, then glared at him and said, "Like I said, I didn't know you were in here."

"Sure," he replied, grabbing a lock of her hair. He leaned in close and she could smell his breath, which reeked of liquor and cigar smoke. "If I had a woman like you, I wouldn't let her out of my sight, but as you can see, your fiancé's not here…"

"He'll be here in a minute," she lied. She had just walked out of the party where Jackson was busy chatting with his ex, so she doubted he even knew where she was.

"Well, he's not here now, is he?" stressed Xavier, his hand now traveling down the lock of hair he held in his hand. "You need a real man to teach you what love is all about." His hand brushed against her breast as he reached the lower portion of her tresses, and that's when she lost it.

"Trust, Jackson is as real a man as they get," she retorted, pushing him away.

"Please," he said, biting his lower lip. "I taught him everything he knows. Why settle for the copy when you can have the original?"

"Xavier, you're drunk. How about you and I walk out of here and pretend this never happened?"

"Or, how about we stay here and do something we'll both never forget?"

"I'm warning you," she said, holding up her hands, her palms facing forward. It was a self-defense tactic she had learned, but had never actually used. It was supposed to appear as though she were surrendering, when she was really preparing to hit, push and block her opponent—or at least that was what she had been taught in the one thirty-minute session she had taken a few years back at the Y. She had no idea if it would even work, but was sure praying it would. "You're drunk and just need to cool off," she added before quickly scanning the room in a desperate attempt to come up with an exit strategy.

Seeing Jasmine prepared for battle made Xavier laugh, for he had never dealt with a woman as feisty as she was. He found it arousing and humorous, all at the same time. "Believe me sweetie, I ain't drunk. Matter of fact, why don't you bring your pretty little ass over here, and I'll prove to you just how sober I am." He leaned into her, and she kneed him in his groin while using her greatest defense mechanism yet…her voice.

Letting out a blood-curdling scream, Jasmine threw herself on top of the large oak table and scurried across it while Xavier hunched forward, attempting to recover from the pain she had just inflicted upon him. She had screamed so loudly and in such a high pitch that he swore he saw the glass liquor bottles that were sitting on top of the wet bar shake. Luckily for her, it didn't take long before she saw the doors to the den swing open, as Caleb and Jackson rushed inside.

"What's going on?" inquired Caleb, who had instructed Jackson to check on his fiancée after seeing how upset she appeared upon spying him with his ex. The two had already begun making their way down the hall, but hastened their steps upon hearing her scream, the shrill of it heard over the music and chatter surrounding them.

"Nothing," replied Xavier, throwing his arms up in the air and smiling. He was doing his best to ward off his two brothers, who were at the end of their rope with his shenanigans. "We were just taking a break—"

Jackson stepped out from behind Caleb and punched Xavier square in his jaw, cutting the conversation short once he saw Jasmine standing on the other side of the table, frazzled with her back against the wall.

Caleb and Jasmine watched Xavier fall against the large oak table, the impact of the punch jarring his inebriated mind. He flailed around for a moment, but soon regained his balance. Once back on his feet, he charged at Jackson like a bull, wrapping his arms around his waist as he pushed him toward the French doors to the den, which were now wide open, giving the guests a clear view of the chaos taking place inside.

Being of sound mind and therefore having full control of his motor skills, Jackson planted one foot behind him, and used it as leverage to plow into his brother. He pushed him back toward the table, and it wasn't long before he had him laid out on top of it again. Just when he was about to drive his fist into the side of his face once more, Caleb pulled him off. "That's enough!" he shouted, struggling to contain Jackson, who was full of rage. It was then that some of the guests began heading toward the den to see what all the commotion was about, including Mr. and Mrs. Taylor, and Jamal.

"Let go!" shouted Jackson, as he tried throwing Caleb off of him. Xavier used the distraction as an opportunity to charge at him again, but Jamal, who had just entered the room, stepped in between them and took hold of Xavier.

"What the hell is going on in here?!" demanded Mr. Taylor, shocked and embarrassed by the barbaric behavior displayed by his nephew and sons. The music and chatter that had once filled the house ceased, and you could hear a pin drop.

Jamal and Caleb restrained Xavier and Jackson respectively, as they stared each other down like two mountain lions, each one trying to assert himself as the alpha male. There was silence for a while until Jackson said, "Ask him," finally responding to his father's question, his nostrils flaring as his chest heaved in and out. His dark eyes, now razor sharp, sliced through Xavier.

"Well?" asked Mr. Taylor, glancing at his eldest son.

"You would question me, wouldn't you?" Xavier retorted, now angry with his father. "Never questioning 'the golden child.'"

"Grow up!" yelled Mr. Taylor.

"You think I don't know what's going on here?" asked Xavier, pointing at his brothers and then his father. "I know all about your private meetings and plans to cut me out of the business. I may be a lot of things, but I'm not dumb."

"That has nothing to do with this—"

"That has everything to do with this!" growled Xavier, cutting Jackson off. "All my life I've busted my ass for you, but that's not good enough, is it?" he asked, turning his attention back on his father. "The prodigal son returns, and you're ready to bestow all your riches upon him?! I guess being married to a stripper didn't fit the picture perfect image you wanted to portray, so as her son, I'm now paying the price."

"What are you talking about?" insisted Mr. Taylor, looking perplexed. "Jackson hasn't squandered his money on women and liquor like you have, so your analogy makes no sense! And as for your mother," he began, a furrow forming in his brow, "You can't begin to know how I felt about her."

At that, Mrs. Taylor, who had been consoling Jasmine behind the oak table where she stood, decided it time to take her back to her room. Yet before getting whisked away, Jasmine noted the pained look on Xavier's face. Seeing tears in his eyes suddenly made her feel sorry for him, despite the fact he had tried to violate her just moments earlier.

Mr. Taylor, also noticing Xavier's wounded look, softened his tone and said, "You have worked hard, Son, but you need help."

"Riiight," said Xavier, cutting his eyes at Jackson.

"I have no intention of taking anything from you—never did. I just don't understand why you would take this out on her—" Jackson stopped abruptly upon scanning the room to discover that Jasmine was no longer there. Blinded by rage, he hadn't seen her and his mom walk out.

"I was doing you a favor," said Xavier with a smirk. "Women are a dime a dozen. That little tramp will bring you nothing but trouble—just like all the rest."

At that, Jackson lunged at his brother, again, knocking him back down onto the table. He was so revved up that it took both Caleb and Jamal to restrain him this time. Once they had succeeded at pulling him back, they watched Xavier stumble to his feet before using the back of his forearm to wipe his mouth, which was full of blood. His pain and anger proved more potent than any alcoholic beverage he had ever consumed, for he spat out one final remark before his father tossed him out.

"You think you're hot shit. *Please.* You used to want to be me."

"Perhaps once," began Jackson, struggling to catch his breath. That third round almost depleted his reserves. "But," he continued, "not anymore."

"Go home," said Mr. Taylor, placing a hand on Xavier's shoulder, which he knocked off, causing his father to stare at him in disbelief.

"I thought I was home," he said before storming out.

*****

Jasmine sat at the foot of the bed inside the guest bedroom of the Taylor household as she and Mrs. Taylor attempted to make sense of all the chaos and madness they had just escaped.

"I'm so sorry about this," said Mrs. Taylor for the third time.

"It's not your fault," said Jasmine, confused as to why she seemed to be taking an unnecessary amount of responsibility for Xavier's outrageous behavior.

"I knew he'd fly off the rails one day," said Mrs. Taylor, now pacing the floor. "When the boys were growing up, I did my best to reach out to him. I knew he had a mother and therefore didn't need me to assume that role, but I tried to establish some type of bond so that there would be cohesiveness between our two families." She took a seat next to Jasmine on the bed and hung her head low. "No matter what I did or how much I tried to reach out to him, I just never seemed to make any progress."

"I'm sure it didn't help that you're not that much older than he is," offered Jasmine, who was aware of the thirteen year age gap that existed between she and Mr. Taylor, making her less than a decade older than his eldest son.

"True," agreed Mrs. Taylor. "However, looking back on it, I don't think my age would have made a difference. That child resented my mere existence."

Having grown up a motherless child, Jasmine could definitely relate to Xavier's resentment toward his stepmother, as she too found any attempt of outreach by an outsider intrusive. Even now at the age of twenty-two, she was finding it extremely difficult to accept her father being in a relationship.

"I never felt comfortable with Xavier being around my boys," continued Mrs. Taylor. "Kit, his mother, never seemed to have a firm grasp on him when he was a teen. She let him run the streets way more than I ever allowed my sons." She paused for a moment, and appeared as though she were trying to choose her words carefully. "I hate to say it, because he is my husband's child, but I always feared he would be a bad influence on my boys. And since he's much older, I just never felt comfortable with them hanging out. But, whenever I tried to voice my concerns, I got shot down. 'They're brothers,' Samuel would say. So, I just learned to keep quiet because the last thing I wanted was for him to feel as though I was trying to isolate his child."

"I see," said Jasmine, who was starting to gain a better understanding of the dynamics that existed between the brothers—a perspective she wouldn't have gained by talking to Jackson, for he himself had yet to come to terms with things.

"Jackson thought Xavier hung the moon," said Mrs. Taylor, rolling her eyes. "I think the toughest thing about being a parent is that you can spend countless hours teaching your children right from wrong, but in the end, it is ultimately up to them to decide how they will live their lives. But, I must say I always knew Jackson would be okay, despite whatever negative influences may have been impressed upon him. Aside from God's love, he has his nature to keep him safe; Jackson is determined and bull-headed, just like his father."

Before Jasmine could respond, there was a knock at the bedroom door. "Are you okay?" asked her father, stepping inside.

"Yes."

"What happened?"

"Nothing."

"Nothing?" he asked, peering at her over the rim of his glasses.

"I'm fine."

"Nothing around here seems fine," he retorted, taking a step toward her. "What was all that fussing and fighting about?"

"My sons may have gotten a little beside themselves tonight," interjected Mrs. Taylor, "and for that, I apologize."

"Sweetie, pack your bags," said Mr. Fairchild, immediately dismissing Mrs. Taylor's apology.

"But Dad—"

"Please," begged Mrs. Taylor once more. "We were all going to go to church in the morning—"

"You can fly back to L.A. with Angela and me and stay home for a few days," he interrupted, staring at his daughter.

"No thanks," replied Jasmine, who had absolutely no desire to spend the rest of the week with him and his new fiancée. "I'll stay here until tomorrow, then fly back to Berkeley as originally planned. I'm fine Dad, really."

Mr. Fairchild hesitated for a moment, as he wasn't quite sure whether or not to believe his daughter. But, knowing that she was indeed grown, he knew there wasn't much he could do. "Okay," he said, finally relenting. "Give me a call if you need me."

Jasmine watched her father exit the room with Mrs. Taylor, the tension between the two permeating the air. Now alone, she found herself growing more and more upset as she recounted the night's events, the image of Jackson chatting with one of his exes now at the forefront of her mind.

"Who is it?" she asked, after hearing a knock at the door.

"It's me," said Jackson, rushing inside as soon as she opened the door. "I'm so sorry about everything. He didn't touch you, did he?"

"No," she replied, glancing down at the floor.

He let out a huge sigh of relief then said, "I would have come sooner, but I had to help my father do damage control after Xavier left. I apologized to the remainder of our guests before ushering them out. Thank God my boss and his wife left early—"

"Did you walk your friend to her car?" she asked, referring to the woman with the cocoa brown complexion she last saw him with.

"What?"

"Never mind," she said, heading toward the bed. He grabbed her by the arm and spun her back around.

"No. What are you talking about?"

She looked up at him with tears in her eyes. "The last time I saw you, you were chatting with your ex-girlfriend. You left me all by myself! I then went inside the den to cool off, and that's when I almost got attacked by your brother!"

"I'm sorry about that," he offered, unable to dismiss the visible hurt, anger and frustration now marking her countenance. "I was heading your way when she stepped in front of me. We were just talking—"

"So! I didn't know exes were on the guest list. If that was the case, I could have invited everyone I dated. We could have turned this into one big, fat reunion!"

"It's not like that, Jasmine. Lena and I grew up together."

"Well, that's just great," she said, throwing her arms up in the air. "I'm glad you get to make up all the rules."

"I wasn't doing anything except talking to an old friend—"

"An old friend you undoubtedly slept with," she said, shaking her head in disgust. "You and I have different definitions of friendship."

"You know what?" he began, rubbing a hand over his goatee, "I'm not going to keep defending myself to you. Xavier was dead wrong for what he did, but I had nothing to do with that."

"You're right," she said with anger in her voice. "Why defend yourself when you're perfect. I'm the crazy one. Crazy and insecure."

He just stared at her for a moment, and she took his silence as his way of affirming her sarcastic remark.

"Forget this," she said, climbing into bed.

Now equally upset, Jackson turned to her and said, "So, when are we going to finish talking about this? Tomorrow? Next week!"

"I don't care if we never talk about it," she shot back while glancing over her shoulder, her back now facing him.

"Fine," he replied, turning to leave. He too was tired...and pissed. Grabbing hold of the knob, he slammed the door shut, the harsh sound causing Jasmine to sit up and glance back at the closed door he had just stormed out of.

Chapter 28

The following morning, Jasmine attended church service with Jackson and his parents as planned. The morning was quiet, and tone somber, thanks to the eventful evening they experienced the previous night. Although they had yet to make sense of it all, much of the silence was due to embarrassment and anger—mainly on Jackson's part. He was ashamed for having taken part in all the commotion that put an abrupt end to what had otherwise been a joyous occasion, but that didn't stop him from being angry with Xavier, as there remained quite a bit of unfinished business between the two.

The sanctuary of Victory Baptist Church was brimming with members and guests, and Jasmine felt at ease, despite the fact it was the first time in years she had stepped foot inside a church. She had stopped attending religious services after high school, and hadn't taken the time to seek any out since having moved to the Bay Area, as college life had consumed the majority of her time. During those four years, her Sundays were either spent as a day to cram before a big test on Monday, or volunteering at Pleasant Beginnings. Although she hadn't been sure what to expect, the church service actually served as a pleasant distraction from all the thoughts that were crowding her mind. For those two hours, she didn't think about the previous night's events, her ambiguous feelings toward Jackson, or all the mayhem that awaited her back at work. Instead, she focused on the minister who, ironically, delivered a powerful sermon about uncertainty. He talked about the failing economy, massive layoffs, and a future that seemed to be growing more and more unpredictable. He also talked about an increased fear of the unknown, and used Proverbs 3:5 to drive his point home: "Trust in the Lord with all your heart and lean not on your own understanding." Jasmine found the message to be very timely, given how unsure she felt about her future, the direction of which seemed to be growing more uncertain as the days passed by.

After the service, she and Jackson lingered around the atrium of the church as they waited for Mr. and Mrs. Taylor to finish making their rounds. It was the church Jackson and Caleb had attended since adolescence, so his parents knew a lot of the members quite well. When a few decided to walk over to the young couple to congratulate them on their engagement, the pair smiled faintly and said "Thank you," while secretly wishing for them all to hurry up and go away. Jasmine however straightened up a bit once she saw the minister approach.

"Good to see you again, Pastor," said Jackson, shaking his hand.

"Likewise," replied the minister, his eyes drifting toward Jasmine. "This must be the beautiful bride-to-be."

"Nice to meet you," she said, shaking his hand. "That was a great sermon."

"Thank you," he replied before adding, "congratulations on your engagement. Have you two found a church home?"

The pair glanced at each other, then back at him and said, "No."

"Well, no rush," he assured. "I told Jackson we offer pre-marital counseling. Hopefully you two will come see me sometime."

"Thanks," said Jackson. "We'll keep that in mind."

Once they returned to the Taylor household, Jasmine retreated inside the guest bedroom to prepare for the trip home, and almost instantly, all the trouble and chaos she had forgotten about earlier in the day came rushing back. Feeling heavy, she took a seat on the edge of the bed and began pondering once more, all the issues surrounding her and the life she thought she wanted. As if it wasn't tough enough dealing with all the changes that came along with growing up, she was now faced with the toughest decision of her life. Should she take that trip down the aisle and pursue the life so many dreamed, even if it meant having to overlook the numerous doubts that were now lingering in the back of her mind?

Deep down, she knew that men like Jackson didn't come along very often, so the last thing she wanted was to lose him and the bond they had established. Yet, a part of her was scared stiff, for she still wasn't sure he could be trusted. He had already admitted that before her, he had never been faithful to anyone, and recent events made her further question his loyalty. And it didn't help that she couldn't stop thinking about Bianca's recent allegations, which she had yet to confront him about.

Nervously twisting the sparkling engagement ring that adorned her finger, Jasmine couldn't ignore the unsettled feeling that was slowly rising from deep within the pit of her stomach. After placing the last item inside her weekend bag, she zipped it shut, then took a deep breath, for she dreaded doing what she knew needed to be done.

"Knock, knock," she said upon stepping inside the den, the doors to which were wide open.

"I was just about to come see you," said Jackson, watching as she took a seat next to him on the leather sofa. "Look," he began, turning to face her, "I'm really sorry about what happened the other night. I don't know what got into my brother, and I hate to think about what could have happened if Caleb hadn't told me where you were."

"It's okay," she said, glancing at the liquor bottles sitting on top of the wet bar across from them. "It's not your fault."

"I hope we can put all this behind us and move forward," he said, reaching for her hand, but she pulled it away.

"Can I see your phone?" she asked, her voice calm and eyes steadied on his.

"What? Why?"

"Because, I need to see something."

"What do you need to see?" he asked, a scowl now plastered across his face. She ignored his angered expression and simply held her palm out in front of him. Sighing, he rolled his eyes, dug deep inside his pants pocket, and pulled out his phone. "Here," he said, shoving it into her hand.

It took just a few seconds for her to access his photo gallery and instantly, one provocative picture after another appeared across the screen. "We're done," she said, shoving the phone at his chest.

Jackson fumbled with the phone as he quickly tried to ascertain what it was that had set her off, and once he saw the incriminating photos, he shot up out of his seat. "I don't know what the hell this is," he said, his breathing now heavy, "but I had nothing to do with this."

"Yeah right," she said, springing up off the couch.

"Wait," he said, grabbing hold of her arm after she made a move toward the door. "This doesn't prove anything. I have no idea how these got on here."

Jasmine ripped her arm free from his grasp and said, "I can't believe I trusted you. I can't believe I almost gave my whole life to you!"

"This is a set up, and I know who did it—"

"Save it," she said, placing a hand in front of his face. "I'm done listening to your stories, your false promises. When we get back to Berkeley, I don't ever want to hear from you again!"

"Jazz—"

"You're a liar and a cheat," she continued, her anger mounting. "I knew from the moment I met you that you would bring me nothing but trouble. I can't believe how stupid I've been—how dumb I was to fall for you. I see why you wanted me to give up my job now. How easy it would be for you to play your games while I'm forced to rely on you."

"What? Jazz, you know me. You know I wouldn't do anything to jeopardize this relationship. I'll prove to you that this was a set up."

"Good luck with that," she said, removing the sparkling diamond engagement ring from her finger. She slammed it down onto the wet bar then stormed out. It wasn't until she made it within inches of the guest bedroom that she heard the sound of glass breaking.

Frustrated, Jackson hurled a cup from the wet bar across the room and watched as it exploded against the wall, shards of glass scattering everywhere. He peered down at the jagged bits on the floor and couldn't help but feel like it was his heart lying there, shattered into a million pieces.

Chapter 29

"Hello?"

"Bianca…it's Jackson." He heard a loud sigh on the other end of the line.

"What do you want?"

"You know what I want," he replied, his voice sharp. "I want you to tell my girl the truth."

"What? That you're a dog and it's only a matter of time before she gets bitten?"

"I know you planted those pictures on my cell phone," he said, ignoring her insult. "You're the only person who had access to it, and a motive. You wanted to get back at me, and you did. Now, I'd appreciate it if you'd call off this war you've waged against me."

"And what if I don't?"

He hesitated for a moment, unsure of how to respond. Then, after taking a deep breath he said, "If you don't, I'll be forced to tell my father what you've done."

Bianca shrieked with laughter. "You're going to run and tell daddy what I did? You tried that already remember? If memory serves me correctly, things didn't work out too well—"

"Please," he said, losing patience. He was trying his best to hold his tongue, for he wanted nothing more than to annihilate her on a verbal scale. Yet, he knew that retaliating would only incite further animosity.

"Please?" she asked, puzzled by his last remark.

"Yes," he confirmed, shaking his head. He knew she was enjoying this all too much. "I'm asking you nicely."

"Hmm," she said, unfazed by the desperation she now heard in his voice. "Now look who's begging."

After that, all he heard was a dial tone.

*****

Jasmine refused to see or speak to Jackson, so the two started the New Year off single. Although Lisa had invited her out to a New Year's Eve bash, she declined and instead chose to celebrate alone on her couch, eating an order of Wing Stop and toasting to Foxy. Yet, her solitary celebration was anything but quiet considering Jackson had been blowing up her cell phone ever since the two made it back to the Bay. After failing to obtain an admission of guilt from Bianca, he decided to relinquish his pursuit of her and instead began devoting all his time and energy toward convincing Jasmine that he was indeed the same faithful, caring man she had fallen for.

His initial plan of action involved a seemingly endless stream of voicemails and text messages. The phone calls were fairly easy to dismiss, but Jasmine found it increasingly difficult to resist the urge to read some of the text messages that flooded her inbox. At first they were long:

> Baby, answer your phone. I know you're upset but I just want to talk. You have to believe me when I tell you I was set up.

> Jazz, please, let me explain. I promise you I've been faithful. I would never do anything to hurt you, ever.

And then they grew short:

> I love you.

> I miss you.

`Miss me?`

Despite the fact his messages failed to yield a response, he refused to let up. All he wanted was for her to allow him the opportunity to explain things, like how Bianca had been threatening to sabotage their relationship all because she was still angry and bitter about how things had gone down between them years ago. Jasmine however, had no intention of hearing him out, for she feared he would only approach her with lies. When she wouldn't engage him by phone, he took things a step further and showed up at her doorstep. Even after she had shut off all the lights, retreated inside her bedroom, climbed into bed and pulled the covers over her head, he continued to rap on her door. A part of her felt tempted to open it just to get him to stop knocking, but the last thing she wanted was to see him, for she knew all he would do is stare at her with those dark, magnetic eyes of his and say the right words and she would melt. The man was walking, talking kryptonite, and there was no way she was going to let him sweet talk his way out of this one...not this time.

The only thing that kept her from obsessing over the breakup and giving in to his pursuits was work—or more specifically, the trouble she was still facing with Morgan. She had succeeded at digging up the old emails Lisa thought would help prove that they had indeed come up with the ad concept in question, and by the end of the first week in January, the two were finally ready to present their case to Carl.

"Good morning," stated Carl, greeting the two opposing sides as he entered the conference room in which most of their team meetings took place. He took a seat at the head of the long, oval-shaped table with Jasmine and Lisa sitting to his right, and Morgan to his left. "I wish we were meeting under different circumstances," he added, glancing between the two parties. "In any case, it appears we have quite a dispute on our hands. Morgan, would you care to start us off? After all, it was you who reported the matter."

"Sure," she replied, straightening her posture. "A few weeks after the company announced acquisition of the Bella Cosmetics account, I began toying around with some ideas for their campaign. No one was assigned to it yet, but since I'm quite familiar with the brand, I was confident I could present the client with an ad that would target their primary customer base, and help boost sales. I had jotted some notes down, which I left on my desk the weekend before I took my vacation. When I returned two weeks later, the notes were gone, and Jasmine and Lisa had presented their concept, which closely resembled mine."

Jasmine rolled her eyes at Morgan's outrageous claims, for she and Lisa had never experienced any sort of block when it came to brainstorming ideas. They therefore neither needed nor wanted to steal anyone's notes, especially hers. And besides, Morgan was an art director, not a copywriter, a fact she had the tendency to forget. Although Jasmine thought her to be very talented and competent in her role, it appeared at times she was overly confident about her visions, often overstepping her bounds and micromanaging others.

"May I speak?" interjected Jasmine, who was growing increasingly agitated. Her nerves were already shot, thanks to her now fractured life, and she wanted nothing more than for this circus Morgan had created to come to an end.

"You'll have your chance in a minute," stated Carl, allowing Morgan to continue pleading her case.

Lisa shot Jasmine a look and laid a hand on her forearm, a gesture that conveyed compassion, and a desire for her to keep cool.

"As I was saying," continued Morgan in her usual, dictatorial tone, "the concept was stolen. I should therefore receive credit, and appropriate disciplinary action should be taken."

"Now, let's not get ahead of ourselves," replied Carl, who was used to Morgan's insubordinate behavior. "Let's allow the accused to speak."

Lisa took the floor first, as she could sense Jasmine's anger and frustration still boiling, and wanted to allow further time for it to simmer down. "I'd like to start off by saying that Jasmine and I have worked together on several campaigns, and it has been our partnership that has enabled us to develop strong, compelling copy to complement the artwork created by our artists. Morgan has served as the senior art director on a few of our assignments, overseeing and unifying the creative visions of both the artists and copywriters. However, we were assigned to this account under Steve's direction. He was the art director in charge at the time. Once assigned, Jasmine and I immediately began brainstorming ideas for the copy—"

"Yes," interjected Jasmine, who felt she was going to explode if she weren't given the chance to speak. "I have here several emails that Lisa and I sent back and forth to each other over a period of days that shows how we were bouncing around ideas. I also have a few comps we submitted to the printer, and the dates they were delivered." She passed the supporting documents over to Carl, who immediately began examining the evidence. He appeared deeply engrossed in the material as Jasmine continued to speak. "I find it odd that the complaint was filed months after the comps had been received, and the creative team approved them," she added, cutting her eyes at Morgan, who turned her gaze on Carl.

Carl remained silent, for a while…a long while, as he continued to scan over the documents he held in his hands. Then, after what felt like an eternity, he turned to Morgan and asked, "Do you have any evidence you'd like to submit?"

Jasmine and Lisa watched as Morgan drew in a sharp breath, as if Carl's question had knocked the wind out of her. "My—my evidence was stolen," she stuttered, shifting uncomfortably in her seat. "As I stated earlier, the notes I had were removed from my desk."

Carl pinched the bridge of his nose then said, "Unfortunately, there's no way for us to prove that Jasmine and Lisa confiscated your notes, Morgan. It could have been any co-worker who took them, or you may have simply misplaced them. In any case, they have presented me with some factual data that I must carefully consider. And since cases are judged based on one's ability to prove one's argument, I must side with Jasmine and Lisa on this one. A serious accusation such as this cannot be pursued based on assumption, so there will be no further action taken at this time. This meeting is adjourned."

Jasmine let out a sigh of relief, while Morgan, completely humiliated and defeated, slithered out of the office.

"We did it!" exclaimed Lisa, jumping for joy once Morgan and Carl exited the room. She calmed down after noticing her friend wasn't sharing her enthusiasm. "What's wrong?"

"Nothing."

"It's Jackson, isn't it?"

Jasmine remained silent, then slowly nodded. Although she and Lisa proved victorious in solidifying their credibility and ultimately their positions at the agency, the triumph couldn't mend her broken heart.

"You still don't want to hear what he has to say?"

"What is there to say?" she replied, fighting back the tears that were now welling up in the corners of her eyes. "He lied to me. The evidence was right there, in his photo gallery. It wasn't like the pictures had been sent to him as an attachment. They had been taken with his phone."

"Give it time. It's only been a few weeks. Maybe he'll come up with the proof he promised you."

"I doubt that," said Jasmine, suddenly feeling an overwhelming sense of despair. "Thanks, for everything," she offered, changing the subject. "We beat Morgan at her own game, just like you said we would."

"That we did," replied Lisa, smiling faintly. "I'll be at my desk if you need me."

Lisa exited the conference room, and Jasmine stayed behind, feeling more alone than she had in a long time. Although it had been her decision to call things off between she and Jackson, she couldn't deny the fact that he had in many ways become her best friend, the first person she wished to share her good and bad news with. Thus, her and Lisa's triumph over Morgan didn't leave her feeling anywhere near as victorious as she thought she would, considering she didn't have him to share it with.

Upon returning to her cubicle, she took a seat and laid her head down at her desk, but no sooner than her forehead met the cold wood, her cell phone started ringing. Instantly, her head shot up, a small part of her wishing it was Jackson on the other end.

"Hey, you haven't returned any of my calls. Had you not answered, I would have thought you were avoiding me."

Jasmine held the phone for a moment then said, "Sorry Richard, I've been dealing with a lot."

"Oh, sorry to hear that," he replied. "Trouble in paradise?"

She hesitated slightly then said, "Yeah...you can say that."

"Well, if you ever need a friend," he offered without skipping a beat, "I'm here. In fact, if you're not doing anything this Friday, I'd love to take you out."

"I don't know..." she said, her voice trailing off as she stared at the computer screen in front of her.

"Well," he began, after hearing the hesitation in her voice, "there's no pressure, so you can just call me when you're ready. But, if it helps, I must say you'll have an extraordinary time."

Giggling softly, Jasmine struggled to contain the tears that were still fighting to break free. Then after glancing down at her ring-less finger she replied, "Okay, I'll keep that in mind."

Chapter 30

One week had gone by since Jasmine and Lisa proved victorious in their battle against Morgan, and the tension at Infinity fizzled. The environment had cooled considerably thanks to Morgan's probationary status, as it was the first time anyone had been reprimanded for his or her underhanded ways at the agency. Her punishment therefore sent a strong message to all the employees, and although there was still competition for assignments, it became easier for everyone to better focus on their performance now that there was less interference from scheming co-workers. The only person who had trouble focusing, however, was Jasmine.

"Ahem," said Lisa, jabbing her in the side in an attempt to alert her to the fact that the new client they were meeting with had asked her a question.

"Yeah, yes?"

"I asked, when can you have the ad copy ready?"

"Oh, just give me a few days—one week, tops," she replied, hoping that would be the only question directed at her. She had tuned out most of the conversation and had fallen into a trance. Lisa thought she had been following along closely since she had been jotting down notes the entire time, but when she peered over her shoulder, she saw it was nothing more than doodles that decorated the pages of her notepad.

Once the meeting adjourned, the two headed back to their cubicles, and Jasmine noticed every eye in the office seemed to be glued on her. *Am I paranoid?* She thought, suddenly wondering if some of her peers were now blaming her for the disciplinary action Morgan incurred. *I'm trippin'*, she thought, choosing to dismiss all her silly notions. Yet, when she finally made it to her workstation, it instantly became clear why she had suddenly become the center of attention.

"What in the world…" With eyes wide and mouth agape, she stared in shock at what appeared to be over one hundred long-stemmed roses pouring out of her cubicle. Every inch of her desk and parts of the floor was covered with vases overflowing with the beautiful flowers. After noticing a note tucked inside one of the vases that stood front and center atop her desk, she reached for it and read it silently:

I'll never stop loving you. --Jackson

"This one's a fighter," said Lisa, staring at the flowers in amazement.

"Whose side are you on?" asked Jasmine, shooting her a dissatisfied look.

"I'm on the side of love, and this man definitely loves you."

"Either that or he feels incredibly guilty for being a liar and a cheat," she retorted, forcefully grabbing hold of one of the vases that sat atop her desk. She marched straight over to a nearby trashcan and turned the vase upside down, dumping the flowers inside. Before she could turn the vase right side up, she spotted another co-worker who had been passing by at that moment, throw his head back as if he were stunned by what he just saw.

"Help me get these out of here!" she whispered loudly to Lisa, embarrassed her failed relationship had become the topic of office chatter. If she thought Jackson was going to let her walk out of his life without a fight she was sorely mistaken. After all, Persistent was his middle name, and she was about to discover just how far he was willing to go in order to win her back.

Two weeks later, while heading into work on an early Friday morning, Jasmine, as well as every other person who entered the high-level security building in which she worked, was surprisingly greeted by violin music upon stepping inside. At first, she thought the entertainers were provided courtesy of one of the companies that conducted business there, but as soon as she spied a familiar set of dark eyes staring at her from across the atrium, she immediately became aware that the entertainment was for her pleasure, and her pleasure only.

Oh. My. Gosh. she thought, her eyes still fixed on his. It was the first time the two had seen each other in over a month, and the trembling sensation she felt building inside the pit of her stomach made her feel as though she were looking at a different person, and not the man she had once planned to marry. Feeling the prying eyes of strangers bore into her as they passed by on their way into work further added to her angst, and she suddenly felt an overwhelming urge to escape.

Bolting toward the elevator doors, Jasmine made it within inches of freedom when suddenly, she felt Jackson's hand clasp her forearm. "Wait," he said.

"Get your hand off of me," she demanded sharply, glaring up at him.

"Miss Fairchild, is everything alright?" asked the now very concerned security guard, who had granted Jackson's request to set up the surprise serenade. He had agreed to allow him and his band of minstrels access to the building, having figured the surprise would be greatly welcomed and appreciated. Yet, after seeing the very upset recipient, he now thought otherwise.

"Just give me five minutes, please," said Jackson, his dark eyes begging her to give him a chance.

She hesitated for a moment, but then noticed that the security guard was advancing in their direction, his hand moving toward his walkie-talkie. "Everything's fine, Jimmy," she assured. "I promise this will all be over, soon," she added, nodding in the direction of the violinists, who had yet to end their performance. "Five minutes, that's it," she said to Jackson, gesturing toward the entrance to the stairwell. He maintained his hold on her arm as they slipped away, disappearing behind the door. Once they were alone, she yanked her arm free. "Are you out of your mind?!"

"Not at all."

"Whatever this is, it has got to stop. All these shenanigans—"

"Shenanigans?" he asked, frowning.

"Yes, shenanigans" she said, stunned by his ignorance. "The countless voicemails, text messages, and late night drive-bys. You think I don't know it's your headlights flashing through my windows late at night?"

"Well, perhaps if you answered your phone or opened your door, I wouldn't have to resort to such drastic measures."

"Speaking of drastic, let's not get started on all those flowers you sent. Thanks a lot for embarrassing me by the way."

"Embarrassing you? I thought it was romantic."

"More like creepy," she said, folding her arms across her chest. "It's bad enough I have to explain to everyone we broke up, and then you send all those flowers like you're some kind of madman. I don't want my co-workers in my business like that."

"Who cares what they think," he said, taking a step forward. "I've missed you, Jazz."

She hated to admit it, but she missed him, too. The thought of which was becoming increasingly difficult to deny as he took more steps toward her, his scent washing over her like a wave as he closed in on her in the tight corridor of the stairwell. He smelled…different. Pleasant, but different. Although she had told him several times that his signature cologne reminded her of her no-good ex boyfriend because it had also been his favorite scent, he never ceased to wear it. Yet, now that they were broken up, he had finally decided that a change was in order.

Focus, Jasmine… "I want you to leave me alone," she said, taking a few steps back, yet he continued his advance until she found herself standing up against the wall.

"I'll never leave you alone," he said, his voice deep and rich like molasses. She hated how easily he could affect her.

"Stalker," she said, trying to sound insulting.

"No," he replied, shaking his head as he moved in even closer. "I'm just a man that goes after what he wants and doesn't stop until he gets it."

Suddenly, she felt her anger return. "Is that what this is to you, some kind of game? What, I never gave it up so you're waiting for me to fall into bed with you so you can check me off your list?!"

"What?!" Jackson began laughing so loudly that his voice echoed inside the stairwell, causing her to glance up one flight, for she hoped no one was on their way down, listening to their conversation. "Who's crazy now?" he asked, still laughing.

"Excuse me?" she replied, frowning.

He placed a hand against the wall above her head, bracing himself as he leaned into her. "No offense, sweetheart, but I don't have to work this hard to get laid. If sex was all I was after, I would have been gone a long time ago. Trust."

"How do I know you haven't been getting a cheap fix to tie you over?"

"I haven't been with anyone since we've been together. And, I don't want anyone but you. Besides, if I were getting some, you wouldn't have me so wound up."

Jasmine looked at Jackson and actually believed he was telling the truth. The redness in the whites of his eyes suggested he had lost several hours of sleep, and she could tell by the stubble on his face that this situation had thrown him off his game. Normally, his goatee appeared neat and polished, but today, not so much. Although he was still decked out to the nines in a sharp suit and tie, it seemed his face hadn't seen the sharp end of a razor in weeks. Unfortunately for her, however, his unkempt facial hairs in no way detracted from his good looks. If anything, they just gave him a more rugged, feral appeal, and that, combined with his new scent, made her want him more.

"Where's the proof you're supposed to be providing me?" she asked, her voice cracking as she peered deep into his eyes. Man, did she wish he had it…

"I'm still working on it," he replied, staring down at her. "But, in the meantime, I want you to know how much I still love you."

"Love?" she asked with a skeptical look, her thoughts drifting back to the nude pictures she had found on his phone.

"Do you know why I sent you all those red roses?" he asked, ignoring her snarky remark. "I sent them because I'll never forget how your eyes lit up when I showed up at your doorstep with a fresh bouquet on our first date."

Jasmine recalled that evening and how nervous she had been. The last thing she wanted was for him to get the best of her, so she tried to pretend that nothing he did that night impressed her.

"Hmm," she said, shrugging. "I don't recall."

"Do you remember the first time we met?" he asked, running a hand down the length of her hair.

"Nope," she replied, lying. He was standing so close and looking so good...smelling so good, that the last thing she needed was to take a trip down memory lane, her mind getting tangled in some romanticized version of their union.

"Well, I do," he stated firmly, his eyes steadied on hers. "We were at the student bookstore when I suddenly spotted you from across the room. I thought you were absolutely stunning, and it was like for a moment, time stopped. I continued to watch you, hoping you would look my way, and when you did, our eyes locked. No words were spoken, but I knew we had made a connection, and I wanted to approach you, but you turned and walked away. I should have known then that this wasn't going to be easy."

Jasmine's breathing grew heavy as she stared at Jackson's mouth, listening as the words flowed from his lips. He remembered that moment exactly as she recalled it. The only difference, however, was that she knew despite whatever attraction she may have felt for him that day that he was trouble, and she had tried her best to stay away. How crazy it was to think that he had succeeded at charming his way into her heart.

"Have dinner with me tonight," he said, knowing he had gotten to her. She didn't have to say a word, for he could tell by how her cheeks had deepened in color, and her breathing grew heavier that she was just as out of sorts as he was.

"Absolutely not," she replied, fighting to hold her ground.

"Why not?"

"Because," she began, trying to control her breathing, "I have plans."

"Break them."

"You always have been an egotistical jerk, haven't you?" she asked, glaring up at him in disbelief. "What makes you think I'm just going to drop everything for you?"

"What could you possibly have going on that you can't get out of?"

"Ha!" she laughed, humored by his flippancy. "Not that it's any of your business, but…" she hesitated slightly, as she quickly tried to gather her thoughts, then suddenly, the conversation she had with Richard a few weeks prior came to mind, and she finished with, "I have a date."

Jackson stared at her incredulously. "With who?"

"It's *'With whom,'*" she corrected, "and, wouldn't you like to know?"

"Well," he said, straightening out his tie, "I feel sorry for *whomever* it is."

"Sorry? Why?"

"Because, you're not going to do anything but torture the guy."

"If you honestly feel that way, like I've somehow tortured you, then why don't you just beat it?"

Grabbing hold of her biceps, Jackson pinned her against the wall then said, "You're going to torture the guy because no man wants to go out with a woman who's in love with another man."

His nostrils were flaring and she could see the vein in his neck pulsating, as if the mere thought of her being with someone else was driving him mad. Swallowing hard, she replied, "What makes you think—"

Before she could finish her sentence, he kissed her, and instantly she felt a tingling sensation start to build in her lower abdomen. For a moment, it felt like her feet had been lifted off the ground, and as his tongue danced inside her mouth, not only did she feel weightless, but also like her memory bank was being completely wiped out. Suddenly, those nude pictures she had found on his phone became a distant memory, and only the feelings he conjured up in that moment remained.

Once the kiss finally ended, he slowly pulled away from her and took a few steps back. He too was stunned, having felt the same electricity she had felt. And, he was surprised she had shown no resistance given how hostile she had acted towards him moments earlier. Noticing the stunned expression that had swept across his face, she watched as it soon became replaced with the devilish grin she had grown accustomed to seeing, and instantly, she was pissed.

"I hope you know this doesn't change a thing!" she shouted, glaring up at him. Even she knew she sounded ridiculous.

With his hand hovering over the doorknob, he replied, "Sure," that annoying, triumphant expression still gracing his visage as he headed out the door.

Chapter 31

Jasmine called Richard as soon as she made it to her desk to let him know she was finally ready to take him up on his offer. Although she had been somewhat amused by his use of hyperbole, a part of her hoped he could deliver the "extraordinary" experience he had promised, for she needed something that powerful to take her mind off Jackson and their encounter inside the stairwell.

After the workday ended, she headed straight home and started preparing for her night out with "blue eyes." She had decided to sport an Hervé Léger number she had purchased online at a discount along with a pair of three-inch stilettos, for nothing spelled revenge better than a body hugging bandage dress and killer heels.

"You look breathtaking," said Richard, expressing his approval of her outfit the moment he arrived at her doorstep.

"Thank you," she replied, smiling.

The two hopped inside his cherry red mustang then headed to the city, where he had dinner reservations for them at the Supper Club. Upon arrival, he asked for permission to place a blindfold over her eyes, then escorted her inside the venue, which was different from any restaurant she had ever been to. The Supper Club wasn't just a restaurant, but rather a culinary experience accompanied by unique, top of the line entertainment. Diners didn't sit on chairs in front of tables, but, instead lounged on comfortable beds, where waiters and waitresses supplied them with one delectable course after another.

Once seated, Richard removed Jasmine's blindfold and allowed her to take in the scene before explaining how he wanted her to get the most out of the experience, and particularly the food, which was prepared by some of the best chefs in the city. Replacing the blindfold, he proceeded to feed her samples of each course as it arrived. With her sight impaired, he wanted her to focus on the enticing aromas and mouthwatering flavors that had been infused into each dish. He of course made sure to remove the blindfold whenever a trapeze artist, dancer, or other eccentric performer appeared throughout the evening to provide entertainment.

Jasmine enjoyed every minute of their outing, and felt that the date was truly as "extraordinary" as Richard had desired it to be. Yet, it still hadn't proven powerful enough to erase Jackson from her memory, for she couldn't stop thinking about how much she missed spending time with him. True, he too had treated her to some extravagant outings, but just being in his presence made her feel good. She recalled how much fun they had doing mundane activities together, like eating takeout while sitting on the floor of his condo, or just hanging out watching television, chatting and laughing about random things.

"So, what do you think?" asked Richard, interrupting her thoughts as his clear, blue eyes peered into hers.

"I think this is absolutely fabulous," she replied, struggling to shake off all thoughts of her ex. But, doing so proved impossible, especially when the dessert plates arrived and the two were presented with a peach flambé, the rising flames reminding her of the burning sensation Jackson had roused inside her lower abdomen when he kissed her inside the stairwell.

"Is it good?" asked Richard, as she took a bite out of the confection. When she didn't respond, he said, "Hello, earth to Jasmine."

Stunned, she sat before him frozen, her eyes glued to a figure sitting in the opposite corner of the room. *I must be hallucinating*, she thought.

"Is something wrong?"

"No, sorry," she said, struggling to maintain her composure. "I um, I have to go to the restroom," she announced, rising from her seat. "I'll be back."

"Okay," said Richard, watching as she headed across the room. Luckily, he didn't notice when she gestured toward the restrooms, beckoning Jackson to follow.

"What the hell are you doing here?!" she asked when they made it into the hall where the bathrooms were located. "You followed us?!"

"I can't believe you're actually out on a date," he said, looking dismayed. "And, I can't believe you're wearing this—this dress!"

"You have a lot of nerve, you know that? You have no right to impose on me like this. You lost that privilege when you cheated on me!"

"Dammit I didn't cheat on you!" he shouted, the harshness of his voice causing her to jump slightly. "What is it going to take for you to believe me? You know I wouldn't hurt you, Jasmine. Why are you doing this?"

"Me?!" she shouted, tears springing forth from her eyes. "I'm not the one with opposite sex friends that feel they can show up at my doorstep whenever they feel like it. I don't have ex boyfriends suddenly reappearing in my life, and I damn sure don't have any nude pictures on my cell phone! You ripped my heart out, and yet you expect me to show some respect for you!"

Jackson clasped his head with both hands, as if their conversation was causing his head to ache. "Jazz, I swear to you, nothing happened. You know me. You know I've changed. You have a lot to do with why I am the way that I am now. I already have enough people in my life thinking I'm the same person I was three, four—five years ago, and as much as it pisses me off I'm okay with it. I'm okay with the world betting against me, but not you. I need you in my corner. You know me!"

With tears now pouring forth from her eyes, Jasmine gritted her teeth and said, "No, I don't know you. That's the problem. I don't know anything anymore."

"Listen, I know things look bad, but I promise you, nothing happened. I wish I could prove it to you, but I can't." She started to walk away and suddenly, a feeling of desperation swept over him. "Wait," he said, stepping in front of her.

"Move out of my way, Jackson. I've given you enough chances already. You said yourself you can't prove anything."

"Maybe I can't but you can," he said, causing her to stare up at him, perplexed. "What does your heart tell you? What would Missy want?"

Now furious, she replied through clenched teeth, "How dare you speak her name."

"I'm sorry, it's just I...I just said it because I know she's the only person you would listen to right now." He let out a heavy sigh, glanced down at the floor then looked up at her and said, "You can't possibly believe that I would ever do anything to hurt you." His eyes now glistening, he reached for her hand then placed it over her heart and begged, "Baby, please, just follow your heart."

Seeing Jackson on the verge of tears made Jasmine feel more conflicted than ever. She wanted to trust him, but couldn't ignore the fact that she felt completely and utterly spent. "I stopped following my heart a long time ago," she said, pushing his hand away from her chest. Wiping away her tears, she stormed past him and out toward the restaurant.

After expressing her desire to call it a night, Richard asked for the tab, and the two then headed back to her apartment. They pulled up in front of her place a little after midnight, and she watched as he removed his keys from the ignition. "Thanks again, Richard. I had an incredible time," she said, looking at him and smiling.

"My pleasure," he replied, leaning towards her. Their eyes locked and for a moment, she wanted to know what it would be like if she were to truly move on from Jackson. So, when Richard placed a hand behind the back of her head, she didn't hesitate to lean in as he brought her mouth to his.

"That was nice," he stated with a smile that soon faded once it met her bewildered expression. "Is something wrong?"

Jasmine had spent the entire evening trying to erase Jackson from her memory, but even Richard's kiss hadn't proven effective. In fact, all it did was make her miss him more, for it didn't come anywhere close to making her feel the way she did when she and Jackson's lips collided.

"Listen, Richard, I had a great time, but—"

"Uh oh," he said, cutting her off. "That sounds like the beginning of a long goodbye."

"Sorry, but I just got out of a serious relationship, and I thought I was ready to move on and start dating again, but...I'm not." Richard averted his eyes for a moment and sighed, a reaction that was not lost on Jasmine. "I'm so sorry," she continued, attempting to soften the blow. "I didn't mean to lead you on."

"It's okay," he replied, smiling faintly as he returned his gaze to her. "You were up front about everything. I guess a part of me was just hoping that it wasn't too late for me to have a chance with you."

"Thank you so much for understanding," she said with a weak grin. "And, thanks again for a wonderful evening. It truly was 'extraordinary,'" she said, mimicking his previous words to her.

"Well, I aim to please," said Richard, stroking the side of her face with his hand. "Your ex is a lucky man to have your heart."

Smiling, Jasmine stepped out of the vehicle and closed the door behind her. Just when she was about to head toward her apartment, she heard Richard call out to her.

"If by chance you and this mystery man aren't able to work things out," he offered as a last ditch effort, "feel free to use my number."

"Okay," she replied, watching as he drove off into the night. She turned to resume heading toward her doorstep when suddenly, the brightness of two familiar headlights shone in her direction. Glancing over her shoulder, she watched as the car pulled away from the curb. Despite how upset Jackson had been to see her out on a date, that apparently hadn't stopped him from making sure that the woman he loved made it home safe.

Chapter 32

"Who is it?" asked Jasmine before peering through the peephole of her apartment door after hearing a knock one lazy Saturday afternoon.

"It's Lisa. Open up!"

"Hey…what are you doing here?" she asked upon opening the door. She took a step back to allow her friend room to enter.

"We've barely had a chance to talk at work, and I've been dying to hear how your date with Richard went last week," she said, rushing inside. Jasmine watched as she headed straight for the couch and began spreading some items out on the coffee table. "You can't just leave me hanging like that—is this a new fashion statement or something?" she asked, suddenly taking note of her friend's humdrum attire.

"I'm just trying to be comfortable," said Jasmine, glancing down at the grey, oversized sweat suit and very comfortable yet beat up pair of house slippers she was wearing.

"Well, if you've given up on that fabulous wardrobe of yours, you know who to call."

Jasmine plopped down on the couch next to Lisa and couldn't help but think of how she probably would have thrown her out had she not come over armed with a mouth-watering order of lollipop chicken, lumpia, and a few DVDs so they could veg out in front of the t.v.

"Here, pick one," said Lisa, pointing at the movies she had scattered all over the coffee table. "I'm going to go get us some plates," she said, springing up off the couch.

"Just make yourself at home," said Jasmine with sarcasm in her voice as she watched Lisa head inside the kitchen.

Lisa soon returned with plates and utensils in hand. "So, how did it go—and spare no detail."

"It was a beautiful disaster," said Jasmine before taking a large bite out of a chicken wing. She headed over to her DVD player, put in one of the movies from the pile and pressed Play.

"Disaster?"

"Yes girl, a disaster. Richard's great, but we won't be going out again, and Jackson and I are done, for good."

"Wait, what?" asked Lisa, frowning. "Explain."

Jasmine recounted her encounter with Jackson inside the stairwell, her wonderful outing with Richard, which left her feeling empty, and the fact that Jackson showed up at the tail end of their date, making things even more confusing.

"Wow," said Lisa, shaking her head in disbelief. "That sounds like a scene straight out of a movie. Makes my life seem like a bore fest."

"Well, I'm happy to have entertained you," she replied, not the least bit amused.

"I'm sorry," said Lisa, taking note of how insensitive she sounded. "How are you feeling?"

Jasmine stared blankly at the television screen in front of them and said, "I know it sounds crazy, because I broke up with him, but it's like no matter how much I want to hate him, I can't. Even with evidence of him cheating, I still want to be with him." Suddenly, she clasped both sides of her head with her hands and Lisa watched as she shook her head, tears now welling up in her eyes. "I feel like I'm cursed to love a man who isn't good for me," she said, a tear rolling down her cheek. "I swore after my relationship with Demetri that I would never fall for a jerk like him again, and now look at me. Here I am, hopelessly in love with one of the biggest players I've ever met. It's like he has super powers, and he's cast some sort of spell over me and now I'm cursed."

Smiling, Lisa placed a hand on her good friend's shoulder for comfort and said, "You're not cursed, Jasmine. And, Jackson doesn't have super powers. He's just a man—a very attractive, sophisticated, and charming one, but a mere mortal no less." She heard Jasmine giggle softly as another tear rolled down her cheek. "You're in love," she continued, "and that's what love does to us; it makes us say and do crazy things, like forgive people even when we don't feel like it."

"Yeah, I guess you're right," agreed Jasmine, wiping away her tears.

"You know there's still a chance he's telling you the truth about those photos. I mean do you really think he'd be dumb enough to cheat and then carry the evidence around on his phone? You said yourself he's wronged a lot of women. Perhaps one is trying to set him up like he said."

"I don't know," she replied, still not convinced.

"Well, try not to stress. I'm sure you'll get the clarity you need soon enough."

"Thanks," said Jasmine, smiling faintly.

She and Lisa spent the rest of the afternoon and early part of the evening watching movies, engaging in girl talk, and laughing about everything and nothing at all. At one point, Lisa grabbed a book off one of the shelves, placed it on top of her head and gave her best impersonation of stiff-necked Morgan, bragging about her latest endeavor. Her impression was spot on, and it caused Jasmine to laugh so hard that her ribs started to ache. It was the first time in a while she had felt some sense of normalcy, and she thanked Lisa for her company and friendship upon her departure.

Later that night, while cleaning up the mess she and her friend had made, Jasmine picked up the book Lisa had placed on her head while mocking Morgan and realized it was the Bible. Holding the good book in her hand reminded her of the sermon the minister delivered the Sunday following her and Jackson's engagement party. She recalled the scripture he used about uncertainty, and realized he was right in that the only person she could fully place her trust in was God. She didn't know if Jackson was telling the truth about not having cheated, or if the pictures she had found on his phone had been planted. Yet, she did know that it was time she stopped fretting over things she had no control over. After all, Lisa was right: the truth always seemed to have a way of coming out. She had no idea how things would ultimately unfold, but prayed she would receive the confirmation she so desperately desired…she just hoped the much-needed information would arrive sooner rather than later.

Chapter 33

A few weeks passed by, and Jasmine hadn't seen or heard from Jackson. Despite the fact she had been assigned to a new project and was knee deep in work, she couldn't stop thinking about him. The sound of his voice, the warmth of his embrace, and his masculine scent were just a few things about him she missed. And although she didn't enjoy public displays of affection nearly as much as he did, she found herself longing for the way he would grab hold of her with no regard for peering eyes, as if they were the only two people in existence that mattered.

She tried her best to dismiss her nostalgia by engaging in things that she had, at a certain point and time found comforting, but nothing proved effective. The cigarette she tried to sneak in during one of her breaks actually made her gag, and her recent retail therapy session left her feeling empty. All the shoes and handbags in the world couldn't fill the void that was now present, and it pained her to think of how she and Jackson's beautiful time together would soon become nothing more than a distant memory. There was no doubt her life had changed, for she now realized that without him, nothing was the same.

There had once been a time when she couldn't wait for the lunch hour to roll around because she'd usually be starving after having spent most of the morning either conjuring up copy for new ads, meeting with clients, or engaging in an intense brainstorming session with Lisa and the rest of the creative team. Lunch was also the time Jackson would call to see how her day was going, but now that he was no longer in the picture, her desire for food waned, and the loneliness from his lack of support was crippling. Getting through the workday was a challenge, and she was finding it increasingly difficult to stay focused.

"Excuse me," she said to her co-workers before exiting the conference room in which yet another staff meeting was taking place. A call had just come through on her cell phone, and she stepped out into the hall to answer it. "Hello?" she asked, cupping the phone to her ear.

"Jasmine?"

"Speaking. Who is this?"

"Caleb."

She felt her heart jump inside her throat. "Hey…what's up?"

"Well," he began, hesitating slightly before continuing, "I know I'm probably the last person you expected to hear from, but I have something to tell you—something I think you should know."

"What is it?" she asked, her heart now racing.

"Well…a few days ago, I stopped by my father's house to discuss a recent sale and I overheard Bianca talking on the phone to someone inside the den. I don't know who she was talking to, but she was laughing and saying something about some pictures she had taken with Jackson's phone and how she had 'finally gotten him back,' or something like that."

"Really?" she asked, feeling a mixture of relief and regret.

"Yes," he confirmed, hearing the angst in her voice. "I don't know what all went on between you two," he continued, "but based on what little Jackson shared with me, and then after overhearing Bianca's conversation, I knew something wasn't right. And, I can vouch for the fact that she's been acting crazy towards my brother ever since they…well, you know."

Although he was being rather vague and she could hear the hesitancy in his voice, Jasmine understood exactly what Caleb was trying to say. It seemed Jackson had been telling the truth all along.

"Look," continued Caleb, "I don't normally get involved in my brother's affairs, but I just felt you needed to know."

"Why didn't he call to tell me this?" she asked, her heart pounding inside her chest.

"He told me he's been trying to explain things to you for weeks, but you won't listen. I guess he figured you wouldn't believe him now either. Anyway, I just thought that if there was any chance you two might get back together, then telling you was worth the shot."

"Thanks," she said, fighting back tears. "You have no idea how good that makes me feel." Knowing that Bianca had planted those pictures on Jackson's phone as he claimed made her feel relieved. Yet, as her mind flashed back to the pained expression she saw on his face the night she went out with Richard, she wasn't convinced this revelation would prove to be the glue they needed to piece things back together. "I don't think your brother wants anything to do with me though."

"Why would you say that?"

"Well for one, he was pretty pissed about the breakup," she said, choosing to keep her "revenge date" a secret. Suddenly, a lump formed in the back of her throat. "I messed everything up," she said, letting out a heavy sigh. "He probably hates me."

"I doubt that," said Caleb, offering her some ounce of hope. "Look, I know my brother can be stubborn, but I've seen the way he looks at you. The way you two were together—I've never seen him like that before, with anyone. Just give it time. I'm sure he'll come around."

"Thanks Caleb," she said, wiping away a tear that had started to trickle down her cheek. "I really appreciate your call."

"Anytime," he replied before adding, "I'd hate to see Bianca have the victory. You should have heard how she was cackling, just like a witch would before flying off on her broom."

Jasmine laughed and Caleb did too, and for a moment she envisioned him flashing his crooked smile.

*****

Two days later, Jackson was sitting inside his office, sorting through some sales leads when he heard a knock at the door. "Come in," he said.

"You have a delivery," announced his assistant, holding a small gift box.

"Thanks, you can just set it down."

He watched as she placed the box on the table in front of him then exited the room. Leaning back in his chair, he eyed the small package before picking it up. He searched for a note but there was none. He then opened the box and inside sat a perfectly decorated cupcake that had the word "I'm" written on it in frosting. He set the cupcake back down onto the table and eyed it for a moment when suddenly, there was another knock at the door. "Come in," he said.

"Sorry to bother you again, but you have another package."

"Thanks Tammy," he said, as she exited the room. Again, he searched the box for a note, but there was none. He then opened it and inside sat another cupcake, this one with the letter "S" written on it. Before he could set it down on the table, there came another knock at the door.

"I'm sorry," began Tammy, her arms overflowing with small boxes, "They just keep coming in."

"It's okay," said Jackson, rising from his chair so he could assist her with setting the boxes down on the table. After she exited the room, he sat back down and opened them one by one, each containing a cupcake decorated with a single letter scribbled in icing on top. After rearranging the confections on his desk, they spelled out:

I'm sorry and…

Leaning back in his chair, he anticipated another knock at the door, but there was none. After a few minutes passed and he realized he wouldn't be receiving anymore letters, he stared at the cupcakes and rubbed his goatee. The message was incomplete, but it didn't take a genius to figure out who had sent it.

Chapter 34

By mid spring, the birds were chirping and the sun was peeking out from behind the clouds. Although there were many muggy days, Jasmine took every opportunity she had to enjoy the brighter side of the season, spending as much time as possible outdoors. Desiring to break free from the cramped confines of her apartment, she decided to take a drive up the coast one Saturday afternoon. After cruising along the highway for an hour or so, she found herself in Half Moon Bay, where the weather was cool. She knew people would be out walking their dogs, so she kept a close eye on Foxy, whom she had brought along for company.

After taking a stroll along the beach, she took a seat on a rock and nestled Foxy in her lap before staring out toward the water, watching as the tide rose and fell. The image reminded her of her failed relationship with Jackson, as it too had been washed away, much like the waves that swept onto the shore, leaving a mark in the sand before heading back out into the ocean. Despite having left him a few voicemails following Caleb's phone call, and sending him a peace offering in the form of his favorite dessert, weeks passed by with no word from him.

The more time passed, the more Jasmine realized that her relationship with Jackson was indeed over. Yes, she was hurting, and at times the pain felt unbearable, but she knew it would eventually subside. The one good thing about having endured a painful past, she thought, was that it had taught her that God is real and there is light at the end of the tunnel. She knew she would get there eventually, and still had plenty of hope for the future. After all, she didn't doubt that other men would come along. Perhaps she'd be lucky enough to meet a few great ones. She could fall in love again and possibly settle down. Yet, in spite of all that, one disturbing fact remained: there would never be another Jackson Taylor. He was one of a kind. Thus, deep down she knew that regardless of whom she might meet, she would never love any man the way that she loved him.

The only other man Jasmine loved at the moment was her father, and luckily for her, their relationship had drastically improved over the past few months. He had yet to get married, but was keeping her abreast of all the details surrounding his and Angela's impending nuptials. She was learning how to be more supportive of his new relationship while he was doing his best to support her and her newfound singlehood.

"Hello Dad," she said after dialing his number on her cell phone.

"Hey baby girl, how's it going?"

"Pretty good. How are things with you?"

"Not bad, can't complain."

"How is Angela?"

"She's good, thanks for asking."

"That's good," said Jasmine, glancing down at Foxy who was now squirming inside her lap. "I hope things are still going well for you guys. I really mean that."

"They are. And, thank you," said Mr. Fairchild, smiling. He was pleased with the changes he noticed in his daughter, but couldn't help but feel concerned for her considering how things between she and her fiancé had turned out. "Have you heard anything from Jackson?" he asked, eagerly awaiting her response.

"No," she replied, feeling a slight tugging sensation build inside her chest.

"I'm sorry to hear that."

"It's okay. I'm fine Dad, really. I just wanted to check in on you. Keep me posted on your wedding plans, will you?"

"Of course. Feel free to call if you need anything. And Jasmine?"

"Yes?"

"I love you."

"I love you, too."

Deciding to call it a day, Jasmine gathered Foxy in her arms and began heading back to the lot where she parked. To treat herself for all she had accomplished at work, she finally decided to buy herself a car. No longer having occasional access to Jackson's vehicle, she realized she no longer wished to be at the mercy of others when it came to transportation. Luckily for her, the new expense didn't pose a strain to her finances, for she ended up using some of the money she had inherited from Missy to finance the endeavor. She was becoming quite good at managing her money, despite the fact she hadn't been frugal during the years she relied on the "Bank of Dad." Missy would have been proud to see her living more sensibly she thought, a lesson she had learned from her no less. After all, Missy had successfully passed down an inheritance much larger than most would have thought possible, given how modestly she had lived.

Missy had considered Jasmine the daughter she never had, so passing her wealth on to her after she passed only seemed fitting. Jasmine was extremely appreciative, for it was Missy's money that was enabling her to live quite comfortably as a new member of the workforce. When she shared the details of her latest purchase with her father—a silver metallic, Corvette Coupe, he was pleasantly surprised she hadn't asked him to assist with the down payment, or to co-sign. Yet, considering she hadn't disclosed the amount of her inheritance to anyone, including him, he had no idea how easy it was for her to afford such a big-ticket item.

Now happy to be standing on her own two feet, Jasmine had absolutely no intention of blowing the money Missy had so graciously bestowed upon her. In fact, she planned to keep the majority of it tucked away for safekeeping, only to be used when it became absolutely necessary. And to think she had gotten so upset upon discovering hidden truths about Jackson and her father, when all the while she had been harboring a few secrets of her own…

Chapter 35

When Jasmine headed into work that following Monday, she felt refreshed thanks to her weekend outing, which was good considering she needed to be at her best for the meetings she had lined up with prospective clients. She had just sat down at her desk and was about to enjoy her morning cup of coffee when suddenly, the nosey new receptionist informed her she was needed inside one of the conference rooms.

"I thought our first meeting wasn't for another hour or so?"

"I dunno," replied Katherine, shrugging. "It appears a new client is here now."

"Okay," said Jasmine, grabbing her notepad and pen. "I'll go get Lisa."

"He only asked for you."

"Who?"

"The new client."

"Okay…" she replied, just as confused as she had been before.

"Oh, and be careful," warned Katherine, as she watched Jasmine head down the hall.

"Careful?"

"Yeah. This one is fine. You might just fall in love."

"I doubt that, but thanks," said Jasmine, rolling her eyes. She had already dated her fair share of attractive men, and despite her outing with Richard, she had absolutely no intention of ever mixing business with pleasure again.

After taking a short trip down the hall, Jasmine stepped inside the conference room and said "Hello," upon entering, but when the new client turned around, she almost fell down.

"Hi."

"Huh-hi," she stuttered, trying to maintain her composure. Just when she had given up all hope of ever seeing or speaking to Jackson, there he was, looking well rested, clean-shaven and dressed to the nines.

"Long time no see."

It had been an entire season since the two had last seen or spoken to each other—thirteen weeks to be exact, and seeing his face for the first time in months brought forth an avalanche of emotions. A part of her felt happy to see him while another part of her was angry he had taken so long to contact her. "What are you doing here?"

"I wanted to see you."

"Really?" she asked. "You never returned any of my calls—"

"I know," he said, cutting her off.

There was a long period of silence, as the two stared at each other, one not knowing what to say to the other. He could tell upon observing her noticeably smaller frame that she had lost a considerable amount of weight, the stress of their breakup causing her to lose the extra ten pounds she had been carrying around since having given up cigarettes. Finding it difficult to hold his gaze, she too allowed her eyes to wander, and they swept over his entire person until they eventually landed on something familiar.

"I see you're still wearing the watch I gave you," she said, finally breaking the silence.

"Yeah," he replied, glancing down at his wrist. "I think of you whenever I look at it."

Although she was glad to see he had kept her memento, she was still upset about how much time he had allowed to pass by, the minutes literally ticking away on the watch she had placed on his wrist no less.

"Caleb called me a while back," she said, her eyes drifting back up to his. "He told me everything."

"I know."

"I'm sorry I didn't believe you."

"Thank you," he replied, his lips curving into a faint smile.

There was silence again, until she asked, "How's your family?"

"They're good," he replied before letting out a heavy sigh. "Xavier is in rehab."

"Wow," she said, surprised by the news. She had sensed early on that he had a problem with alcohol, despite Jackson's firm denials. "I'm glad he's getting help."

"Yeah, me too. It took some doing though. It wasn't until he awoke one morning, unsure of where he was or how he had gotten there that he finally agreed to go." Jackson paused for a moment and took a step forward. "You were right—you, my father and Caleb all tried to warn me about the trouble he was in, but I didn't listen. I guess I just didn't want to believe it. I can't help but think that had I listened to what everyone was trying to tell me, you would have never been in danger."

"It wasn't your fault," she said, her mind drifting back to that dreadful night.

"When you left, I was so angry I couldn't think straight," he said, staring at her intently. "I felt like you were throwing away everything we had worked so hard for—"

"How do you think I felt?" she asked, growing incensed all over again. "I believed in us...I really did. But then, things started happening. All the run-ins I had with some of the women from your past and present...it was becoming too much." Her gaze drifted toward the floor, but then she looked back up at him and said, "I never felt so unsure about so many things before and I wanted to trust you, but after I found those pictures, that was it. If the shoe were on the other foot, you would have done the same."

"I understand that things may not have looked good, but I had nothing to do with those photos."

"I know that now," she said, her eyes staring back at his. "When I saw those pictures it was like the worst feeling in the world. I felt so betrayed and I guess a part of me wanted you to hurt as much as I was hurting. I went on that date to get back at you, but when I saw the look on your face that night I felt awful. I figured that was why you never called me back."

Chuckling, Jackson took a few steps toward her and said, "I guess I can't blame you for wanting to get back at me, considering how things looked, but I didn't keep my distance because of that date." He shook his head and said, "You and I both know that whoever your rebound was, he could never compete with me."

Giggling softly, she replied, "Well, I'm glad to see your ego is still in tact."

"I know you wouldn't have it any other way," he said, smiling. She watched as his smile faded and heard a shift in his tone. "Look, Jazz, I'm leaving. That's what I came to tell you."

"What?"

"I've been traveling back and forth between here and Nevada for some time now, but am finally ready to make the transition."

"Oh," she said, unsure how to respond.

He moved in closer and placed his palm against her cheek, a move that caused her to look up at him. "But, before I go," he continued, "there's something I have to get settled first."

"What's that?" she asked, the warmth of his hand sending a tingling sensation down her neck and spine.

"I have to come clean about something."

Jasmine could feel a lump starting to form in the back of her throat, and her heart was now racing in anticipation of what he was about to say. A part of her had always feared that he hadn't been completely honest with her, and it appeared her worst fear was becoming a reality.

Jackson peered long and hard into Jasmine's dark brown, almond-shaped eyes, and could see them growing watery at the corners. He knew he had her in suspense, but couldn't understand the pain he now saw plastered all over her face. No words could describe how much he missed her, or how scared he had been to think he had lost her, so he figured that if she had even the slightest inkling of how much he truly adored her, she wouldn't be on the verge of tears. "I lied when I said I wasn't going to keep defending myself to you," he said, watching as tears began rolling down her cheeks.

She blinked hard and stared back at him.

"I'm never going to stop," he continued. "In fact, I plan to spend the rest of my life showing you how much I love you so you'll have no choice but to be convinced."

Jasmine shut her eyes tight and exhaled, finally releasing the breath she had been holding in the moment he said he had something to reveal.

"Look," he began, taking hold of her hand then placing it over his heart. "I'll be the first to admit that my past isn't pretty, but the one thing I know for certain is that this thing that I feel right here," he continued, pressing her hand firmly into his chest, "this feeling I get when I think about you…when I look at you…I've never felt it before. And now that I know how it feels to be without you, I never want to feel that way again."

She could feel his heart beating just as fast as hers, and suddenly, more tears started streaming down her face. "What if I can't give you what you want?" she asked over the golf ball-sized lump in her throat. She didn't know if she could give up her current job, or be the type of wife he wanted her to be.

"All I want is you," he replied, his eyes now glistening. "I just need you to give us a chance—a real chance. And, I need you to trust me. Besides, I have no idea how you could have ever doubted my love. I gave up sex for you—something I'm extremely good at."

Despite the tears that were pouring uncontrollably from her eyes, Jasmine laughed heartily at Jackson's comment, the fact he had said it with complete and utter sincerity making it all the more comical. "I can't believe I actually missed your cocky attitude," she said, shaking her head in disbelief.

"So, does that mean you're coming with me?" he asked, hoping she was finally ready to take a leap of faith.

"Yes," she confirmed, smiling.

He leaned forward as if he were about to lay one on her, but then pulled back abruptly and asked, "By the way, how does the sentence end?"

"What sentence?" she asked, now completely confused.

"The cupcakes you sent. They spelled out, 'I'm sorry and...'"

"Oh," she said, suddenly recalling the last delivery she had sent. "I was going to say I'm sorry and I..." her voice trailed off as she fought back more tears.

"And I what?" he asked, still awaiting the response.

"And...I love you." She could feel herself spiraling head first into the dark pits of his eyes, the depths of which seemed endless. "You have my heart, Jackson Taylor. Don't break it."

"And you have mine," he said, placing his hands at her waist. After that, his mouth was on hers.

Jackson clutched Jasmine tightly, and drew her in close—so close she felt she had been consumed. Like magnets, they possessed the uncanny ability to repel yet attract each other just as strongly. She knew she would never find a man who angered yet excited her as much as he did, and he knew he would never find a woman who frustrated yet challenged him, as much as she did. They were made for each other, and no words could describe how happy she was to have him back. The feeling was almost too good to be true, so she lightly dug her nails into the back of his neck to check and see if his presence was real or merely a figment of her imagination, but it wasn't. He was the realest thing she knew, and she had no intention of ever letting him get away...

Four Weeks Later

Making love to Jackson was like celebrating Christmas on the fourth of July. He gave Jasmine everything she wanted…things she never knew she wanted…and man, was there fireworks.

"Wow," she said, resting her head against the plush pillows that sat atop the king-sized bed of their honeymoon suite. She stared up at the ceiling and blinked a few times to assist her blurred vision back into focus while he lay beside her, his chest heaving in and out from exhaustion. "That was amazing."

"Yes, it was," he said, rolling onto his side so he could cup her face with his hands. That was the second time she had used that adjective that morning, making it a total of five if you counted the three from the previous night. And, no matter how many times she said it, it never stopped being true, and he never grew tired of hearing it.

"So, Mrs. Taylor," he began, peering deep into her eyes. "Tell me again how much you can't live without me."

"Excuse me?" she asked, frowning. She should have known it wouldn't take long for him to say something to ruin her natural high. "You came back to me, remember?"

"Is that right?" he asked with a wry grin.

"That's how I remember it, yes."

"That's funny," he began, narrowing his eyes at her. "If I recall correctly, you contacted me. And, it was only after you apologized for having doubted my loyalty that I decided to return. *And*," he continued, his brows rising high on his forehead for emphasis, "*you* were extremely overjoyed."

Now back to her senses, Jasmine shook her head and rolled her eyes. "Really?"

"Yes, really," said Jackson, knowing he had her. From the start, he had always known exactly what to say and do to get under her skin. Considering she never could ignore his taunting, it had become a tactic he used to reel her in, and she fell for it, every time. "I wasn't pawing myself inside that conference room or saying how much I missed me," he added, a sly smile slowly creeping across his face.

"Yeah, well I didn't propose to myself for the second time," she quipped.

"Oh, you want to play like that?" he asked, now grinning from ear to ear as he climbed on top, pinning her body underneath his. "Well, I never said I *wanted* myself, and I damn sure wasn't screaming my own name last night."

"You're such a jerk!" she shouted, pressing her palms into his chest. She tried scooting her body out from underneath his, but he wouldn't budge.

Laughing, he braced himself so he could remain on top of her, despite her attempt at pushing him away. "I'm your jerk, for life," he said, staring down at her, his expression now serious.

"Yeah, I guess so," she replied, her tone now serious as well. She stared up into his crystal clear, onyx-colored eyes and could see her reflection in them. With her eyes locked on his, she raised her right hand to meet his left and interlocked her fingers with his. She then held his hand out in front of her face and examined it closely. "I still can't believe we did it," she said, admiring the platinum wedding band wrapped around his ring finger.

"Yeah, me neither," he said, glancing at his hand. "These last four weeks have been crazy."

"Crazy and amazing," she agreed with a smile.

"You really like that word *'amazing,'* don't you?"

"Whatever," she said, brushing off his remark as she began to reminisce about the past month and how hectic their lives had become. The two had spent every spare minute of their waking lives feverishly planning their wedding with the help of their family and closest friends, who were elated to hear of their reunion. Jackson's mother helped secure the venue, which wasn't hard considering she and Jackson's father lived in Nevada, home of the quickie wedding chapels. And it was Jasmine's good friend and co-worker, Lisa, who helped her find a wedding gown in record time, the two scouring through catalogs during their lunch breaks and downtime. Even Jasmine's father, who was totally caught off guard by his daughter's off then on-again engagement, participated in the planning process by helping fund the event. No one except them could fully comprehend the sense of urgency tied to their nuptials, some even suspecting that Jasmine had gotten knocked up, fueling a shotgun wedding. Yet, their expediency was due to the fact that they had come to the mutual realization that they were in love and couldn't stand to be apart a minute longer. It was quite simple, really: they were meant to be together, forever, and nothing less than forever would do.

"Do you think we're going to make it out of this room today?" she asked, glancing over at the clock sitting on the nightstand next to the bed. "I'm hungry."

"Me too," he said with a cocked eyebrow and sly grin.

"I mean for food," she said, as they both belted out a laugh.

"I'm sorry, but I haven't had sex in a million years."

"It hasn't been that long, stop exaggerating," she said in reference to their two-plus year sexless courtship. One that, in actuality, wasn't even that long once you factored in the chase and then their breakup—the amount of time she had wasted pining away for her college crush Stacey Fisher, or the many months they had spent apart after she suspected him of cheating.

"Well, in my book, it feels like an eternity," said Jackson, rolling onto his side as he reached toward the nightstand.

Jasmine remained silent and watched as he began flipping through the room service menu in search of much-needed fuel. She knew she couldn't argue with him, for he had demonstrated an exceptional amount of patience and self-control the entire time they dated, given his previous playboy ways.

"Here," he said, handing her the menu. "You should be able to find something to satisfy your hunger in here."

"What are you getting?" she asked, glancing over at him.

"I'll have whatever you're having."

"Okay," she said, quickly eyeing her options. "Make it two burgers and fries then."

"Burgers and fries for breakfast?"

"Um, check the time lover boy," she said, nodding in the direction of the clock. "It's past noon."

"Already?" he asked, glancing at the clock and then back at her in shock. "Wow, I guess I lost track of time."

"Yeah, you did," she said, crawling over him so she could grab the receiver of the phone sitting on the nightstand next to the clock. He swept her mid-back length hair, which was now disheveled, to the side, then began drawing imaginary circles on her back with his index finger while she placed their order. A few seconds later, she returned the phone to its base then looked at him and said, "The food will be here in less than an hour."

"Good. That gives us plenty of time."

"Time for what?"

"To play pirate ship," he replied, grabbing hold of her wrist with his free hand. In one swift move, he had her lying on her back again with her hands pinned above her head, giving him a bird's eye view of her bare, ample bosom.

"What are you doing?" she asked, giggling while squirming underneath him in an attempt to break free. The fact he had enough strength in one hand to render her helpless was both mind-boggling and sexy, she thought.

"I told you, we're playing a game. I'm the pirate and you're the damsel lost at sea—"

"And you're searching for the booty, right?" she asked, finishing his sentence.

"Oh, so you've played this game before?" he asked with a chuckle.

"No, I haven't," she corrected, staring up into his dark, majestic eyes. "I never play games that allow my opponent to have an unfair advantage."

"Well," he said, staring down at her full lips, which he was now longing to kiss. "Luckily for you, the way I play, we both win."

"I like those odds."

*****

Thirty magnificent minutes later, Jackson was heading toward the door of their honeymoon suite, donning a plush terry cloth bathrobe and nothing underneath. "Thanks," he said to the room service attendant who set up their lunch at the small dining table inside their room. He offered the server a tip then sent him on his way.

A few minutes later, Jasmine emerged from the bathroom, freshly showered and sporting a similar terry cloth bathrobe. She started to make her way over to the table where Jackson was waiting, but stopped in front of the window. She stared out of their beach side hotel room, the one with the perfect view of Kauai's natural landscape, and took a moment to enjoy the scenery. "I wish we could stay here forever," she said, her eyes fixed on the sand and water below.

"Me too," he agreed, approaching her from behind. He wrapped his arms around her waist and rested his chin on her shoulder. "But, I have that meeting with my father on Monday," he continued, "and you still need to clear out your apartment."

"Don't remind me," she said, still dreading having to move. She wasn't happy about uprooting her life, although she and Jackson had decided that moving to Vegas, where he planned to take over his father's real-estate business, was the best option for them. She wanted to be with him, and was willing to do whatever was necessary to make it happen.

"You know, it's funny…" she began, still staring out the window at the beach below. "If someone had told me when we first met that this is how things would end between us, I would have never believed it."

Smiling, Jackson squeezed Jasmine tighter and kissed her softly on the cheek. "End?" he asked, shaking his head to the contrary. "No sweetheart. This is only the beginning."

Other books in The Cupcake Series:

How to Bake a Cupcake

www.jgirlpub.com